THE FLAME SEER

BOOK ONE OF THE CRYSTAL MYTHOS SERIES

AUSTEN RODGERS

Copyright © 2019 by Austen Rodgers
www.austenrodgers.com
Illustration and Cover Design by Jeff Brown
Edited by Bodie Dykstra
Interior Images by Stacy Sheppard

First Edition: October 2019
ISBN 978-1-950278-01-5 (paperback)
ISBN 978-1-950278-00-8 (ebook)
ISBN 978-1-950278-02-2 (audiobook)
Published by Hypercube Press
www.hypercubepress.com

HYPERCUBE **PRESS**
SCIENCE FICTION AND FANTASY

CONTENTS

This series is dedicated to my wife, Tessa.
I hope to be as strong as you one day.

PROLOGUE

The dimness of the cave shrouded the councilman's wrinkles as he recollected every memory he could: the creatures he had seen and the horrors his father had told him about. He clutched his robes closer to his bones, tightened the red sash around his waist, then took a deep breath.

"Only twenty-seven Nephilim survived the Anchor Crystal's breaking," he said, "and they lived in bitterness and agony until the end of their days. The Anchor held everything together, and when it shattered, so did their world."

The old man spread his arms outward. "These empty caves were their just reward—their prison—where they spent decades in pain, vigilant in their grief for what they had done."

The boy at his feet bounced on his knees, eyes fixed to the councilman seated in front of him. "Tell me the part where we come in," he begged.

"I will get there, Udug. Be patient."

The child stilled.

"Those that survived hated one another, and while they did not mate in a physical sense, their savagery should be indication enough that most of their offspring were the product of rape. Their children took a different shape and were weak compared to them. Some were let free or escaped, but most were consumed by their parents.

"A few Nephilim tried again and again to keep their bloodline pure and bring about a child like them, and it was a vicious cycle until one of them, on a whim of curiosity, began to look after her deformed child. She tried to learn what it was that made their offspring different in this new world. The boy was given the name 'Dalkhu,' and as the centuries passed and the boy grew, he watched many of his kind being slaughtered."

"That's when we learned their ways, right, Master?" the boy asked.

The councilman sighed at the interruption but nodded. "Dalkhu asked his mother to sharpen his mind, give him control over the soul inside him, and teleport by traveling outside the veils of the world. He thought that if his kind were to offer servitude to their parents and find them food in these desolate caverns, they would become valuable and the killing would stop. So Dalkhu learned and, in turn, taught the others. Thenceforth, we, as a people, were named after him.

"It took years before the Dalkhu, now young adults, lived in relative peace with their parents, but it was short-lived. One of the Dalkhu discovered something in the veil that would change the course of history."

They smiled at one another.

"Earth," the boy said.

"Yes. The discovery of another world just beyond the invisible layers of the veil shocked the Nephilim. They did not know that their world had fractured into three all those years ago and assumed that these caves were all that was left of their world. Anger returned to their hearts. They feared that their Dalkhu servants would flee to this new world and it shattered what little peace there was."

"So we killed them!" the boy exclaimed.

The old man's face straightened. "Not all of them, I believe. There were Dalkhu who wanted freedom and others who defended the Nephilim in search of favor and power. No one clearly won. Some Nephilim fled to Earth and beyond, but those who wished to retain their oppression may still be sealed below. Regardless, the Dalkhu freed themselves and formed leadership in the Council. Laws were created, and we officially became a society of our own."

"So why are we different from the Anunnaki?" the boy asked. "We are both children of Nephilim, right?"

"When the Anchor Crystal broke, more than just the physical makeup of the world changed. Auras and streams of invisible energy separated when the world was no longer held together. In these caverns of Kur, one of those streams settled, and our souls are affected by it. The same goes for the Anunnaki in Dingir. We are both children of the Nephilim, but the energies that give birth to our souls are ethereally opposite. Things between us and our *brothers* got out of control before we even understood these waylines of energy and how they affected our souls, so we accept that things are set in motion and our destiny will remain unchanged."

The boy looked to his hands for a moment as he contemplated this. "We will never stop fighting?"

The old man shook his head. "It is not likely."

"Then we should seek to win: fix the Anchor and

reunite the worlds and the energies in them. Our children would be like the Nephilim, wouldn't they?"

The old man's wrinkled forehead tightened. "The Nephilim had their time. They were cruel and horrifying creatures that deserved the fate that was handed to them."

"But there is beauty in power, is there not?"

"Boy," the old man said, "you know nothing of the monsters you speak of."

CHAPTER ONE

Angela threw her back against the wall and wondered if she really was prepared to die. She'd been accepted, completed the training, said the vows and sincerely meant them, yet she hadn't *truly* understood that dying meant losing everything she cared about. Risks were an accepted part of her life. This mission had been a risk, but she hadn't expected it to be a trap.

Her heart pounded and her lungs ached. It was safe for the moment, but Angela knew that she should still be running. The shaman's "magic" was something she'd seen before, and he wasn't human.

The temple corridor was made of yellow straw and mud bricks and furnished with crackling torches and wooden doors. One last deep breath and Angela willed her shaking legs to move. More prayer rooms lined the hallway around the corner, and nothing appeared out of the ordinary until the sound of rushing feet reached her ears and the wall on the far end of the hallway flickered with an unnatural reddish light.

She cursed under her breath and spun the other way. It was too good to be true, and she knew better. No Dalkhu would give up a hunt so easily. She jogged back down the corridor as light-footed as she could manage in her heavy leather boots and tried one of the shoddy wooden doors. Its black iron handle refused to twist, and she rushed to the next door. It swung open with a loud groan that irritated her, but inside the room was empty other than ceremonial ornaments, crude pottery, and small altars with petty offerings of small coins.

The air smelled like the earth with a tinge of the sharp incense that had been burning there. In the farthest wall, a small window sat several feet above her head. Angela was pissed at herself for wasting time and catching her breath. She had been too confident that she'd lost them. But it didn't matter now. All she needed was another minute of solitude to adjust the mechanism at her waist and she would be gone. The room would have to work.

She closed the door as quietly as she could and reached for the leather bag at her belt, gave it a gentle squeeze to be sure it was still there, then pulled the shifter from her belt. The cylindrical device's outer shell was polished brass, and a pane of glass served as a viewport. By gripping the tube with both hands, she wrenched the top portion off and removed the cap. A small tray connected by a mess of wires slid out the hollow tube, where a green crystal was held in place by springy prongs.

Angela held the empty tube between her knees and brought the rest of it closer to her eyes. Careful not to damage the metal prongs, she pulled at the crystal with delicate fingers until it popped loose, and she stowed the dull green rock in the bag at her waist. At the exact moment she found the blue crystal by which she could travel home, she jumped.

Splinters burst from the door as it flung open and a masculine figure in black robes stepped into the room. Tongues of fire danced under his hood where his skin should have been, and his exposed hands glowed red like hot iron. He was a Dalkhu.

Angela screwed the cap back on with shaking hands and little regard for the machine's fragility. She took off in a sprint and tossed the canister out the window before jumping and grabbing the sill and pulling her chest and head through until her stomach balanced on it. She bent her knees and leaned forward, hoping to tumble down to the sand and dry earth ten feet below her, but she stopped.

No matter how hard she flailed her legs and tried to pull herself through, she couldn't budge. The pack on her back was caught. Frenzied, she unclasped the straps and let it fall behind her. It crashed onto the floor and she leaned forward.

Angela fell from the window and landed on her back in the dirt, kicking up a cloud of dust. A sharp pain rippled through her spine, and she realized she had fallen on her shifter. Her back screamed in retaliation as she tried to roll over, but before she could rise to her knees, something slammed against the back of her head and smashed her face into the ground.

Sand and dirt smeared against her cheeks and into her eyes. She wailed as the pressure against her skull grew heavier and she clawed at the leg holding her down.

"Settle, vermin," a voice said. It was guttural, almost like he was choking on marbles. "This will be over sooner if you stop."

Angela reached for the grip of her weapon, ripped it from its holster, then pointed it where she thought the second Dalkhu was standing over her.

"Yeah," Angela said, wincing. "I know."

The gun hummed for a split second as it drew power from the batteries in her belt and heated the coil inside it, vaporizing water. When the pressure of the steam built up, it popped and hissed as a three-inch prong launched out of the barrel. The spike flew fast, tugging a small wire along with it, and buried itself into the creature's thigh. Waves of electricity pulsated through the wire that attached them together. The Dalkhu groaned as his muscles seized and he toppled over. The weight lifted from the back of her head.

Angela struggled to her feet, wondering if she should leave her gun and batteries behind to continuously discharge into the Dalkhu. But when she glanced over the one beneath her, she realized that this was not the same one as before. Paralyzing one of the two Dalkhu wouldn't buy her any time, and she would leave behind the batteries that powered the shifter, too.

With no greater alternative than running and fighting to the end, she pressed a button on the side of the tether gun. A winch inside the gun whirred, ripped the prong from the Dalkhu's leg, and skittered across the ground. Once the red-tipped spike returned into the firearm, she picked up the shifter and started running again.

Crude earthen homes of dirt, stone, and thatch lined the side of the road. In less than one hundred yards the street split into two different directions. The left fork led toward the late-afternoon sun and into the rugged and uninhabited sand-filled landscape of the central lands of Earth. The right fork led farther into the town, where larger homes and shops of more wealthy humans stood.

Angela veered to the right. The humans were already aware that she and the Dalkhu were not of this world. They had put on a spectacle of flight, fire, and physical prowess above their comprehension, so going into town and causing a bigger fuss with the locals didn't matter. She needed a place to hide and she wasn't going to find it in the wilderness.

People panicked and scuttled back into their homes when they saw Angela running down the street. A few even yelled out at her, averting her search for solitude and forcing her to carry on. She traversed a busy market square, bashing her way through people and dodging wagons and carts. On the other side of the settlement, Angela spotted a home with stones missing from its walls and the door boarded shut.

She slammed her shoulder into it and burst into the house, blowing plumes of dust into the air. Pieces of broken chairs and pots were scattered on the floor. She cringed at the pungent smell of urine, but the desolate home would have to do.

A blast like the cracking sound of thunder erupted a few feet to her side. The rush of air whipped her hair back and crashed against her, toppling her into the wall. The door slammed shut beside her. Her ears rang, her limbs felt numb, and the world spun around her.

The Dalkhu from the temple, shrouded in ethereal flame, stood in the room with her now. His shoulders were broad and defiant, and even through the flames that shrouded him, Angela could see the anger in his yellow eyes.

I'm outnumbered and under-equipped, Angela thought. *If I hadn't been forced to leave my wings on the temple floor, I might have made it far enough.*

The Dalkhu lurched forward and swiftly swung his leg. His sandaled foot swept toward her like a flaming meteorite and connected with her head, leaving her bobbing as she fought to keep herself together. His ember hands grabbed her wrists.

His touch burned hotter than a brand, heat soaking into her skin and spreading up her arm. Her veins carried his fire through her until every fiber of her body boiled. She screamed and shook, sobbed and spit, flailed her arms, and tried everything she could to get away. When she couldn't, she wished she was dead rather than endure it any longer.

"Writhe if you must," the Dalkhu said in a deep voice. He pinned her down like she was a lifeless doll.

Angela saw a flash of silver and felt a pinch in her stomach before she even realized he'd drawn a dagger from his robes. The blade had pierced her leather cuirass and cotton underclothes and buried into her skin. It was all too much; her breath froze and her body stiffened. The blade was just underneath her left lung and warm blood ran down her stomach.

The Dalkhu pulled out the dagger and wiped the blood on her greaves.

"Shedim, the vessel."

The second Dalkhu, the one she had shot, approached from the doorway. He produced a clay cup from a pocket, removed the lid, then crouched before her to press it underneath her wound. When her blood filled nearly half of the cup, he removed it and re-secured the lid.

The Dalkhu that held her to the wall looked up at the cup for a moment, then smiled. "Something to connect us," he said. The heat from his maw distorted the air.

Angela slumped against the wall with her head drooped low. For a moment, she forgot about her city, about her people and her husband, and couldn't help but think how wonderful it would be just to go to sleep. But slowly, her foggy mind realized that the Dalkhu no longer held her wrist. The pain was fading into lingering discomfort, and something cold was nudged under her fingers.

My shifter...

"Run home, lamb," the Dalkhu said. "Delay too much and you won't be well enough to make the journey."

Confusion washed over her mind. Releasing prisoners was abnormal for a Dalkhu—perhaps even unnatural. Sure, draining her blood was something new, but letting her go was something even more perverse. The Dalkhu were known for finishing what they started, oftentimes tracking down wounded soldiers for days until they finally finished the job. Angela couldn't decide if she was lucky or he was a fool.

She groaned as she lifted her head and asked, "Tell me... your name."

Flames billowed between his lips when he smiled. They licked his yellow teeth, and he asked, "Why do you want to know?"

"So I can... kill you the next time we meet..."

The Dalkhu chuckled deep and monstrously. He shook his head. "Go."

Angela frowned, but he was right: she wouldn't be in any shape to concentrate and travel home if she lingered. Her eyes struggled to refocus on the shifter in her hands. With shaking fingers, she unscrewed the cap and placed a blue crystal from her pouch between the prongs. Angela slid the guts of the device back into the tube, then screwed the cap back on until the blue crystal rested behind the viewport.

She tried to read the Dalkhu's expression for the last

few seconds she stayed on Earth, but she could discern little through the disfiguring flames that warped his features. With no answer of a name, but knowledge of her own life fading away, she pressed a button on the device. Electricity drawn from her batteries passed through the cables that connected them to her shifter and into the blue crystal. The machine hummed and flashed blue light that illuminated the room. She vanished from the earthen floor and entered the empty space between the worlds.

Travel was much faster between the worlds' invisible barriers, yet she was unable to move at all. It was a strange stasis in which she watched blurring white and black expanses whiz past her. The veils, as cool as Dingir's crisp air, brushed against her cheeks and arms as a tingling creep surrounded her entire body. The sensation reminded her of diving into a body of water or running between two vacuum-tight sheets.

The seconds it actually took for her to complete her journey would sometimes feel as though a decade had passed. In that space, time's existence was intangible; despite the time she spent stringing sentences of thought together again and again for what could feel like hours or years, she was also in no danger of bleeding to death. Angela would feel no worse, or better, at the end of her journey than she did at the beginning. She couldn't scratch an itch on her nose if she wanted to, but she had the time to engage in deep thoughts and write complete stories in her mind. Even her body's urge to breathe was paused so long as she went in satiated.

Angela's thoughts had gotten off track. Keeping the picture of her destination clear was the hard part, but she did arrive, broken as she was. The grass and dirt caught her weight, and the shadows of the Ascendancy's spires and arches, cast by the low sun on the horizon, covered her. The cold was familiar and welcome.

Sleep took ahold of her before she could yell out for help, but the thunderous sound of her arrival was enough to draw attention. A woman in the beige tunic and laced trousers of an alchemist noticed Angela's slumped figure, then the blood on her hands. She disappeared inside the dark oak doors and returned a minute later with armored men and women. They glided down the steps and raced across the lawn. Sunlight gleamed against the brass machines on their waists and shoulders.

A tall man with curled brown hair and dark eyes dropped to his knees next to her and placed a palm against her cheek. He said her name and rubbed her shoulder, but she didn't hear him.

"Angela," he said again, shaking her. "It's me, Michael. Wake up."

He lowered his ear to her mouth and felt the weakness of her breaths. He pried at the cut in her cuirass and saw just how soaked with red her underclothes were.

Michael shook her harder. "Wake up, Angela. Come on." A tear streaked down his cheek, and in a trance, he shook her again and began to yell.

A hand took him by the shoulder and pried him off her, splaying him out on his back. "That's enough," the man said, pointing a finger down at him.

Michael wiped at the tears on his face but only smeared dirt and blood. "She's my wife!"

The soldier scoffed. "I know. She's not going to wake up with you thrashing her around. Get yourself together and we'll take her to the infirmary."

Michael stood and watched the other soldiers scoop Angela off the ground. He kept wiping at the crud in his eye and murmured, "What happened to you?"

CHAPTER TWO

An insect scuttled along the frozen ground, aimlessly searching for somewhere warm to hide. It would pause where the sunlight gleamed off the gold brick street, but the blowing wind rattled its tiny frame and sent it scampering once more. Earlier that day, it only knew of humid heat, tree leaves, and dangling fruit, but it had stowed away in a crate on its way to the city that floated on air.

The streets shot out in all directions from the center of town, where the earth and rock held strong and stationary. Support beams held up the expanding metal platforms, where buildings made from limestone slabs and mortar stood tall. Beneath the city's streets, pipes and wires twisted around one another and meshed together at boilers and circuit boxes.

Angela had arisen unusually fast that morning. By the time the sun's light poured in through the bedroom blinds, she had already showered and taken to the sofa for a quick chapter in her newest survival book. A courier had informed her the night before that she was being sent out to Earth for a brief mission. He was lax in the details and wouldn't tell her anything beyond that it was a simple reconnaissance mission, and that made her anxious and eager at the same time. But Dingir made her feel alive.

The murmurs in marketplaces, the pangs and dings of metalworkers, and the salutes she threw across her chest to passing soldiers fueled her. She crossed the golden thoroughfare and grass lawn surrounding the Ascendancy with long strides. The cathedral-like structure of sandstone slabs, pillared archways, needle-like spires, and diamond-shaped windows of stained glass was a symbol of the Anunnaki government and the central point of the city.

Angela glided up the whitewashed steps and entered through the dark double doors. The floor shined under the yellow glow of bulbs in the main lobby, and the stale smell of paper gave the place an aura of lawfulness. Padded chairs sat on both sides, and a secretary's desk stood at a T-intersection of hallways. The left hall led to the wing that housed most of the provisions of the Uri Gallus, a division of Ascendancy operations that involved the direct defense of the city. Angela took the hall on the right, which led to where the Etlus, the offensive over-lookers of Earth, were based.

Brass plaques marked the simple wooden doors on both sides of the hallway. After passing the armory, the infirmary, and various rooms used for classes, Angela came to the office of Kushiel Valadine, the Grand Etlu. The door squeaked as she pushed it open and stepped inside, and as she turned to close it behind her, his voice called her name.

"Angela," he said. "You're early."

Kushiel, an older man with wrinkles on his forehead

and gray hair that reached his shoulders, smiled politely from his seat behind his maple desk. As Angela took the seat across from him, he shuffled papers out of their way, some of which were maps, long equipment lists, and after-operations reports.

"Just ready to go, sir," she said.

Kushiel nodded, his copper eyes looking her up and down. He pushed his chair back and said, "Well, not yet." Bending, he searched through a drawer and placed a folded wad of brown- and tan-colored armor on the desk: her cuirass, molded specifically for her size, gauntlets and greaves, followed by her bulky pauldrons. Lastly, he retrieved a thick belt dangling with her tools of trade and placed it on the desk, too.

"Your armaments," he said.

Angela pulled them closer, then immediately went for a small bag that hung from the belt, pulled the drawstring, and stuffed her hand inside. Two blue and green crystals glowed in her palm. One of the blue ones pulsed, as some shards naturally did.

"No red?" Angela asked.

"No," Kushiel said. "You're on reconnaissance, remember?"

"Well, yes, but it would be nice in case I run into trouble."

"I assure you, you won't. It's a pointless mission in all reality."

Angela narrowed her eyes. "Why do you say that?"

Kushiel leaned back in his seat. "A few weeks ago we received word that there was some kind of traveling shaman performing enchantments for coin in the central region of Earth. Nothing much to think of it, but a few days ago we received another rumor of a fire that lit up a residential area when the shaman began performing harder tricks, such as vanishing and producing elements from thin air."

"Definitely seems Dalkhu. No rogue of ours would care for human coin in the first place, let alone have the equipment to pull off something like what you're describing. It could be dangerous."

The Grand Etlu held up a hand. "This is an investigation, Angela. You have direction not to engage. Just confirm or disprove that the shaman is a Dalkhu. And it's not a priority, but try to figure out why it's after human currency."

Angela sighed but said, "Very well, sir." She scooped her things into her arms when a question came to mind, and she paused. "I don't mean to be rude, sir, but when will you give me a more meaningful assignment? It seems as though it's been ages since I've done something that requires a great effort."

Kushiel ran a hand down his face, rubbing fatigue and possibly giving himself a moment to think, then said, "It's just how the cards fall, Angela."

She didn't accept that answer.

"Besides," he said, "you should be happy you're not put in direct danger on a regular basis."

Angela bit her lip and glanced away for a moment. It was clear to her, and in frustration she said, "You should treat me like any other soldier and let me do my part."

Kushiel shrugged. "I don't know what you want me to say. Someone has to do these kinds of missions."

Angela shook her head. "You act like I can't see it, but I don't want your favoritism."

When Kushiel had no response, she marched into the hallway, kicking the door shut on the way out.

MICHAEL RUSHED UP THE WHITE STEPS AND PUSHED THE oaken doors open. The soldiers carrying Angela stormed through behind him, then passed the front desk and veered down the right hallway. The farther into the Ascendancy they carried her, the quieter the halls seemed to become and the more eyes that seemed to watch them.

The infirmary was lined with short beds that offered little padding and cotton sheets not quite thick enough to stave off the cold. As Angela was placed down on the closest mattress, Michael couldn't help but notice that she was the only patient, and seeing his wife there struck him.

Two healers in dull red robes rushed to Angela's side. "Shoo!" the woman said. "Anyone who isn't directly involved with this woman needs to leave the room!"

The soldiers who knew Angela and Michael grumbled, but the crowd began to trickle out. Some nodded to Michael as they passed, placed a hand on his shoulder, and offered their condolences. His eyes locked onto his wife on the bed, he barely heard them. Not until the healers had unclasped the pauldrons from her shoulders and removed the cuirass did Michael see her wound in clarity. He knew her wounds would be bad, but he hadn't expected the gash to be three inches wide or her underclothes to be as soaked as they were.

The surgeon took a silver knife to her abdomen and peeled back loose skin while the other held a light overhead. Michael looked away while they worked. "There's no damage to the lung. Just the muscles and the intestines, which won't be too hard for her body to heal."

"Sir," the healer said, turning to Michael. "The only severe problem seems to be the amount of blood she's lost. We'll apply thin cloth to the worst places on the intestine to help stay the internal bleeding, then sew her up. Given a few days of rest, she should be just fine as long as no infection takes hold. She's strong. Maybe lucky."

Michael only nodded, then turned his gaze back to Angela. Irritated, he brewed as the healers continued their work.

Lucky? he thought. *There is no luck in this!*

The door to the infirmary creaked open, and a man with gray hair that touched his shoulders stepped inside. His eyes bounced warily between Michael and his wife.

"Kushiel," Michael said. He clenched his fists and stormed toward the old man, his boots clomping loudly as he crossed the silent room.

"Kushiel," he said, "what kind of mission did you send her on?"

Kushiel held up a hand. "We can talk about this in private. I came to see how she was doing."

Michael's nostrils flared. "Well, she's nearly dead, thanks to you."

"This has nothing to do with any failure on my part." Sweat beaded on his forehead.

"I'll have you know she's been stabbed by a Dalkhu. She was *battered*. There are bruises all along her body, and now they're worried about an infection." Michael motioned to the healers, who tried their best to avoid the confrontation. "What kind of fucking mission did you send her on?"

Kushiel clenched his jaw. "Reconnaissance at a village

close to one of our outposts. She wasn't cleared for any combat."

"What went wrong then, huh? What were you thinking? What stupidity took hold of you to send her on a job that risked her life this much?"

Kushiel crossed his arms. "Outside. *Now.*" He turned and exited, and Michael was quick to follow.

Kushiel and Michael leaned against the wall in the hallway, glaring at one another as a group of soldiers passed.

Once they were alone, Michael leaned closer and whispered, "Did you forget our deal?"

Kushiel's lip curled for a moment, but he calmed himself and stared blankly from behind a few disarrayed strands of his gray hair. "No, Michael, I have not," he whispered. "But you have to realize that I can't control everything or be held responsible for accidents like these. People make mistakes. Reports get inaccurate from time to time, and there's nothing different that I could have done to prevent this."

Michael shook his head. "You can't tell me this is blameless. If it is out of your control, then your reports were wrong. Whoever *wrote* those reports is responsible for what's happened to Angela, and I expect you will punish that person accordingly."

Kushiel rolled his eyes. "That is for me to decide, Michael."

Michael paused as another group of soldiers walked past them. When they were gone, he pointed at Kushiel and whispered, "Regardless of who is truly at fault, I still hold you accountable, and you are going to do something for me."

The Grand Etlu raised an eyebrow.

Michael smiled. "Don't forget how devastated your wife would be if secrets slipped from my tongue."

Kushiel's jaw tensed. "I'm getting tired of your threats. Some days I'd wish you'd just do it and destroy me so I can do the same to you."

Michael laughed. He knew the old man would probably go as far as trying to murder him if it came to that. "Let's be realistic. You've held your end of the bargain for a very long time, and I imagine that has been a challenging thing to do. Policy will force Angela out of the Etlus to give her time to recover and be evaluated. My guess is that she'll sign up for the Uri Gallus. She'll spend some time learning those ropes, and should she want to pick up being an Etlu again, she'll have to be retested. I want you to do two things for me. The first is that I want her partnered with me once her training is done."

Kushiel scoffed. "Like I have any control over what managerial decisions Ja'noel makes over there. You should bring this up with him, not me."

"No, you two are close. He respects what you say since you've served the city side by side for as long as you have."

Kushiel sighed. "The second thing?"

Michael grinned. "If Angela does decide to retry her role as an Etlu, I want you to fail her test results, deny her —I don't care as long as she does not become an Etlu again. I won't have her facing danger in a different world any longer. I've feared this day would come, and now that it has, I will be sure that it will never come again." Michael leaned in closer. "If you fail to do these specific things I ask of you, I *will* tell your wife."

Kushiel scowled. His jaw clenched, his lip curled, and his fingernails bit into the mortar in the wall. Michael knew the Grand Etlu wanted to explode on him, and he relished the man's pain almost more than he did Angela's company. He felt empowered by it. Assuredly, that was his number two.

Kushiel relaxed and shook his head. "You know that my wife's life is in your hands, don't you? The woman adores me much more than I am comfortable with, thinks I am too good a person to do harm. I am afraid if you tell her she will be too devastated and take the fall. So how long are we going to play this game, Michael? You hold old deeds over my head and threaten my livelihood every day I still breathe. When will you let this go?"

Michael's lip curled as he whispered, "Never." He turned and began to walk back toward the infirmary door.

"You're reaching the point where you are controlling her life. That's *sick*. She deserves the life she wants."

Michael stopped and spun. "You do not tell me what is best for her."

Kushiel rubbed his temples. "She's beginning to think that I am favoring her by my own choice. I don't know if she thinks the reason is because she's a woman or because she believes I have affection for her, but how long do you think it's going to be before she figures out you've been blackmailing me all this time?"

"Do you?" Michael asked, glaring at him. "Do you have affection for her?"

Kushiel's eyes fluttered for a second. Then his lips tightened. "No."

They stared at one another.

"Are we done here?" Kushiel asked.

Michael nodded. "Don't you ever forget how much she means to me. The list of things I wouldn't do is rather short."

MICHAEL AND ANGELA SETTLED ONTO A FIRM GREEN couch along the wall farthest from the door. A variety of sweet treats—little lemon tarts and strudels stuffed with glistening red chunks—covered the short table in front of them. With no delay, Michael snatched a brown cupcake from the bounty and ate half in one bite. He rolled his eyes in some kind of gasm as an avalanche of brown crumbs cascaded onto his lap and the floor. Angela laughed.

He turned to her, eyebrows raised, and asked, "What?"

"Nothing," she said.

The room was alive and boisterous. Fifteen others had gathered in the small apartment, and while each of them had at least acknowledged Angela and Michael, she could tell that some did not care to be there, and others couldn't seem to keep their eyes off her. She hardly ever wore dresses, let alone the light blue that went so well with her eyes. Dingir was always too chilly for exposed legs unless the occasion was special.

Angela was speaking with Michael when the hostess, her old friend Lailah, returned to the room with two cups in her hands. "Here," she said from behind her brown curls. "It's a new batch."

Angela wanted to pass on the drink but took it with a smile. The beer was an amber color, and the smell of it reminded her of tree nuts. She brought the cup to her lips and sipped gingerly. It went down smoothly, but the dark taste of it tainted the experience.

"Thank you," Angela said, trying to exhale the smell from her mouth.

Lailah nodded and turned her attention back to the rest of the party.

Michael nudged Angela with his elbow. "You don't like it," he whispered.

Angela shook her head. "Is it that obvious?"

"Nah," he said as he lifted his cup. "I just know you." He cringed once the liquid touched his tongue, too.

"All right, everyone," Lailah said. Her smile spread from ear to ear as she stood in the middle of the room and motioned for a man on the edge to join her. Just as giddy and red-cheeked as she was, he wobbled to her side on inebriated legs and wrapped an arm around her waist.

"Thank you all for coming. It's absolutely wonderful to be surrounded by such warm friends that we can share this important moment in our lives with. As you all know, Jophiel and I have decided that it's time we bring a new child into Dingir."

A flurry of clapping and boisterous cheers filled the room. Angela clapped her free hand against her wrist. Michael cheered.

"So," Lailah continued, "we just wanted to pull together a small celebration for tradition's sake. Please, help yourselves to the food and drink. We understand that some of you can't stay long. So stay, leave, eat a while, and be happy with us while you can. It doesn't matter. Thank you for your support and your presence tonight."

There was one more round of clapping before members of the party resumed their conversations with one another and Angela and Michael melted into the background again. A half hour passed, and in that time, Michael downed two more treats and both of their drinks, after which they agreed it was time for them to leave. Their final goodbyes were said, and Angela and Michael stepped out into the brisk air.

As they marched home, Angela held her coat tightly

with one hand and held Michael's with the other. The streets of golden brick led them past the center of town, where earth and rock of the floating island held the Ascendancy sturdy, and back onto the metal sheets held by the undercity's support beams. When the wind was just strong enough the platforms beneath their feet would bob and flex in places, but they were never afraid of it. They walked along the city's jagged metal edge. There were no handrails to stop someone from falling into the blue expanse below.

"Tell me," Michael said, looking up from his feet. "Do you want a child?"

She tried not to laugh by keeping her mouth shut, but her lips vibrated as the air escaped her. Michael glared at her seriously, and she felt a little bad.

"Um," Angela said, looking away to hide the grin at her own foolery. "Sorry. You just took me by surprise. I don't hate the idea, but I don't think it's a good time for us."

"There will never be a perfect time. We just have to make it work. Are you afraid?"

Angela bit her lip as they walked. "Don't get me wrong, I love kids, and I think the idea of having one with the person I care most about is absolutely wonderful, considering how creating another life is something larger than either of us, but it just seems like it should be a very planned sort of thing."

Michael was quiet, and it took Angela a moment to finally come to terms with how she felt, then a few more for her to put it into words.

"It's just... I watched my parents die, and it's not like they lived dangerously. I just don't think that we're in the right line of work to have a child. I don't want our kid to have to go on without a—"

"Don't," Michael said. He put a hand on her shoulder,

stopping her, and waited for her to look into his eyes. "Don't even say it. It's not going to happen."

Angela exhaled through her nostrils slowly. She shrugged. "Okay."

Michael nodded and they resumed their walk home under Dingir's ever-twilight sun.

CHAPTER THREE

On his hands and knees, he tried to recover his breath. With each inhale, a spark of rage in his chest grew hotter as he grew more and more aware of what had happened with each passing second—or, more precisely, what had *not* happened. It was an outcome he had not expected.

"I'm still here!" He rammed his open hand onto the stone floor, splattering the spilled blood. "Why?"

The middle-aged man with a short gray beard pushed himself from the ground with a grunt. The candles sprinkled about the room reflected against his yellow irises. He shook the blood from his palms with violent swings, wiped the sweat from his brow on his robe, and stepped away from the puddle at his feet.

He stooped for a rag and wiped his hands. Across the chamber, two others watched him so silently he couldn't hear them breathing underneath the hoods of their black robes trimmed with blue cords. He wondered if his students were more speechless from confusion or their fear of the spell's unknown effects. Even Udug didn't know what went wrong.

He tossed the rag aside and walked to the edge of the dark chamber, his sandals clapping on the hard stone. A desk, carved from the rock when the chamber was first opened, protruded from the wall. Intricate symbols of history and saints had been carved in the surface and traveled down the face to where the stone legs merged with the floor. Thick fiber parchments were strewn over the table's expanse.

He scanned the pages for specific symbols and pictograms, looking for anything that might tell him what went wrong. After scanning each page, he discarded them onto the floor.

"I wonder if the passage was copied inaccurately, teacher," a smooth voice said from behind him.

Udug crumpled the page in his hand without knowing and slowly turned to face the voice. He knew which of the two students it was. His eldest pupil, Shedim, would have never spoken against him or his knowledge of the old language.

"I doubt it, Anzu. I was the one who translated these," he said.

Anzu, the shorter of the two men, scoffed and raised his chin. His skin was soft and hairless.

"Perhaps you were out of touch, then?" he asked.

Udug clenched his jaw and tilted his head. "Do not anger me further, Anzu. Do you even understand what was at stake? What was to be accomplished? Now, more so with the outcome of that spell unknown to us, we walk a line even more perilous and narrow than before."

"Yes," Anzu said. "I knew the risk and the cost and moved forward with you, thinking that it would work. But now, considering your failure, I've half a mind to report this to the Council while a punishment below banishment or death is still available to us."

His face twisted in anger. Spit flew from his lips. "You will not, Anzu! We will try again once we are certain what went wrong. There is no turning back from this. We've attempted the forbidden already. The only way now is forward."

Anzu shook his head and shifted his weight anxiously. He looked up again and said, "For a good cause? Yes, undoubtedly. But there is no way we'll keep this hidden for long. I will do what is best for us in the long run: confess."

"If your foot touches the threshold of this chamber, I will break you."

Shedim, finally breaking his silence, spoke. "Udug, is there not a way to end this without violence?" He turned to Anzu beside him. "Why can we not try this again? It is apparent that nothing has gone awry. I see no harm in trying a second time."

"Shush, Shedim," Anzu said. "We both know that we can't take another risk like this. Our teacher has endangered our lives enough already. By doing so, he has failed our people and us. Confession to the Council is our only option for absolution. There is no other action that will absolve us, as his pupils, of his evils."

Udug stood poised, waiting to see if Anzu would move against him, and when he stepped backward, Udug howled. His muscles tightened. He lunged forward with incredible speed and charged across the chamber and slammed into his student, sending them both to the floor.

A heavy strike across Anzu's cheek dazed the boy before Udug gripped his throat and lifted him into the air.

He coughed and choked, tried to pry Udug's fingers from his neck, but his teacher was much stronger than him.

With a furrowed brow and a sneer, Udug turned his gaze inward. He focused on his soul and sought to pull upon the energies within him, but something wasn't right. It didn't feel the way it should; he felt empty at first, and when the energy did arrive, its force was weak. It was taking him longer than it should have.

"See," Anzu gasped, "you *are* out of touch."

Udug tightened his grip, and he suddenly found the resonance he sought. With another yell, he released the energy from his soul and pushed Anzu through the veil. He vanished from sight, along with Udug's arm from his fingers to his mid-bicep. Water gushed from the hole his arm created, soaking his clothes and rushing onto the chamber floor.

Udug gritted his teeth as his stub of an arm jerked around wildly. "You will not flee this, Anzu," he said with grit in his throat. He held him there, drowning him in a world he could not see. The room was beginning to flood to his ankles. Candles were knocked over one by one, darkening the room.

When the thrashing stopped and Udug was certain the boy was dead, he released him and slowly removed his arm as he knitted the veil's hole back together with his mind.

Shedim's voice wavered. "You left him on the other side?"

Udug felt calm, unfazed by what he'd done as he wrung the water from the sleeves of his robes. "No one will find him there."

He sloshed through the water to the stone desk and sighed. The papers he had thrown to the ground were now waterlogged and ruined, and he loathed translating the old symbols again. It had taken him weeks to accomplish it the first time. Then there was the problem of finding some way to remove the standing water in his chamber. The old man grumbled as he bent and scooped up a soggy parchment.

There was something peculiar; a feeling in his chest, dull and painful, had made itself known. The sensation grew as he picked up what he could until it became unbearable.

"Shedim," he said, "help me with this. I do not feel like myself."

Perturbed, Shedim nodded and made his way to Udug's side. He bent, grabbed a handful of waterlogged papers, and quickly reached out for his teacher as the old man slipped and began to fall. He groaned in misery as Shedim pushed against the desk to pin him upright.

"Something isn't right," Udug said, clutching his chest. There was nothing natural about whatever was happening to him.

Shedim's eyes widened. "Do you think there was a delay in the effect?"

"No, this is something entirely different. Something went wrong." Udug writhed and screamed, slipped, and fell into the water.

Shedim dropped to his knees and removed his hood, exposing his shaved scalp. He quickly held his teacher's head above the water and watched his eyes flicker.

"What would you have me do?" Shedim asked.

Udug found it difficult to breathe, let alone speak the words "hide me" as he slipped into sleep.

CHAPTER FOUR

I t was a rocky place etched with canyons and fissures.
The multicolored stones of brown, black, and beige
appeared to waver and shift under the heat of the
three suns. In yellow and orange, they stared down at the
world with a deathly gaze, determined to snuff out any life
that tried to emerge onto the surface. And even though
Angela had no concept of time and had never been to this
place before, she knew that the suns never moved.

She swooped downward, unable to control her direction
as she soared toward the surface. Angela moved her hands
in front of her face, but she couldn't see them—or the rest
of her body. It was as though she were invisible on this
uncontrollable flight or wearing a mask that portrayed this
reality to her paralyzed body.

The closer she flew to the surface, the hotter it became.
She squirmed and fought to somehow direct herself away
from the heat of the stones below, to find cover from the
stare of the suns above, but she couldn't steer herself
anywhere. She glided along the surface for some time, then
dipped into the largest canyon she had ever seen.

In the shade of the tall canyon walls that grew all around her, she saw the mouth of a cave. Sounds she did not hear with her ears, but with her mind, came from the darkness. A deep reverberation echoed through her head like a long and dreary musical note. She passed through the cave's opening, and a rhythmic clanging grew, pulsing against her consciousness. She stretched out an arm to touch the walls of the cave, tried to find something to grab onto and stop herself, but she couldn't feel the rock against her skin, even though she knew she should have.

The sporadic and natural stone tunnel transitioned into a wider, smooth surface that appeared cut with intelligent precision. She passed pillars and artwork etched with symbols she couldn't read, and blazing torches in sconces whizzed past her head. While she had never seen this place before, a strange sense of familiarity, like a long-forgotten memory finally resurfacing, came to her.

Unintelligible whispers seemed to come from the darkest crannies of the cave. They surrounded her and grew louder with each passing second, muffling her own thoughts. Angela tried to plug her ears, curl into a ball, and clamp her eyes shut, anything to distance herself from this vision. She thought of Michael and of home, hoping that those thoughts would whisk her away.

She stopped and turned to face an arched doorway decorated with hand-carved symbols she vaguely recognized, but she couldn't remember what they meant. A red drape made of soft fabric hid the opposite side of the threshold, and Angela began to pass through it.

A man's blank face was only a few inches from hers. Every wrinkle, every detail of the scar on his cheekbone, and every fiber in his yellow irises were clear to her.

There was another man dressed in the same hooded

robe farther back, but Angela could only see the stubble on his tilted chin. Her heart raced as the feeling of vulnerability grew. Somehow, she knew these two, and they did not possess goodwill for her. Even though she could not see the flames of their souls, she knew they were Dalkhu, and she was seeing their world.

GASPING FOR AIR, ANGELA SAT UP, A SCREAM ON THE EDGE of her lips. A sharp pain in her torso forced her to lie back down and rest her head on the pillow. Her eyes darted around the room as her lungs pumped furiously to catch up. There were beds and nightstands with small lamps. Sunlight cast flecks of color through the stained-glass windows in the far wall.

The anxiety in her chest faded as her mind came to grips with reality. Angela couldn't tell if the bumps on her arms were her body's way of fighting the cold air or her own fright's physical manifestation. It poisoned her mind like volcanic ash in the atmosphere, spreading and settling over everything. It rumbled and shook her, but everything seemed to steady when she saw Michael asleep on the bed closest to hers.

"Michael," she croaked.

He didn't stir.

She cleared her throat and said his name a bit more clearly.

A quiet groan came from his bed, and he rolled onto his back. His eyes opened, then closed, and opened again. He looked confused and tried to find who said his name. When he saw Angela awake, he flung his feet to the ground and stumbled to her side. The back of his palm was warm against her forehead, and his smile and soggy eyes made her smile, too.

"Hey," Michael said. He bent his knees and kissed her cheek. "You're awake."

He held the back of her neck softly and placed his lips on hers. Angela weaved her fingers in his hair, plunging herself into every feeling he gave her. She had almost lost this moment. It was just them, and he made her feel free of everything that wanted to harm her. She felt safe.

Angela sniffled and wiped her eyes. "How long have I been asleep?"

Michael hummed. His eyes locked deep into hers. "About a day, I'd guess."

Angela nodded.

"What happened?"

"I—" She paused. "I don't really know."

Michael's lips tightened.

"No, I mean I know, but I don't understand."

"Well, neither do I," Michael said. "So start explaining."

Angela shook her head. "You'd better get the Grands. I don't want to repeat myself."

"Angela, just tell me."

"Michael," Angela whined, looking at him sincerely.

He sighed, then stood. "All right. I'll see if I can't get someone to make you a meal, too."

"I don't want to eat. I'm fine."

Michael stood there for a long moment, trying to gauge her, but he eventually nodded and left the room. She lay there for the better part of an hour, replaying the memories of her mission in as much detail as she could. By the time Angela had come to the few small conclusions she could manage, Michael had entered the infirmary.

The Grand of the Uri Gallus, Ja'noel, walked into the room on quick strides. Angela had deemed him a decent man a long time ago, though she had never been under his command herself. He'd been a leader at the Ascendancy for almost as long as Kushiel had, but he was not quite as old. Ja'noel kept his shaggy hair from dipping below his ears and didn't shave the scruff from his cheeks, and his green eyes always scanned the room around him, even in mid-conversation.

Behind him was Kushiel, whom Angela paid little mind except for the papers in his hand. Lastly, a woman by the name of Sarosha entered the room and shut the door. Angela knew even less about her, the Grand of the Dubah, whose importance to the Ascendancy was debatable. The woman was in charge of maintenance-like things and had nothing to do with combat in any shape or form. Vital, yes, as she was the one who literally held the city together, but she was not as well known for her service. Sarosha was the pup of the three Grands, but rumors of the tan-skinned woman said that she was as much of a spitfire as the others.

"Angela," Ja'noel said in a smooth voice, "glad to see you awake. Quite a surprising event, no?"

"Yeah," Angela said, pushing herself upright to lean her back against the wall behind her. A groan escaped her lips, but she was glad no one tried to stop her.

"So," Michael said. "Now will you tell me?"

Angela nodded, and the four of them took seats on the beds around her. It was difficult for her to admit her mistakes. She should have changed the crystal in her shifter instead of catching her breath, and she confessed that she'd been spotted and ambushed rather quickly, which was the hardest for her to admit. She was one of the most experienced scouts in the Ascendancy.

Angela told them everything she could remember: the two Dalkhu bold enough to cause a scene in a human settlement, the chase that ensued, how she was eventually cornered and bled, then not just allowed but *instructed* to return to Dingir. This fact, out of all of it, unsettled the others the most. By the end, they were just as confused as she was.

"You think it was planned?" Kushiel asked.

Angela thought about it again before saying, "Yes."

Sarosha repositioned herself on the bed and pushed the angled cut of her short black hair out of her eyes. "You're sure the two Dalkhu you encountered weren't extremist rogues searching for some freak sense of enjoyment? Getting a thrill out of your pain?"

"They were far too fast, too skilled to be run-of-the-mill exiles. I honestly suspect that they were part of the Dalkhu Council. At least at some point."

Kushiel hummed in thought. "I agree with Angela. I know that her intuition is spot on, and with the suspicious reports we previously received, it does sound a lot like a trap now." He looked to Angela. "I'm sorry for what has happened. It's my fault."

Angela shrugged. "This was going to happen sooner or later, Kushiel. Let's not pretend."

"Well," Ja'noel said, "letting you live is certainly something very odd, and we may never understand the purpose behind it."

Michael opened his mouth for the first time and said, "Maybe we were lucky and all they were trying to do is send a message. Things have been increasingly active on Earth. Right, Kushiel?"

The old man nodded. "That may be all there is to this, but until we know for sure, all we can do is move forward."

Everyone agreed. Getting revenge was certainly something that Angela would enjoy, but she knew that there was no possible way for her to find the Dalkhu who accosted her. While the red crystals would help her pass through the veil, no Anunnaki had ever returned from the Dalkhu world of Kur. It was a hostile place, and she wouldn't know where to enter. The risk of her arriving somewhere she couldn't survive, like a cave devoid of air or full of water, was too great.

Angela remembered the dream as she thought about Kur. The rumors she had heard and the visions she saw in her dream came together, and she wondered if she had seen something that no other Anunnaki had.

"Angela," Michael said. He was standing over her, touching her wrist. "Are you all right?"

"Yeah," Angela said. She rubbed her eyes. "I'm fine."

"Well," Kushiel said, "if we have nothing else to speak of, I suggest we look forward and discuss what's to happen now."

Angela nodded.

"I'll be heading out," Sarosha said, standing. "I'm aware of protocol. Thank you for informing me, and let me know if anything changes." Her intense brown eyes settled on Angela. "Best of luck, and a swift recovery."

"Thank you," Angela said.

Once Sarosha closed the door behind her, Kushiel stood and passed the papers to her. The top page was a form that read "Incident Report," and most of it was blank. Angela groaned. Michael chuckled.

"Looks like you have to repeat yourself," he said.

Angela smiled a little. "Yeah, I guess."

She flipped the page to the back and looked at the next

form, then let her arms plop onto the bed as she stared at Kushiel, unenthused.

"Really? Do we have to follow policy to that extent?"

Kushiel shrugged.

"Can't I just go on leave for a while and come back?"

Ja'noel stepped forward. "You will, for a few days, but we've found that keeping a busy mind and body helps with recovery. That policy exists to ensure that you are truly ready to go back to Earth. We don't want you going on missions if you can't handle it, mentally or physically. I'm sorry, but you have to transfer to the Uri Gallus, the Dubah, or drop out entirely."

Michael touched her hand. "I think the most important thing you need to realize is that not every Etlu gets to see these papers. Be grateful you're alive to sign those."

Angela scowled. "Fine. I'll sign up for the Uri Gallus." She pointed a finger at Michael, then at Kushiel. "But don't think that I won't be going back."

Kushiel nodded, and Michael smiled thinly.

"Good," Ja'noel said. He turned to the nightstand and handed her a pencil. "Welcome to the Uri Gallus."

After nearly twenty minutes of hand cramps and signatures, she passed the papers to Ja'noel. The deed was done, it seemed, regardless of if Angela liked it or not. She hoped that it would be a fast recovery and an even faster process of returning to the Etlus and eventually Earth. The landscapes, the stars at night, the feeling she got when she fought for something bigger than herself—Angela missed it already.

The Uri Gallus played an important role, too, but their duties were boring. The kind of excitement they experienced, a Dalkhu attack on Dingir itself, was a rare thing. The Shardwatch, the armory, all the rest of it was just busy work in her eyes. But that was something she'd have to adjust to for a while, she knew.

"There is one last thing I'd like to discuss with you," Ja'noel said.

Angela looked to him. "What's that?"

He scratched the gray scruff on his cheek. "I know this isn't something you want to hear right now, but you must know that there are going to be rumors about what's happened. Most of them are probably false, and it's only a matter of time before the public hears word of it and becomes unsettled by this mysterious Dalkhu activity."

Ja'noel held up a hand. "Now, this is entirely up to you, and regardless of what you decide, we will understand, but we think it would be a good idea if you consider giving a public speech as 'a woman who escaped her Dalkhu assassins.'"

Angela raised an eyebrow. "I didn't really escape."

"No," Kushiel admitted, picking up the conversation. "But they will believe it if it comes from you. What lens do you want the people to look at you through? You have a chance to use this disaster to bolster the city's morale and potentially alleviate the people's worries that their leadership has no clue what is going on."

"I see," she said quietly.

"You know how paranoid the tradesmen get, Angela," Kushiel said. "They travel to Earth, too, and if they stop because they're afraid, Dingir loses its supplies."

Angela shrugged. "I mean, if you think it's something that will help the city, then of course I will do it."

"You are a great asset to your people," Kushiel said.

Ja'noel smiled. "Yes, thank you very much." He held up her signed forms. "And since we've got these and nothing else to discuss, I think we should leave you to your rest. Welcome to the Uri Gallus."

Angela nodded. "Then—" She stopped and thought about it. "I'm not sure if 'thanks' or 'you're welcome' is called for."

Ja'noel chuckled.

"I know being an Etlu is important to you," Kushiel said, rising to his feet. "Just keep that same passion you had the first time you tested and you'll be back before you know it." He turned to follow Ja'noel out.

"Thanks," Angela said.

Michael watched Kushiel as he left.

ANGELA'S FIRST DAY IN THE INFIRMARY HELD LITTLE excitement. It would have been unbearable if Michael had not kept her company until the late hours of the day. The healers consistently checked on her and took notes of her progress and anything of concern.

The next morning Michael returned to her with a new book to ease her boredom. He was dressed sharply in full uniform before heading off to attend to his own duties. They had managed to get Michael two days off work, but with Angela's recovery progressing well, the time had come and he was needed in the Shardwatch again.

The book Michael brought kept her mind busy but didn't satisfy her entirely. She would read for an hour and an itch under her skin would pull her mind back to her dreams of leaving the infirmary. Eventually, she gave up reading, asked the healers to bring her paper and a pencil, and she began writing the speech Ja'noel had asked her to give. By spending the majority of the day working on it, she pumped out what she imagined was three-fourths of the entire thing.

An immense feeling of fatigue still held on to her tightly, despite her being bedridden. She tried to describe it to one of the doctors as "the feeling before sickness kicks in." The doctor didn't disregard her, thankfully, and even offered her supplements of various plants to help reinvigorate the body, but they didn't seem to make a difference.

Michael returned in his armor, having just finished working for the day, and Angela was glad to have company again. With his help, she tried to stand and walk around the room. Bending and turning her torso still hurt, but she could move if she had to. Still, the fog over her mind and her constant exhaustion refused to subside.

Angela found twisting quite a bit easier by the third day. The healers inspected her torso and found that her wound was closed enough to remove the sutures. She was grateful the itching sensation had mostly subsided, and through debate and a one-legged balancing act, she proved she was capable of taking care of herself again. She did mention, however, that even on the third day of her recovery, she still felt as though she hadn't slept. They brought her forms to sign and offered her more supplements for her feelings of illness, attributing it to the blood loss.

By the time Michael had stopped by to visit her in the infirmary, she was ready to leave, which was a pleasant surprise for him. With her written speech in her left hand, and Michael's arm in her right, she finally walked out of that damned room.

They received a few salutes, a few handshakes, and even an awkward pat on the back as they walked down the hallway. Angela beamed under the attention; it was an unusual thing for her. Michael was just glad to be walking with his wife again. He had taken her for granted before and vowed to cherish her more frequently.

They made a quick stop at Ja'noel's office and informed him that Angela was nearly done with her speech.

"Great," he said, smiling from behind his desk. "Perhaps we should schedule a time for it to commence, then?"

Angela shrugged. "Sure."

Ja'noel eyed a calendar pinned to the wall, humming as he scanned it. "How about tomorrow just before prismal time?"

Angela blew air through tightened lips. "Yeah, I guess that's fine. I'll be ready by then."

Ja'noel nodded. "Good, I'll see you then, just outside. We'll have a podium and a simple platform set up, spread the word around, and see if we can get a good-sized crowd."

A nerve in her gut struck a chord.

"Until then," Michael said, smiling as he turned Angela by the shoulders.

They exited the building through the wooden double doors, and Angela took the stone steps down to the grass outside the Ascendancy. She pulled her coat tighter to shield her exposed skin and watched the cold breeze carry the fog of her breath away. Beams of light reflected off the brass edges of sandstone buildings and the gold streets. The clouds floated lazily against a background of bright blue.

All of it felt good. The calling of tradesmen, the blowing air surrounding her, stretching her legs and arms to work the knots and strains in her muscles. Angela hated the staleness of the infirmary more than ever, and she wondered how she'd managed to tolerate it.

"Ready?" Michael asked from behind her.

"Yeah," she said, smiling.

"Then let's get you home," he said, and they left.

She took him by the arm, and she could tell that he was just as happy as her. They were content and joyful. Their boots clomped against the streets, and the ever-circling sun led them home with its bright reflections. The sky was bluer and clearer than Angela remembered it ever being. She felt like the world was trying to tell her "welcome back."

They weaved their way through people carrying business necessities or simply enjoying a stroll around the city. Between the rows of sun-bleached buildings, a man limped as he carried a linen sack punctured by a dull steel pole at the bottom—scrap metal to be re-forged into new machinery. Another man pulled a small wooden cart filled to the brim with glass vials, beakers, jars containing both liquids and solids, and alembics. His clothes, and his cart, gave him away as an alchemist.

"What do you think it's like?" Angela asked.

"What is what like?" Michael said.

Angela motioned to the man. "Being a tradesman or even a hunter."

"I don't know, really. I suppose it would be less stressful, but I wouldn't do it."

Angela tilted her head. "You mean to tell me, Mr. Room Full of Toys, that if the opportunity arose you wouldn't be interested in being an inventor?"

Michael smiled. "Well, yeah, I'd like it, but then I'd have to deal with traders and I'd get frustrated when my stuff didn't work the way I wanted it to. I would have to live with that every day."

Angela couldn't help but nod.

"Besides, you know I'm not a good 'peopler.'"

She laughed. "Yeah, it would be all right, I think, but boring after awhi—"

Angela's feet slipped out from under her. She threw her arms in the air, but just before her back hit the ground, Michael caught her, his hand instinctively wrapping around her healing torso.

"Careful," Michael said. "There's ice there."

Angela sighed, relieved she wouldn't be going back to the infirmary.

"Oh, goodness!" a voice said from the other end of the street.

Michael turned and groaned. A larger man walked toward them, hand raised and wearing a wide smile.

"Donny," Angela said as she righted herself. "Good to see you after so long."

"Angela! You as well, dear," he said.

Donny's nose was small and smashed, and the buzzed hair on his head connected with the stubble on his cheeks. It gave her the impression of a chipmunk. His bulbous figure was covered in brown leather bibs splattered with blotches of black oil, and he wore a thick wool sweater underneath his blue coat. He was, by a reasonable set of standards, not the most attractive man Angela had ever met.

"I saw that," he said, pointing to the ground. "Must have missed that spot. Sorry."

"It's fine." Angela smiled. Michael faked his well enough. "So, how has the Dubah been treating you? Haven't seen you since classes."

Donny lifted the tan knit cap from his head and ran his fingers over his stubble-haired head. "Oh, you know, same as always. Goin' round and round where the sun don't shine." He grinned, then froze for a moment as though he remembered something and looked Angela over. He took a step closer and quietly asked, "How are you holding up?"

Angela's heart dropped as fast as Michael's jaw.

"Really, Donny?" Michael asked. "I don't think it's any of your business."

Angela grabbed Michael's wrist. "It's fine."

Donny held up his hands. "No, come on now, Michael. It's just… rumors, you know? I'm curious."

Angela loathed the situation. Surely, if someone was already asking her about what happened on Earth, there would be more to come. Someone in the Ascendancy, most likely a healer, had a loose tongue and Dingir had already begun to speculate.

In the nicest tone she could manage, Angela said, "Look, I'll be speaking outside of the Ascendancy tomorrow before prismal, okay? You'll get all you need to know then."

Donny nodded timidly. "I'm sorry. I didn't mean to be intruding, it's just—you know—it's not normal for a Dalkhu to not finish the job, am I right?" His eyes were like microscopes, examining every tiny change in Angela's expression.

"No, it's not typical," Angela said.

"I thought not," Donny said. He shrugged. "Anyway, sorry again." He smiled. "I hope you'll be back to your old self and doing what you love soon enough."

"Me too," she said, and she led Michael forward by the hand.

They were nearly twenty feet past the man when Donny yelled from behind them and they turned to face him again.

"Maybe we should meet up for lunch sometime?" Donny asked. "It's been too long since we've really chatted."

"Sure, I'll talk to you later," Angela said, resuming her walk.

Once they were farther away, Michael leaned closer to Angela and said, "That guy annoys me so much."

Angela patted Michael's shoulder. "I know, but he's not a bad guy. Just odd."

Michael shook his head. "I don't know. Ever since he came back, I get this funny feeling..."

As they left the main thoroughfares and emerged into the outer ring of Dingir, the buildings changed from two to three stories high to squat homes packed tightly together. The smell of wood-burning chimneys was strong, and their house was almost identical to the homes next to it—hand-sculpted bricks made of brown and red clay, shuttered windows painted white, and not a single blade of grass surrounding it. They stepped off the golden road and through the gated fence to their plot of metal and stone.

Angela ran her fingers over the mortar between the rough bricks as she had hundreds of times before. Michael pecked her on the forehead and fiddled with his keys. A small potted pine tree sat next to the door, and she held her palms to it, feeling the prickle of its pines. With a finger, she lightly prodded the soil, ensuring that it was still some-what moist.

Michael was leaning against the doorframe, watching her, and she smiled. With a waltz up the steps, she kissed him lightly and said, "Thanks for remembering my tree."

He smiled and kissed her again before pulling her gently into their home. Angela removed her boots and coat, then proceeded to chuckle at Michael's immediate perusal of the kitchen cupboards. He shrugged at her and resumed his search as Angela looked about their home.

Past the short entryway, the space opened into the main

living area. A wooden table for two stood underneath the kitchen window. Lightly stained pine flooring made its way from the kitchen to the living room. There was a wooden bench with green cushions, a rocking chair that happened to be Angela's favorite place to read, and bookshelves that sat near the fireplace. She breathed deeply, savoring the smell of earth, wood, and smoke.

In silence, she roamed about the house, refamiliarizing herself with her belongings. Even though it had only been a handful of days, everything felt new. The books on the shelves were still in alphabetical order, and the brass knick-knacks that Michael had made for her were lined in undisturbed rows. The bathroom and shower were still tidy. Michael's toy room looked as cluttered as she had seen it last. Scrap metal tubes and sheets leaned against the far wall. Pliers, sheet cutters, heat wands, and other tools hid the steel table. The window was open even though the melon-sized smelter wasn't lit, so Angela shut it.

A mountain of clothes piled atop the bed blocked her advance, but with one wide swoop of her arm, she plowed them to the floor and jumped onto the bed. The headboard crashed against the bedroom wall as the bed bounced her in retaliation. She beamed and stretched herself out, admiring the softness of her sheets, which just begged her to slip between them. Just as she went to oblige their call, Michael rushed into the room.

"What happened?" he asked. "Are you all right? I heard a noise. Did you fall?"

Michael bent over the bed to take her hand, but she gripped his shirt and tugged him down the third time she told him, "I'm fine."

Angela eagerly nestled up against him with her head on his chest. The silence grew heavy while they enjoyed one another's touch, and Angela, staring off into the cracks and lines between the brick walls, let her mind wander as she slipped back and forth between consciousness and sleep.

"So," Michael said, "how do you feel?"

Angela sighed quietly. She wanted to sleep again, but with both perplexity and sadness, she said, "Definitely not the same as I did before."

"How so?"

"I feel…" Angela trailed off, trying to think of the perfect string of words that would best describe it. "I don't know if it's nerves or what, but I feel sick."

"Well, it should get better soon. There's a lot less stress in the Uri Gallus. Not as much fighting for your life."

"Michael," Angela said, looking up to meet his eyes. "I know you don't like that I'm in the Etlus, but it's where I want to be."

"I know it's what you want, but I don't know if I could take losing you."

Angela tried to think of something to console him but shrugged. "You knew this is what I wanted when we first started dating. Even before then, during classes."

Michael went quiet, and Angela started feeling a bit regretful for not acknowledging his care for her. She placed her palm on his cheek and forced him to look at her. "I love you, Michael, but I've got my own path to walk. If I can get back into the Etlus, I'm going to, so you have to promise me that you're not going to take it personally. You under-stand what pushes me. I want to defend this city, same as you, but in a different way."

Michael nodded and looked away. "I know," he said. "But how can you stand Kushiel?"

Angela laid her head back down on his chest. "I love being an Etlu, I guess."

"After all he's done?"

Angela shrugged. "The past has passed us. I'm not going to let your bad relationship with him ruin it." Angela scooted away from Michael and lay on her stomach. "Besides, it's not like he's going to be the Grand Etlu forever."

CHAPTER FIVE

Angela ran her hand along the relief on the desk, feeling the bumps and curves under her fingers. Even though the flickering candles surrounding her lit the symbols well enough, she couldn't read them. She knew the language, but it was a strange feeling when her brain couldn't register what it was telling her.

The chamber walls were hidden behind barriers of darkness the candles' light couldn't pierce, but she was certain that she was in a room. It seemed familiar, like it was a home to some small part of her that she couldn't quite remember, and it bothered her.

We're linked, you and I.

Angela's skin crawled and she felt sick in her gut. The voice was distorted, low, and it spoke *into* her head. She spun in a circle, trying to see through the black shroud around her.

"Where are you?" Angela yelled. "What do you want?" Her voice seemed to trail off into the distance. She felt small and fragile.

There was no response for a long enough time that she

began to believe the voice was gone, and when it spoke for the second time, she jumped.

These worlds are meant to be together, just like us.

Angela shook her head and plugged her ears. The ground next to her feet glowed red. The darkness in front of her had changed colors, and an aura of swirling red mist flowed out of it. A red orb glimmered and hovered toward her, just inside the candlelight, and it reminded her of the way the moon glowed on a foggy night on Earth.

Don't run. Don't hide. I won't let you, the orb said.

"What are you?" Angela said. "Answer me!"

We will be one.

Angela gestured at it. "Screw off."

We will be one.

The orb passed over the candles, and she bumped into the desk.

We will be one.

"Get away from me!" Angela ducked underneath it. She stayed there, crouched, and watched the orb float to where she had been standing. Inches from her face, the glow was crackling energy that swirled inside it. She could feel it. It was anger, it was contempt, and it wanted her.

We will be one, for our children, and their children, will be whole.

ANGELA JOLTED AWAKE. HER EYES SNAPPED OPEN, AND THE fog began to lift from her mind. On her side, she stared at the wall for an hour, trying to comprehend what she had just seen. Not only had the dream frightened her, but it was odd for her to have a second one so quickly. Only a handful of times did she remember her dreams, and she never had nightmares.

Angela thought of the floating thing, and the Dalkhu in the last vision, and blamed it on stress. There was no other way to rationalize it. She was recovering from the second-worst incident in her entire life, and she wondered if it might affect her for the rest of her life. The cold sweat on her skin made her shiver, and she rubbed the bumps on her arms, but she couldn't fall asleep.

The blanket came off and she sat up as quietly as she could without waking Michael. The knickknacks sat on the dresser, a mirror hung on the closet door, and the black blinds blocked sunlight from entering the room. Everything was in order except for her, it seemed.

The cold floor and early hour of the day were uninviting, but she stood anyway and searched for clean clothes from the dresser. Considering she would be in full uniform later, she took thick green cotton pants and a sweater into the living room and dressed.

It was too early for stress, and a book on the shelf seemed comforting. She nestled under a woven blanket on the padded bench and spent a few hours reading. The book was titled *Lost on the Adrift*, a common nickname for Earth, and it was the newest survival story by one of her favorite authors, L.A. Matta. As she scanned it, she forgot why she was up so early, and by the time Michael stepped out from the bedroom, she had nearly burned through half of it.

"Hey," he said as he rubbed his eyes. "Up early?"

Angela nodded, then returned to her book.

"Nervous about today?"

Angela thought about it. "No."

He half smiled and chuckled, uncertain of how to

respond. He stood there for a moment, scratching his stomach, then turned to the kitchen. Angela watched him over her book. He rinsed his face at the sink, stretched, then went for a drink.

"Do you ever feel like something is wrong with you?" Angela blurted.

Michael spat in the sink and shut off the faucet. He wiped at the water on his face with a rag and looked confused and slightly offended.

"Not you specifically, like I'm calling you out, but at yourself, I mean," Angela said.

He relaxed and said, "I mean, sometimes maybe I second-guess myself. Sometimes I have regrets, but I don't think there's anything wrong with me more than anyone else."

Angela nodded slowly. Michael didn't help, so her eyes returned to her book.

"Something wrong?" Michael asked. He took a step into the living room.

Angela thought about it again. "No, I'm fine." She closed the book on her lap. "You're right. I'm just nervous, and I don't feel very well."

His head twisted to the side like that of a dog. "Really? You still feel sick?"

Angela shrugged. "Sort of."

He placed his hand on her forehead. "Your heat feels fine."

"I don't know. I'll be all right," Angela said, sitting upright and throwing the blanket to the side.

Michael held her shoulder, keeping her from standing until she looked him in the eyes. "If you don't feel right, you let me know, all right?"

Angela nodded, and Michael released her so she could

stand. She walked to the small kitchen table under the window and sat.

"I'm going to need your help with this," Angela said, picking up the few pages of the speech she had written thus far.

"Yeah," Michael said, turning down the hall. "Let me take a shower first."

ANGELA SPENT A LARGE PORTION OF THE DAY PACING about the kitchen and living room. She would speak aloud, both to herself and Michael, and when her tongue would stumble on another sentence, they would rework it together. Even though she had planned on reading the speech, she recited it over and over, trying to engrave it into her brain.

It wasn't the whole truth, but some of it was in there. She still didn't like the idea of lying or embellishing, but she came to accept that there was no way around it. The Grands didn't want Angela's words to frighten the public, and she understood that.

Late in the afternoon, Michael left their home for a short while and returned with all of Angela's gear from the armory. She was to look official, like the soldier she was. Her leather armor had been cared for: coated with a fresh dosage of beeswax and the brass buckles, snap buttons, and machines properly polished to a shine.

She looked good in the bathroom mirror, almost as though she had pulled herself free from her heavy thoughts. The uniform felt *right*, and she was proud to wear it. Everything that had happened was a thing of the past, and she imagined that she was already heading back to her duties on Earth, where she could watch the curious creatures from afar and spend hours next to a fire, staring up at the dark sky. Night was something she could never experience in Dingir, and she loved Earth for letting her see it.

Michael looked good, too. It wasn't every day that he took the time to shave the stubble on his face. He looked clean, trim, and spiffy in his own armor. When Angela thought about it, she was surprised by her own physical attraction to him. He always looked good in his uniform, but for whatever reason, his allure melted her heart.

The time came, and they stepped out of their home. As Michael locked the door, she waited on the side of the road, sucking in the cold air with deep breaths and relishing in the refreshing feeling it gave her. The sun had begun to reach the moisture towers on the edge of town. They loomed over the entire city, and the sun shined through the cloud-cutting nets, damp with beads of water, and cast speckles of colored light over the city. Prismal hour, as it was called, marked the end of the day for most Anunnaki.

A sick feeling grew in her gut as the Ascendancy's slanted roof and spikes came into view. More crashes of teleportation than usual cascaded throughout the city, and she took it as a sign that word had spread to her fellow Etlus on Earth.

The lawn surrounding the Ascendancy was crowded with people from a multitude of professions. There were alchemists in breeches and aprons, dirty metalworkers in bibs, and hunters and tradesmen with shifters and knives on their belts. She wondered if she could deliver the speech in the fetal position behind the podium.

Some of the common folk nodded to her as she passed, and others appeared to have no clue who she and Michael were. Etlus and Uri Gallus saluted them, and Angela saw the small wooden stage and podium as they reached the front of the Ascendancy. Ja'noel, Kushiel, and Sarosha stood next to it.

"You must be nervous," Kushiel said, smiling as they approached.

"Yeah," Angela said. "Must be at least a few hundred people here." She took a deep breath. "I'll be fine, though." Angela retrieved the parchment from the front pocket on her cuirass. "Besides, if it does some good, it's worth it."

"That's it," Kushiel said, smiling. "Just head up to the podium and don't think about it too much."

Angela took a deep breath, pecked Michael on the cheek, and began her march to the wooden platform. The stage creaked under her weight, and she was just high enough that she could see the back of the crowd beginning to flood onto the street. All of a sudden, the crowd was quiet and looking at her. She put her papers on the podium, breathed deep, and spoke as loud and clear as she could manage.

"Good evening," Angela said.

A few people in the crowd responded to her in the same manner, and Angela smiled, feeling some tension relieve.

"Anunnaki of Dingir, like me, many of us here have braced our lives and our bodies against threats both physical and ideological, defending our city, our neighbors, our way of life, and our right to live. Today, we'll talk more of the recent events many of you have already heard about, as well as a plan of action moving forward."

Angela peered up at the crowd for a moment, then resumed.

"It is because of the gift of life my parents bestowed on me that I have come to be a part of this great city. From this love, I have developed my own affection for all of you. As many of you know, I recently suffered a great injury. Four days ago, on a reconnaissance mission to Earth, I was attacked by two Dalkhu. I barely made it home. Since then, rumors have spread of upcoming battles and increasing Dalkhu activity on Earth."

She lifted her head and scanned the wide-eyed crowd.

"I am here to tell you that these are false words. While there will always be skirmishes and fights between us, Dalkhu and Anunnaki relations are the tamest they have ever been. After human interrogation, thorough recounting of events, and partnership with the Grands of the Ascendancy, we've come to the conclusion that those who attacked me were rogue Dalkhu and no longer affiliated with their own people. Many of their characteristics—their rather unpolished fighting and manipulation of the veil, their clothing—have led us to believe that they worked alone and without their Council's blessing."

Angela cringed as the half-truths came from her mouth. She wanted to stop but steadied herself.

"The Dalkhu threat is not one that we experience often these days, but when we do, we see the people gather together under the common desire to protect one another. In these past few days, applications for the Uri Gallus have surged tremendously, and this, I believe, is proof that we stand taller than those who would do us harm. Each and every person contributes to this fantastic city and the peace and security that it thrives on. Those of you who make hard journeys to Earth for resources give to it. Those of you that stay in your shops, tanning leather and smelting metal, give to it, too. I, and the Etlus and Uri Gallus I stand with, thank you."

Angela smiled, and a few people in the crowd clapped. Once she had forced herself to begin, it got easier, and she was happy that it was over already. Michael smiled and nodded, and the crowd began to talk and disperse into the city. Then something stood out of place on the edge of Angela's vision.

A man cloaked in a black and red robe stood perfectly still in the middle of the crowd. The shadow of his hood shrouded the upper portion of his face, but she could see his smile.

Angela scoffed. *That bastard! What a sick, cruel joke!*

He lifted his head and stared at her with yellow eyes. She studied every wrinkle on his forehead and every stray hair. Then the aura of him shifted. Sparks sprayed from his nostrils with every exhale, igniting the grass beneath him. An inferno crawled up his fingers and under the robe until it spread across his face, and Angela recognized the man.

It's him.

No time to think, no time to speak, Angela *moved*, toppling the podium over as she bounded off the stage and sprinted toward the Dalkhu. Michael yelled behind her as she charged through the crowd, but she didn't care. She pushed and shoved, and she found the intruder standing in the middle of the crowd. Flames burst from his crooked smile, cracks of dry skin formed along his face, and his eyes lit up like torches.

Her hand zipped down to her belt and her fingers slid through the brass knuckles with practiced accuracy. She thumbed a button, creating an arc of electricity between two nodes on the striking part of the device, and swung. Just before her fist made contact, the Dalkhu twisted in place, and she missed. He reached out quickly and grabbed her wrist. They exchanged glances for a moment. He smiled, and they disappeared from the lawn.

Angela could feel that they were moving between the veils incredibly fast. The surge of energy that pushed her forward was stronger than that of any shifter, and she knew the Dalkhu was behind it. They were stuck in timeless stasis, staring at one another as they traveled. There was no point in trying to overpower the Dalkhu, so she waited for them to reach wherever he was taking her—waited for the fight to resume.

They broke through. The cataclysmic boom of their arrival brought Angela's head to a spin; she wasn't in any condition to be teleporting about, and she was twenty feet in the air and falling fast toward a rooftop. The Dalkhu had released her, but reality kicked in too quickly for her to do anything about it.

Her knee crashed into the stone building, and while her greaves absorbed some of the blunt force, she still winced and struggled to return to her feet. The Dalkhu was already standing over her. Angela could see the Ascendancy only a few blocks away. The people were scattering in panic in every direction.

"What are you doing here?" Angela asked, still gripping the brass knuckles in her left hand.

The Dalkhu continued to smile, irritating Angela to no end. More than anything, she wanted to punch the smirk off his face, then beat him to a pulp and maybe break a few of his bones in the process.

"Opening your eyes," he said, his voice rumbling.

He lunged forward at such a speed that the hood blew off his head. Angela swung her fist up, trying to connect with his cheekbone, but again he skirted away far more limberly than she anticipated. He sidestepped and came around her, and without anything to catch the momentum of her fist, she staggered forward. His arms quickly scooped underneath hers, and his hands gripped the back of her neck, putting her into a headlock. Angela pulled down as hard as she could and bent forward, but the man arched his back and held her tightly, keeping her upright.

The heat from his hands burned Angela's neck, and she growled through her teeth. The blaze sunk into her skin and soaked her muscles. Everything felt like fire. Yanking at his arms and thrashing her body didn't help; she couldn't break free.

"Hold still," the Dalkhu said into her ear. "Let's be done with this quickly."

A surge of energy prodded her, and with it came a strange sense of both familiarity and perversion. Breathing became difficult as something dormant sparked to life inside her.

"Soothing, isn't it?"

"Get off me," Angela grunted, trying again to shake him.

Pain lanced through her leg, and she dropped to her knees. He wrapped his arm around her neck again, pinning her there, and said, "Look at it. Look at your city for the first time."

Her sight flickered, and like the flip of a switch, the metal of buildings burst and sputtered as they transformed into molten, oozing liquid that poured out over the ground. The platforms of the city grew red hot, melting into great holes where the blue sky was visible beyond. The building she kneeled on combusted, and the flames began to lick her legs. The skin bubbled under her armor. She let out a blood-curdling scream that tore across the city as she tried to pat her legs and soothe the horrible pain, but she couldn't stop it from spreading across her flesh.

She thrashed free of the Dalkhu and stood, frantically searching for somewhere the fire couldn't touch her, but even the sky had changed to a dull red color. She rushed to the edge of the building and watched the people below shift into creatures she couldn't have imagined.

"Now," the Dalkhu said as he approached her, "go to your people."

He kicked her, and she tripped on the lip of the roof and tumbled over. The world slowed for a moment, and she watched the Dalkhu on the rooftop grow farther and farther away. He was still smiling. There was a crunch as her back fell onto the railing of a fire escape. Her body fell away, spinning her until she finally hit the ground on her stomach. The only thing that kept her conscious was the pain in her back and the flames that now burned her face and hair. She rolled, screaming as she tried to beat the flames off herself. Skin melted from her cheeks.

Something gripped her arm and shook her roughly. She jerked away and realized that something was looming over her, and it wasn't the Dalkhu. Angela gripped the tether gun at her belt and pointed it as she tried to scoot backward, still fighting the flames.

"Back!" she growled.

It spoke, but Angela couldn't understand. There was another figure behind the first, then another, and another, all surrounding her with the same cloaks of flame and red eyes. Veins of lava burrowed underneath their skin, and some grew wicked black horns. The barrel of her gun bounced between each of them, and Angela's trembling hand danced on the trigger when her vision went black.

THE LIGHT HURT HER EYES AND SHE WINCED. HER HEAD erupted in pain and her heart fluttered. Panic took hold, and she touched her cheeks where old pain still lingered.

A dream?

She kicked at the blanket and realized that her armor and equipment had been removed. The stained glass and rows of beds told her she was in the infirmary again. Angela cursed.

No. It was too real...

Three figures came into view as the blurriness resided and sounds became clearer. It was Michael, Kushiel, and Ja'noel.

Angela pushed herself upright, wincing at a twang of pain in her back.

"What happened?" she asked.

"I wanted to ask you the same thing," a voice said. Angela looked up from rubbing her eyes. It was Kushiel.

"The Dalkhu, did you find it?" she asked.

"That..." Michael paused. "That wasn't a Dalkhu, Angela."

"What? Of course it was."

Kushiel shook his head.

Dumbfounded, Angela's mouth hung open. "The black robe, the flames. Come on."

"Angela," Michael said, "it wasn't a Dalkhu. Black robes, yes, but the person wasn't a Dalkhu. There were no flames about him."

Angela chuckled. "You're messing with me. I clearly saw it."

The room was quiet for a moment, and Kushiel and Ja'noel glanced at one another.

"What?" Angela asked.

Michael sighed and took a knee before the bed. He took her hand in his and looked somber. "Angela, all we saw was you rushing into the crowd and throwing a fist at a man wearing a robe. Next we knew, the two of you were gone, and when you were spotted again, you were pointing your gun at people." Angela could see pain in his eyes, and she didn't understand what he was saying. "Are you all right, Angela?"

Angela shoved the blanket the rest of the way off. "Yeah," she said, slowly twisting her body and putting her feet on the floor. "I'm completely fine."

"It doesn't seem that way," Ja'noel said plainly.

"What are you trying to say?" Angela asked.

"We're wondering if you just experienced a kind of mental break," Ja'noel said.

"What?" Angela was pissed.

"Maybe you're too stressed after what has happened," Michael said as he rubbed her arm. "Seeing someone dressed like a Dalkhu, a twisted and disrespectful joke no doubt, appears to have triggered you in some sense."

Angela pressed her lips together and blew. She shook Michael's hand from her arm and said, "Good one," then pushed herself to her feet, steeling herself from the pain as she tried to hide it. "I'm *fine*," she said as sternly as she could. "Believe me or not, that was a Dalkhu."

"It's not like you to point a gun at your neighbors, Angela," Kushiel said. He didn't look her in the eyes.

Angela raised her shoulders and held out her palms. "What do you want me to say?"

Michael stared at his hands blankly for a moment, then faced Ja'noel and Kushiel. "I'm with Angela," he said. "Whatever this was, it's over, and if she says she's fine, I believe her."

Kushiel and Ja'noel turned to one another for a moment.

The room was quiet until Ja'noel looked down the bridge of his nose. "Angela, if it happens again, I'll have no choice but to remove you from the Ascendancy's forces altogether."

Angela grumbled at first, then nodded. "Understood." She needed to be there. While she wanted to argue, risking her chances of getting back into the Etlus wasn't worth it.

Ja'noel scratched at his beard again, relaxed a bit, then held up a finger. "But you're no longer authorized to carry a tether gun or clamp."

Angela wanted to argue but only nodded again. "What, uh…" She started speaking before the words in her mind could form coherently. "What are my orders, then?"

Ja'noel's eyes still discriminated her, picked her apart. He didn't trust her now, and she wasn't sure how she would be able to change that. He took a deep breath. "We'll start you in the armory, two days from now, when Barrat returns for his shift."

"All right," Angela said. She nodded and began walking toward the door with her head down. All she wanted was to find a place to lie down in privacy. Ja'noel gripped her arm as she passed, stopping her.

"Get some rest," he said quietly. "When you come back, I'll be watching."

Angela wasn't sure how to take the conversation. On the one hand she was incredibly grateful that if she truly had experienced some sort of mental breakdown, she was being given another chance. On the other hand she didn't believe that her mind had played tricks on her in the first place. It wouldn't fabricate things to confuse her, lie to her —it just wouldn't. To admit it would be admitting she was crazy. The things she'd seen and the things the Dalkhu had said were real. But she understood that, for now, keeping her head down was her best approach.

"I will, sir," Angela said without making eye contact.

Ja'noel released her, and she walked from the room. Michael's footsteps followed her down the Ascendancy's halls, but she didn't wait for him to catch up. She kept her pace, and Michael stayed behind her as they went through Dingir's streets. They were quiet, and being practically alone helped her think. Sometimes, though, she swore the common folk were watching her.

The first thing Angela did when she stepped inside her home was make her way to the bookshelf, grab her survival story, and very carefully lay herself down on the couch. Michael watched her quietly like a phantom hovering in the room until he was satisfied that she was all right. Or maybe he just couldn't think of anything to say. Her back ached now, and she felt like a bag of garbage. Even the couch's padding and the blanket prickled her skin. She tried to push everything aside and clear her mind by burying her nose in her book, but she caught herself drifting off and not even paying attention to what she was reading.

What the hell is happening to me? she thought. *First the dreams, and now I apparently snapped and attacked a man. Am I losing my mind?* She tossed the thought aside. *No, there's no way. That man was a Dalkhu. I'm positive, and I'll find a way to prove it.*

"Hey," a voice said.

Angela put her book down. Michael stood in the hallway.

"Are you going to sleep?" he asked.

Angela raised an eyebrow.

"It's getting late."

She shrugged and picked her book back up. "I'm not tired."

"Do you want to talk?"

Angela put her book back down again. "No, I don't

know what there is to talk about. I had a moment," she said, even though she didn't believe it herself.

Michael grumbled. "I don't know if 'a moment' is the best way to describe it. Maybe you should take it easy for a while. Call off your training in the armory until you're feeling better."

"I'm sure I'll be fine soon enough," she said as chipper and confident as she could. "I think I just need some time to relax, is all."

Michael took a step into the living room. He rubbed his arms, thinking for a second. "I just don't want you rushing yourself before you're ready."

Angela nodded. "I understand, Michael. I just need to push through this. That's all. It'll be fine."

He exhaled through his nose and rested on his knees in front of her. "If you need anything, just ask. If there's something you want to talk about, you need to tell me."

"I know, Michael." She looked into his eyes and felt sorry for a moment. She kissed him. "Thank you."

He nodded and stood. "I'm going to go to bed. I have Shardwatch duty in the morning. Want me to bring you a new one?" He pointed to the book in her hand. "Looks like you're almost done with that one."

Angela smiled. "Please."

"Okay," Michael said, kissing her on the forehead. He turned and said, "Sleep well."

She watched him leave the room. Her head was swimming in thoughts, and she barely understood half of them. It was easier to bury them in her book until she fell asleep than to deal with them.

CHAPTER SIX

The following morning was much like the previous one: miserable. Disturbed, Angela awoke, albeit much later in the morning than she usually did, which was somewhat nice. Too bad it didn't help the fact that she had experienced another sleeping vision and strolled about the home still in the same clothes she wore the day before, brewing on what she had seen.

This time, the images were garbled, mixed up into thirty seconds of incoherency. She didn't remember much other than an occasional word or a still picture in her mind. But by midday, she came to recognize what she believed to be the most important aspect of the dream: the nature of it.

This dream had been fast, like she was flipping through the pages of a book with her thumb. Not only that, but there was emotion to this one. Her own emotion. It wasn't like before, when she had awoken from the dreams in fear; she remembered that in this dream she was angry. She felt stifled, like there was an immense weight put on her for the only purpose of holding her down, and she had to do anything in her power to push it off. She had felt bold. She felt dangerous.

A few knocks at the door pulled Angela from her trance of heavy thought. She moved to the door and cracked it open. Donny stood just outside.

"Hey," he said, grinning.

Angela opened the door a bit more. "Hey."

"I was in the neighborhood and I'd thought I'd stop by. You want to have that lunch and catch up?"

Angela bit her lip. She had completely forgotten about Donny and the last conversation they had when she first got out of the infirmary.

"If it's not a good time, that's fine," Donny said. He reached under his gray knit cap and scratched. "I get it."

Angela shook her head. "No, it's all right. Some fresh air would probably do me some good." Angela half smiled. "Just give me a minute to change, okay?"

"Sure," he said.

Within five minutes, Angela went through her dresser and closet and decided on a white sweater, two layers of tan cotton breeches to slide into her tall black boots for extra warmth, and a jacket to top it off. A quick brush of her hair and she returned outside, greeting Donny again and locking the door behind her. They stepped onto the street.

"Where are we headed?" Angela asked.

Donny shrugged his big shoulders. "Wherever you like."

"Well, I don't eat often, so I would say that you're probably the most informed."

Donny looked at her inquisitively. "Don't eat much?"

"Yeah," Angela said. "Not that I don't enjoy tasting things. It's just that… I don't know. We literally don't need to consume, so I don't. And I don't like taking the time for bodily movements later."

Donny laughed. "Yeah, I get it." He rubbed his belly. "But I don't mind dropping the brown hail, obviously."

"Donny!" Angela exclaimed, laughing.

"What? You ever been down under the city? It's what it is: brown hail falling into the distance."

Angela shook her head. "No, and I don't think I'd care to see, so don't invite me."

Donny snickered. "Fair enough. Anyways, I know a place just a bit farther that has some great tea."

They walked to a shop with huge painted glass windows. Chairs and small tables sat out on the side of the street. For it being a time of day when most people were working, it was quite busy. Others had gathered there, and while some sat inside to avoid the chilly outdoors, Angela and Donny chose to sit under the sun once they had acquired their tea from the counter inside.

Angela picked a lighter strain that Donny suggested she try: a harmonious mixture of berries and spices that Angela admitted smelled appetizing. They settled themselves in their seats, watching the passersby, the warm sunlight on their backs, and Angela took a sip. At first, a rush of delightfully tangy berries flooded her tongue. She coveted the warmth of the liquid as it slid down her throat and into her belly, but then came the somewhat unappealing taste of the spices. While she wasn't particularly knowledgeable about spices, she pegged the taste down to ginger.

Donny saw her slight look of distaste. "Don't like it?"

Angela shrugged. "It's all right. I've tasted worse." She took another drink, trying to show him that she didn't hate it.

"Well aren't you just hard to please," Donny said.

"I won't argue that," Angela admitted. She held her cup in both hands, letting the heat of it warm her fingers. "So, what have you been up to all these years?"

Donny smacked his lips as he placed his cup down on the table. "Well, to be real honest, after our classes I started to fall off the edge a bit. Never completed my schooling to be a tradesman, you know, so I found myself a shifter after a bit of hunting around Dingir and just freed myself."

"What?" Angela interjected. "You can't just *find* a shifter."

Donny laughed. "Here's the funny thing: it might have been an old model, but I struck a deal with a guy who had his hands in the pot, if you know what I mean. Told me I could use it with no charge up front if he got a cut of everything I brought back from Earth, so I took him up on it."

Angela took another drink. "Ah, an illicit trader, I see."

"Precisely. Good times, too. I enjoyed it for a few years but ran into trouble eventually. Got tangled up with some bad news on Earth. Learned a lot there, and it took a few years to make it back, but I haven't left Dingir since. Took some more classes and got accepted into the Dubah under Sarosha. To be real, though, I think they only accepted me to keep a closer eye on me." Donny chuckled.

"Yeah," Angela said, "I had heard you went missing for a while, I suppose. That was a while ago."

"What about you? What have you been up to?"

Angela shrugged. "Same thing I've always wanted—" She stopped when she remembered she wasn't an Etlu anymore.

He was quiet for a moment as Angela tried to think.

"Don't worry about it," Donny said. "It's fine if you don't want to talk about it. Maybe now's just your time to fall off the edge. Nothing wrong about it. Just sucks."

Angela watched the specks of spice swirl around in her cup when she moved it in circles. "Yeah…"

It grew awkwardly silent until Donny sighed. "You seem a bit off. Not like I remember you. Energetic and determined and all."

Her gut sank, and she faked a laugh to hide it. She could trust an old friend, right?

"I feel like shit, honestly," she admitted.

"After yesterday?" Donny asked.

Angela looked at him. He held his cup up to his lips and sipped. The steam floated off into the distance. "You saw?"

Donny nodded. He swallowed his tea and said, "Do you want to talk about it?"

Angela took a drink herself. "Not really, to be honest."

"That's fine. You're talking to Michael about it, though, right?"

Angela couldn't bring herself to lie; she was bad at it, so she nodded in silence instead.

"That's good. He's always been very…" He thought for a second. "Protective of you. Cares a lot."

"Yeah," Angela said. "I feel safe around him like no one else does. Probably why I love him so much."

Donny looked at her peculiarly. He could see enough to recognize that she was hiding something, but not enough to know for sure what was bothering her. Finally, his curiosity grew until it got the better of him. "Something tells me you are fighting this by yourself."

She sighed. "I tell him what I think he'll understand. Beyond that, it's up to me to figure out what's going on."

Donny's glare didn't let up until she felt his pressure to tell him more.

"I get the feeling that something's not right with me,"

she admitted, "and I'm afraid if I tell Michael what's going on, I'll just alienate him or make things worse."

"I understand," Donny said. "When I returned from Earth after those two years, I got a lot of strange looks, too. People didn't trust me, either."

Part of her wanted to spill everything, lay it all out in front of him to be dissected and examined. Most of her just wanted it to go away, and she thought that by not acknowledging whatever it was, it would slowly fade away.

"It's not just the way people look at me, it's what I see." Angela wanted to take it back immediately after she said it. Her emotions took her too far, and she immediately became worried that she would only make things worse by telling him.

Donny bit his lip, and his eyes looked over the road in front of them for a moment as he pondered things. He looked back to Angela and said, "Do you know that the Dalkhu believe that our place of birth dictates our soul's nature?"

Angela shook her head.

"It's the same way with the crystals we use for teleportation. Our world that contains our lustrous city has a certain *tune* to it, if you will, like a harmonic frequency. Anyone born in it, naturally, is affected by that frequency. Then there is Kur, which, as the Dalkhu also claim, is of the exact opposite frequency as Dingir. That's where the soul flame we see on them originates. The people, the crystals, the soul, and the dimension they are from may all be connected to one another. But some Dalkhu also think that the worlds used to be one big one held together by an anchor, so—"

"What are you trying to say, Donny?" Angela asked, cutting him off.

He grumbled, somewhat annoyed with the interruption. "I have an odd feeling," he said, then finished the last of his tea. "And that usually means I'm right." He sat forward in his seat and spoke in a lower tone. "Do yourself a favor and break into the old record room. Poke around, see if there's anything in there for you."

Angela scoffed. "Why would I break into there?"

"Better question is, why is the record room locked?"

Angela furrowed her brow. "Because there are spells in there."

Donny grinned. "Exactly."

A switch flipped in her mind.

Spells! Of course it's a damn spell! Why in the world didn't I think of it before? The Dalkhu on Earth that collected my blood, it was for a spell!

Angela suddenly felt stupid and agitated at herself. Her mind began to race and her heart fluttered as something told her to just move and do something about it. She wasn't sure what, but action was vital.

And then Donny's eyes turned red. The table in front of her lit aflame, and the tea boiled in her hand as the city caught on fire. Donny, the shopkeeper sweeping just outside the door, people down the street—all of them burst into disfigured creatures of molten rock and metal. But as quickly as it came, it also disappeared. She placed the cup on the table and stood.

"I have to go," she said.

"Wait," Donny said as she began walking away. "What's the matter?"

Angela looked back at him and opened her mouth to talk, but she couldn't bring herself to say any more and turned away. Donny leaned back in his seat again, confused and pouting slightly. He was too engrossed in his thoughts to notice Michael standing on the corner across the street and tightly gripping a new book.

Shedim rapped his fingertips on the floor and stared at the far wall of the chamber. It felt like he had been sitting on that blue cushion for days, and no matter what he tried to fill his head with, he could not seem to speed the slow creep of time. He tossed his weight against the wall behind him, sighing in agitation. Lit candles barely illuminated the black rock of the walls, and papers were still scattered about the room.

Some of them were spells, as humans called them. Truth was, those spells were much more conceptual than he imagined most people assumed. Humanity didn't have even the slightest taste of what a soul-powered spell could accomplish: destroy, alter, create, murder. Shedim wished Udug would have taught him more, as he knew just enough to know he hardly knew anything.

I wonder if this partnership is truly best for my own aims. I'm well beyond graduation now, and I am not tied to Udug any longer. I am not required to be his messenger or servant, yet I stay and help him. Why is that? Is it because I believe, as he does, that this should be done at all costs? Should every hindering law of the Council be circumvented in hopes of accomplishing this?

Shedim shook his head.

Maybe it's because I am afraid. Afraid of what Udug would do should I leave him. I know all of his secrets and certainly he would—

A crashing boom filled the room, pounding Shedim's eardrums and wrenching him from his thoughts. He cursed and plugged his ears out of habit, even though it was already too late. Udug flowed into the room through the red cloth drape over the doorway, a grin stretched across his face.

"What happened?" Shedim asked. He opened and closed his jaw in hopes that his ears would pop.

"It's unbelievable! It's marvelous!" Udug laughed aloud.

"What is?"

He crouched before him. "They didn't know! The Anunnaki didn't know that I walked among them!"

Udug leapt into the air and clapped his hands together. Shedim had never seen his teacher act this way before.

"Other than the odd looks I received for wearing this robe, they never suspected a thing," the councilman said.

"I don't understand what this has gained us," Shedim said. "Perhaps you could explain it to me."

Udug nodded enthusiastically. "While the outcome of our spell hasn't worked to the extent we wished it, we can compromise and move forward with another strategy." He paused and turned to Shedim. "I was able to awaken our Anunnaki, if you will."

"The woman?" Shedim asked.

"Yes. It's only a matter of time now, so we must act on our end of things."

Shedim raised an eyebrow as the old man paced the room. "I'm not fully grasping the situation, Master."

Udug stooped and grabbed Shedim's robe by the shoulders, smiling. His breath washed over Shedim as he said, "You will."

CHAPTER SEVEN

I just need to be alone...

Angela ran into the alleyway lined with rows of double-story buildings. It was quieter there, and there were fewer people to look at her. She squatted against the wall between two dumpsters, closed her eyes, and breathed deeply. With her fingers pressed against her neck, she monitored her heart rate.

When she felt that she was relaxed enough—and a bit more certain that being alone was helping—she stood and made her way back to the street. The sun determined the time: it was just before the spectral hour, and the streets would be busy soon.

She walked the roads quickly and avoided greeting anyone between her and the Ascendancy. Donny was right; she needed to get into the record room, even with the risk of being caught. Any sentence or price they would throw at her would be fine as long as she could find something to point her in the right direction.

The dreams, the visions of fire, the Dalkhu—they were real. Only now did she realize that they were a genuine threat to her way of life. She had already pointed a gun at common folk, and she was afraid it was only a matter of time before it happened again.

Angela crossed the grass, climbed the stairs, and stepped inside the Ascendancy's doors. The receptionist behind the front desk was packing papers into a hand case, and a group of soldiers walked past her and out the door.

Good. People are already beginning to leave for the day.

Angela walked through the lobby, then rounded the corner and followed the long stretch of hallway. Luckily for her, this was the Etlu wing of the building, and Etlus operated most during the day if they weren't on Earth. When she reached the storage room she was looking for, she paused and watched other soldiers pass her by, throwing up awkward salutes and hoping they wouldn't ask her what she was doing. Soon, she was alone again and took hold of the doorknob.

Locked, of course. She glanced down the hallway, then pushed her shoulder into the door. It held firm. Angela tried again, crashing into it loudly, but the door only wiggled slightly in its frame. She checked around again.

One more try or I'm walking away. That's it.

Angela charged into the door and the lock snapped free. Once she was inside, she shut the door quickly, but it cracked back open. The floor was slanted, and the broken latch wouldn't hold the door shut. The slam and crack noise was loud enough that someone had to have heard it, so she grabbed a chair from a desk and propped it against the door, swearing that she would be in and out.

Wooden lattices lined any wall without bookshelves. Tables sat in the center of the room, and every cranny that had space to hold parchment was stuffed. The smell of dust and age permeated the air, and Angela had no clue where to begin in the trove of old history. Books about alchemy and metalworking rested on the closest shelves, and guessing by the dust, she assumed they were outdated and left to sit in storage.

The diamond-shaped holders that looked like wine racks were filled with scrolls. Some were sealed with red wax. When she reached the farthest wall from the door, things began to interest her.

Books with titles such as *The Collected Knowledge of the Nephilim* rattled her memory. Angela had heard the term before, but she couldn't place a finger on what it meant or where she had heard it. Another was called *A Study of the Veil,* and she knew she was getting closer. She stepped to the side, removed one of the sealed scrolls from the lattice, and broke the wax.

The scroll was stiff and fought against her as she unfurled it, and a large-lettered word appeared at the top in a dialect that took her a moment to decipher. To the best of her ability, she guessed it read "sweet water" or something like it. In the body of the scroll, she only understood words out of context, like "refresh," "revivify," and "scrapings of copper stone." Merely one scroll in and her head was already aching from trying to understand, but it was a spell, and she was looking in the right place.

Angela rolled the parchment up and stuffed it back in its home before grabbing another. Big letters read either "death" or "dead speech." She scratched her nose and eyed it for a moment, then stuffed it away, too. The next scroll read "heat sight," and the fourth was something along the lines of "soul mother's favor," which seemed more like a prayer than a spell.

Angela groaned as she put that one away. Five feet of

the wall was stuffed with scrolls like those, and she imagined there were at least a hundred there. Five minutes had
already passed, and she had only been able to decipher four
of them. She wasn't going to have enough time to check
them all, so she stepped forward a pace, grabbed a scroll at
random, and broke the seal on it. The word "possession"
was faded at the top.

Angela squinted when she read "to overtake another
being." She cleared her throat. Another phrase read "mind
and soul to the victim, destroying the original occupant."
The scratch in her throat started to burn and she coughed.
Then again—and harder. She covered her mouth, unable to
stop the feeling that she was choking.

"Someone's in the record room," a muddled voice
shouted.

Angela cursed, clenched her jaw, and frantically stuffed
the scroll into her pocket. The spells and texts were locked
in there to keep people from using them for a reason. Being
discovered might earn her a seat in a cell and no chance of
ever making it back into the Etlus. Angela wished she'd
have thought a bit more before she broke in.

The door to the record room creaked open and pushed
the chair aside. Angela dropped to her hands and knees and
crawled underneath the tables in the center of the room. A
pair of armored legs stepped closer, paused, then twisted at
the heels and walked around the table.

Pale fingers hanging at the waist flexed, and in a flash
they burst alight with fire. A dread unlike any she had ever
felt washed over Angela, and she almost cried out. She told
herself it was just a vision and that the fires weren't really
there, but every part of her still knew they would burn her.

Drops of melted skin trailed along the floor, setting
small fires around her. They grew larger, threatening to

consume Angela entirely, and reached out for her like clawing hands. Angela tried to shake the memories of the fire's awful pain from her mind, but she failed. She stumbled out from under the table and bolted for the door. A cough escaped her, and her boots clomped against the stone floor.

"Hey!" a voice called from behind her as she stepped into the hallway.

There were offices, the infirmary, and the armory. No place felt safe. Three figures rounded the corner and screamed.

They pointed at her and yelled "Dalkhu!" before breaking into a sprint toward her.

Angela couldn't recognize who they were underneath the flames that shrouded them. She ran the other way. Who they were didn't matter. She needed to get out of there ten minutes ago, and the father she ran, the more the burning in her throat grew. Around the next corner and behind another door, she locked herself into a storage room, then noticed a ringing sound filling her ears.

Surrounding her were boxes of parchment, hides from Earth, and crates filled with broken equipment waiting to be smelted. She shoved one stack, toppling the wooden crates and barricading the door. Everything was quiet for a moment, and she began to catch her breath again when the doorknob wiggled. Someone slammed against the door. She wouldn't be taken to jail; they called her a Dalkhu. It wasn't just that she was seeing *them* cloaked in flame; they saw *her* the same way, too. Angela knew, without a doubt, that her visions weren't just in her head.

First, they would shock her with brass knuckles or tether guns to immobilize her and remove all possible threat of dimensional projection. There was a chance they would attach their clamps to her leg and drill a hole through her kneecap so she couldn't run. Then they would send her to the Dalkhu home world of Kur with the red crystals in their shifters, as was standard and as she had done a few times before.

That couldn't happen; she'd try to kill them before she let it. Angela knew all their tactics, all their equipment, and the weaknesses in their armor, but she shook her head. She couldn't bring herself to do that, either. Those were people who fought with her. Maybe she even knew them.

Fighting isn't an option, and hiding isn't looking too positive, either. I can't outrun fully geared Uri Gallus, but—

An idea leapt into her mind: she could attempt to teleport without a shifter.

Dalkhu do it all the time.

Her eyelids shut, and she stretched herself outward with a trembling mind when something cold brushed against her. Angela concentrated her mind to a needle's point and thrust herself at it, but the veil flexed with her, completely undisturbed by her prodding.

The mind alone isn't strong enough, she thought, and she searched deeper inside herself for a power stronger than the capacity of her brain.

The soul inside her bucked and squirmed when she tried to take hold of it. There was something perverse about it: a certain ring that did not feel familiar. No matter how hard she tried to grasp it and command its energy, the soul would not bow to her.

The aura of it felt unnatural and out of place. It didn't feel the same as it always did. There was something wrong with her soul.

No. It's... It's someone else's soul.

The rage, the malcontent and hatred for even her, the Uri Gallus' reaction to seeing her outside, the visions she had seen, it all told her that the soul inside her belonged to a Dalkhu.

It disgusted her, but Angela gritted her teeth and begged it to *push*. As much as she hated it, she needed it. And somehow, it answered to her anger. Her hatred of the Dalkhu that dare cast a spell on her and threaten her life and career beckoned the soul's energy. Malice, loathing, and hatred was a language the thing understood.

A burning face emerged in the crack between the door and the frame. The soldiers were getting through. Angela connected the soul's energy to her mind's guidance and pushed, and she vanished from the room. The frozen sensation of the space between the worlds stunned her, and for a moment, her mind stagnated, but she was quickly reacquiring a mental picture of where she wanted to go.

The floor's sudden appearance startled her, and she tripped, landing on her stomach and gasping for air. A queasy sickness washed over her.

It's done. Over. Just breathe, she told herself.

Angela rolled onto her back and clutched herself tightly. Her skin crawled as a cold sweat and tremors took hold. She had expended too much of herself.

Lucky. Very lucky I made it back.

She wobbled to her feet and rushed to the sink to retch. When she stopped, she rinsed and saw that her books, the furniture, and the knickknacks were all where she had left them, and the house was silent.

Slowly, the pounding fire in her chest subsided.

Never again, she told herself.

Even though Angela was proud she had managed the trip, it did little to soothe her; a soul that was not her own lived inside her. Her legs shook with every step toward the front window. Walls of fire thirty feet high waved and washed across the city streets. She searched every corner of every room and was relieved that Michael was not home.

Angela wanted to tell him; part of her trusted Michael to understand, but another part of her was dreadfully afraid. There was no quick and easy answer, no steadfast truth that she could depend on, and no premonition to guide her toward whatever the right decision was. She could die by Anunnaki or Dalkhu hands or figure out how she had come to acquire a Dalkhu's soul and get her own back, but she wasn't sure how to achieve the latter.

Angela stared out the window for an hour, lost in thought, before she struggled to the couch. She glanced at the possession scroll and re-read the words "destroy the original occupant," then stuffed it underneath the cushion, fell on top of it, and cried.

Is my soul destroyed?

"ANGELA, YOU NEED TO GET UP."

"What?" She rolled onto her back.

Michael stood over her, sweat on his forehead and his curly brown hair a mess.

"You have to be at the armory in an hour," Michael said.

Angela jumped upright. She scanned both the room and Michael with wide eyes. Everything was fine. Just them, her house, and no fires.

"You all right?" he asked.

Angela smiled, rose from the couch, and pulled Michael

into a hug and held him there for a moment. "Yeah. I'm fine."

He embraced her, then said, "You need to get ready. Don't you remember your training?"

A sigh escaped her, and she let go. "Is it really that time?"

"Yeah." Michael paused and eyed her curiously. "What's on your neck?"

"What?" She reached up and felt a tinge of pain on her chest.

He pointed to the area around her collarbone. "Go look in the mirror."

Angela walked to the bathroom, and with the aid of the light and the mirror's reflection, the edge of something red emerged from just underneath her collar. She pulled the shirt over her head and tossed it to the floor. At first it looked like a rash had developed at the base of her neck, but when she leaned closer she saw it was a series of crusted scratches and winced when her fingertips touched it.

"What is it?" Michael asked.

"I must have scratched myself in my sleep," Angela said as calmly as she could.

"Do you want help with it?"

Angela shook her head. "It's fine. I'll dress it."

Michael breathed slowly through his nostrils and watched Angela dig through the small cupboard on the side of the mirror. Inside, she retrieved a small glass jar of cloudy saltwater and a long stretch of cloth bandage and placed them on the sink. First, she lightly poured the salt water over her wound and clamped her jaw as it burned, using a towel to catch the excess at her stomach. Then she took fresh water from the sink and rinsed it. Wet, it began to bleed again.

"Where were you last night?" Michael asked from behind her. In his reflection, something about his eyes was hard.

Angela stopped padding the towel against her wound for a moment. "Donny stopped by and we went out for lunch. The fresh air was nice, and I wasn't feeling too great, so I went for a walk."

Michael contemplated it. "Feel better?"

"Not really," Angela admitted.

Michael hummed and leaned in to kiss her temple, and she had to stop herself from pulling away. All of a sudden, she was afraid that his touch would ignite the soul inside her and burn. He pecked her and didn't seem to notice.

"There was a Dalkhu seen in the Ascendancy last night."

Angela turned and put on her best surprised face. "Are you serious?"

He nodded. "It was in the old record room. Ja'noel sent out messengers this morning. The courier even brought my full uniform and all my equipment, so I'll probably be busy for at least these next few days doing searches. Letter is on the counter if you want to read it."

"Well, yes," Angela said.

She started measuring the length of cotton bandage she would need when Michael took the roll from her.

"Sorry," he said. "I just can't watch you suffer."

Angela stayed quiet and let Michael help. He stood in front of her, measured, and cut it at the right length. He used a washable glue to adhere the bandage and cut another strip just below it. When finished, Michael spun her to face the mirror and examine his work, then rested his chin on Angela's exposed shoulder. His scruff poked her sharply.

"Love you," he said.

Angela looked into his eyes in the mirror and reached behind to take his hand and wrap his arm around her.

"Love you, too."

Angela dressed in the highest-necked sweater she could find, and Michael donned his tools and leather uniform. The two of them set out for the Ascendancy. The sunlight was warm on her back and the breeze lighter than usual. The streets were quiet, and Angela took it as a sign that word of a Dalkhu in Dingir had already reached most people's ears. Things would slow down for at least a few days, and as inhibitive as that was, Angela was grateful for the near silence.

Everything past the double doors of the Ascendancy was the exact opposite. People rushed in front of her, bludgeoning each other to get to their business as if they were faced with a life or death situation. There were lines of people waiting to speak with the secretary at the front desk, and the hallways were so full of noise that she couldn't eavesdrop on a single conversation if she wanted to.

Angela tried to wipe her mind clean as they neared the armory. She wanted to be attentive, or at least appear like she cared, when in all reality she didn't. Finding answers to what was going on felt like the sanest thought in a while, and the next best way to find them would be talking to Donny again. But maybe she would find solace in learning how to repair the weapons and gadgets she wore on missions. Maybe it would help her in a pinch, and she was determined to get things back to normal without a big freak-out.

The moment they passed through the door to the

armory the smell of grease and metal filled her nose. The room was circular, but a third of it was cut off by a long countertop. Michael followed her to it and rested his weight against the iron bars that ran from the counter to the ceiling.

Chairs sat on the other side of the room, and there was a single bookcase containing informational packets and books with general information about combating the Dalkhu and animals on Earth. Some were manuals for various pieces of military equipment, there for both required and leisurely perusal. A few charts pertaining to different levels of public alerts hung on the walls, too.

Angela grabbed the golden handbell from the counter and chimed it a few times. Within a minute, a man with a slight limp and one watchful eye came up a set of stairs that led into the basement. His boots clomped to the counter, and a ringed finger scratched underneath his eye patch.

Angela had met Barrat countless times before, and even though those exchanges were exceptionally brief, she had always been fond of how quick and to the point he was when she talked to him. He had never asked too many questions, and she hoped that was still true.

"Angela," Barrat said with his rough voice, smiling courteously. "Good to see you again."

"Yeah," Angela said. "You too."

Barrat reached underneath his countertop and pressed a button. There was a subtle pop as locks released and machinery began ratcheting inside the ceiling. The metal bars rose into the air, pulling themselves up and out of the wooden countertop. They glided upward until the bottom of the bars stopped two feet above Angela's head, and a section of the counter swung outward on hidden hinges.

"Ready to get started?" Barrat asked, motioning her closer.

Angela nodded and stepped next to him. He pulled the countertop together, pressed the button, and watched to make sure that the iron bars fully descended into the counter again.

"If you two got this," Michael said, "I'll be heading to see Ja'noel. I need to touch base with him, considering what happened last night."

"I'm certain we've got our work cut out for us today," Barrat said.

Michael smiled and walked toward the door, then spoke over his shoulder. "Make sure she doesn't lick any batteries, Barrat."

Barrat laughed. Angela couldn't help but smile.

Jerk.

Angela didn't know what to expect below her feet, and she was eager to explore the basement below. She followed Barrat down the flight of curved stairs that jutted from the circular walls of the tower, and once her head cleared the thick floor of the main level, she beheld the armory's treasure in all its glory.

Metal parts and entire hunks of machinery were scattered about the room on desks, benches, and crates. The most common weapon was the tether gun, disassembled and awaiting repair and reconstruction. Tools lay everywhere, and Angela recognized a few from Michael's tinkering.

To her surprise, Barrat led her out of the main room and through one of three arches that led into a larger circle. Here, there were crates labeled with names, big pieces of equipment with wires running up into the ceiling, smelters and forges, and even what looked like what could have been a really big gun.

He bent at a lone bookshelf on the far wall and filtered

through stacks of manuals and pamphlets as Angela looked around. On a table, a gleaming silver ball the size of a marble with screw holes caught her attention. She picked it up and rolled it in her palm, trying to count the holes.

"Here it is," he said, pulling a yellowed manual from the bookshelf. He faced her and pointed at the orb in her hand. "You should know what that is."

"Is it a connector of some sort?" Angela asked. "It looks a bit similar to the ones I've used before, just less holes."

Barrat strode up to the table. "You know how the current soldier get-up requires you to wear eight damned batteries on your belt? This design distributes the weight. Instead of fifty pounds to your waist alone, the newest attempt is to space six smaller ones across your body: two at your ankles, two underneath your arms, and two at your waist."

Angela nodded. "That sounds much nicer to run with, but will there be problems with there only being six batteries?"

The scratch on her chest itched all of a sudden, and she reached up to carefully rub it.

"Don't believe so," Barrat said, stepping to the side of the table and fiddling with a trinket himself. "Tests have found that the silver carries a better charge, and we've reduced the number of output wires coming from the connector." He pointed to the silver ball. "Having everything wired at all times increases the risk of a switch getting bumped and draining batteries before they're needed."

Angela hummed in light disagreement and set the ball down. "I mean, I understand, but I'm worried about not being able to use all of my tools in the blink of an eye when I need them."

Barrat shook his head. "Don't worry. I've been slowly adapting everything to a new magnetized connector, so it'll be easy and quick to reroute power where you need it. Besides, I'm not ready to roll it out all at once, just as equipment returns to me. But it's a good thing you're here now. You can help me finish a few sets when we get you ready." He smiled.

Angela shrugged. "Well, let's get this over with so I can be of use, huh?" She fought the urge to scratch her itch, afraid Barrat would see it if she touched it.

He plopped the yellow manual in front of her. *Armory of the Ascendancy: Supporting Our Etlus and Uri Gallus.* Angela looked up at him dreadfully.

"Can't we just skip this introductory stuff?"

Barrat laughed. "You're the one who said 'let's just get this over with.'"

Angela sighed. "I know."

"Just let me know when you're done skimming it."

Angela watched him head up the stairs to the ringing bell at his counter. When his feet were out of sight, she took one last look over everything. The armory was certainly an interesting place, but it wasn't where she wanted to be, and the booklet in her hand was uninspiring.

A dark brown box with golden engravings sat atop a table next to the steps. It stood out from the dusty wooden crates surrounding it, and Angela, assuming that it held something special, lifted the latch and peered inside. Red velvet lined the inside, and six leather bags sat in neat rows with the drawstrings upright. Angela picked one up and shook it, feeling its weight. It made a noise like rocks rubbing together, and Angela immediately put it back.

Nope. Don't get too nosey, Angela. Best to not be seen poking around with crystals.

The lid settled with a quiet pop, and Angela sat on a rickety chair next to a worktable, then flipped open the manual.

JA'NOEL SAT AT THE DESK IN HIS OFFICE. HE'D BEEN GOING over eyewitness reports for the last three hours. Gathering testimonies was his least favorite part of the job because it usually meant a Dalkhu had entered Dingir, and those incidents almost always involved someone dying.

This time, however, that didn't appear to be the case. No matter where he looked, he couldn't find any recent missing persons claims, a cache of crystals going missing, or any significant evidence that would suggest a Dalkhu had been in Dingir at all.

A knock came from the door and Ja'noel rose and opened it.

"Michael," Ja'noel said. "Come in."

Michael strode into the office and sat stiffly in his bulky armor, leather creaking as it rubbed against the seat. "Any news, sir?"

"No, not much beyond the letter you've already received, I'm afraid," Ja'noel said. "The Dalkhu must have come to Dingir for a very specific and unusual reason. I can't find any evidence that suggests it's been hiding from us for an extended period of time. No one keeps track of the record room's stocks, so I can't tell if anything was taken or not, but some scrolls were tampered with." Ja'noel sighed and stared at his palms. "The worst thing about it is that I don't even know if the Dalkhu is still around."

"I see," Michael said. "Just let me know, sir."

"I will."

Michael began to get up from his seat but hesitated, and the young man's eyes wandered long enough that Ja'noel grew suspicious. "What's the matter, Michael?" he asked.

Michael shook his head. "It's—" He cut himself off and looked away. "It's Angela. I'm worried about her, sir."

"How so?"

"Even I'm beginning to think she may not be fit for service."

Ja'noel's eyes narrowed and he leaned back in his seat, interweaving his fingers.

"I shouldn't be telling you this," Michael said, rising from his seat. "You've got more important things to worry about."

Ja'noel held up his hands. "No, Michael, sit. It's just as important as these reports."

He paused. "You have to promise me that this stays between us."

Ja'noel nodded. "Of course. I wouldn't disrespect you or Angela in any manner."

Michael dropped back into his chair. "She's not coming along very well. She has trouble sleeping to the point where she's slept on the couch the last two nights. When I woke her up this morning, I saw she had clawed herself to the point of drawing blood in her sleep."

Ja'noel's eyebrows rose. "For certain?"

"Yes. And I want to ask you a favor."

"Well," Ja'noel said, smiling, "I can't promise anything, but feel free to ask."

"Can you accelerate Angela's armory training? Or skip it altogether?"

Ja'noel rubbed the scruff on his cheeks. "Maybe, but to be honest I'd be more likely to just relieve her of duty."

Michael shook his head vigorously. "No, don't do that. It'll only make her worse. Getting back in the Etlus is the only thing keeping her moving at all."

Ja'noel sighed. "Very well. Tell me how speeding things up will help, then."

"Just pull her out of the armory and put her on Shard-watch with me. I can watch over her and make sure nothing else happens."

"Ah," Ja'noel said, leaning back in his seat. "I wondered when this question was going to come. Kushiel mentioned your desire beforehand."

"He did?" Michael asked.

"Yes. He said you were rather determined about it."

"Well, things have changed. I need to be by her side *now*."

Ja'noel scratched at his jawline for a moment, thinking. "Do you believe there's a chance she'll have another panic attack like after the speech?"

Michael drooped his head. "I'm not sure."

"Then the restrictions still apply. No tether gun, clamp, or otherwise lethal armaments." Ja'noel sat upright and looked sternly at Michael. "Are you comfortable, at a time like this, to have your wife go about so unarmed?"

Michael nodded. "She won't be unarmed. I will be at her side constantly."

Ja'noel tapped his finger against his cheek. "Very well. As unfortunate and selfish as it is for me to say, I'd much rather have you close by if she does have another episode."

"Thank you, sir. I promise I'll keep her together."

"I know you'll try, Michael, but there's only so much we can do for her. You understand that if she jeopardizes someone's life and you aren't around to stop her, I will authorize the force necessary to capture her, no matter what it takes."

Michael was appalled. Here was a woman, his wife, struggling to come to grips with one of the worst things she had ever experienced in her life, and protocol was going to shove her out or get her hurt. His chest felt like it was going to explode, but he bit his tongue and said, "I only ask that you delay in making that decision."

"Very—"

A bell sounded outside the office. Michael and Ja'noel stared at one another in disbelief. After the initial shock, they rose and rushed into the hallway. Sure enough, a small hammer beat against the alarm bell atop the office door.

EVEN IN THE SECLUSION OF THE ARMORY'S DEPTHS, Angela could hear the faint toll.

An alarm? Angela thought. *That must mean... a Dalkhu has been spotted!?*

Angela stood and burst up the steps as fast as she could push her feet, almost tripping as she reached the main level. Barrat stood with his back facing her.

Placing a hand on his shoulder, she asked, "Is that what I think it is?"

He lifted his head and sighed dramatically. "We're about to get *really* busy."

In less than a minute, six people rushed into the room, shouting and demanding that they get their armor and equipment immediately. They shoved one another out of the way and pressed their faces against the bars like caged dogs.

"One at a time!" Barrat yelled over them. "I'll be giving nobody nothing if you don't calm yourselves!"

Angela stepped closer to the iron bars. An Uri Gallu with short blond hair pointing straight up stood on the other side of the counter.

"What's going on?"

The man continued yelling at Barrat, ignoring Angela entirely, so she reached through the bars, grabbed his shirt, and shook him.

"Tell me what's going on!"

The man swung his hand and hit her arm loose. He bore his teeth and pointed as he said, "Don't touch me, psycho."

She pulled her arm back, ready to smash her fist against his nose. Her blood felt like fire and ice, but she paused.

"What?" The Uri Gallu said. "You going to hit me or what?" He turned his cheek, smiling widely. It took every bit of self-restraint in her to drop her arm to her side, teeth clenched. "Thought not," he said, then spat at her feet through the bars.

Barrat dashed down the steps, shaking his head as he went. Angela took a deep breath through her nose before following him. Downstairs in the dim yellow light, he began searching through the wall of crates marked with names and handed one of them to Angela.

"Take this up there," he said.

"No," Angela said. She placed the crate on a table and stepped next to Barrat. "Where's my stuff?"

"Oh, no," he said shaking his head. "I need you here."

"Barrat, there's no way I'm staying in here. I'd be much more helpful out there."

She pulled down a crate with a brass plaque that read "Angela Ma'at," set it on the floor, and pulled out her armor.

Barrat stood over her, watching for a moment. "Angela," he said calmly. "I can't let you go out there."

Angela paused. "This is my choice."

"Think about what's already happened. The incident with your speech. Your *orders* to learn the armory under me. Stay here. Do you really want to risk it getting worse than that buffoon upstairs calling you names and provoking you?"

Angela bit her lip. She had wished that Barrat wouldn't say anything about what had happened at the speech. "Thanks for caring, but I can handle myself."

His dark brown eye was soft and sincere when he said, "I know you're going through something. Do you really think things are going to get better if you keep sticking your nose into trouble? You need peace and quiet, not—"

She held up her palm, cutting him off. "Don't worry about me. I'll honor my restrictions and leave the tether gun and clamp here."

Barrat raised his hands in the air, irate. "Very well, if you feel that's what you have to do." The stocky man grumbled and turned his back to her without another word.

She strapped the cuirass and greaves loosely over her other clothes, then secured the pauldrons to her shoulders, arranged the wires on her tool belt, fastened the batteries where they belonged, and threw the pack onto her back. The crystal inside the porthole of her shifter was blue, and she thought about asking for a red one but decided against it. If all she could do was incapacitate, distract, or be an extra set of eyes, she would do just that without complaint.

Tightening all of the equipment onto her body took another moment, and when Angela was satisfied, she glided up the steps, back to the main level. The crowd still lingered on the other side of the bars, and with a quick press of the button underneath the counter, she stepped out before reaching back inside to press it a second time. Eyes weighed on her heavily, and the man she almost slugged scoffed at her.

On the Ascendancy's grass, she reached for her lower back and ripped straps from the bottom of her backpack, taking the controller in her left hand. The four-foot cord pulled out of the bottom without a snag, and she pressed a blue button. The bag made a cranking sound, and she jolted as the metal frame of her wings unfolded and burst out to a span of twelve feet. In a single stroke, the linen webbing caught wind, and Angela lifted off the ground. With each press of a button, she soared upward and the city grew smaller below her.

It was her and the wind, nothing else. As far as Angela could tell, she was the first person to spring into action— and the only one in the sky.

Best-case scenario, I beat everyone to the Dalkhu, cripple it so that it can't concentrate enough to teleport me to my death, or flee. I'll hide it somewhere and force it to decipher the scroll under the couch. Hopefully whatever it can tell me will point me in the right direction.

The gloves were off, she decided. No matter the cost, Angela wasn't going to crawl through the remainder of her life with someone else's soul inside her. She shuddered at the thought. The whole situation was sick and twisted, and she vowed that nothing would hold her back.

A small blip moved between a metal-roofed shack and a much larger warehouse. The tiny dot was a barely identifiable outline of a person, and he—or she—slunk to the building's main door, stood there for a moment, then moved on. Without any conscious effort, Angela had already begun gliding closer to the person. The stranger rounded the corner of the warehouse and moved along its perimeter.

A thief? There are no flames at all.

For a moment, the figure vanished from her sight as she neared the building, and then it reappeared on the other end next to a different door. Angela was grateful that it was a relatively windy day; otherwise, the person would have heard her wings beating.

Maybe the person is taking advantage of the alarm's distraction, Angela thought.

The closer she dropped to the figure below, the clearer her sight became. It was a man, and he was dressed in black robes.

Wait, Angela thought. *If I have the soul of a Dalkhu inside me, then I wouldn't see the flame of his soul. We're the same…*

Angela dropped, refusing to flap her wings as vertigo filled her stomach with bubbles and the ground raced closer. She pictured herself splattered across the brass platform like a dropped jar of tomato paste. Yet she waited, knowing that if she could surprise the Dalkhu, injure him enough, he wouldn't be able to get away or hurt her.

I'm so stupid! I should have guessed I wouldn't see his flames!

The fall dragged on, and her insides clenched. Her fingers twitched, slamming the button when her feet reached the top of the warehouse roof. The sudden thrust of the wings jolted her downward, and the backpack's straps slid up under her armpits. The gust of wind blew the Dalkhu's hood off, and he looked up into her eyes. His head was shaved bald, and black scruff grew from his chin. His jaw dropped, and her boots crashed into his shoulders.

The Dalkhu grunted as he fell onto his back. Angela

smashed onto her side beside him. The crash hurt, but Angela hadn't taken the brunt of the blow. She was quick to bolt upright and place a foot on his chest. She discarded the controller, letting it hang from her pack, and took hold of the brass knuckles on her belt.

His eyes rolled as his wits came about him, then snapped open. He reached into his robe to grab something, and Angela bent at the knees and swung downward, but as her fist met his chest, his curved knife sliced the crease of her elbow. Angela winced, then tried to strike him again. The Dalkhu, far more adept than she had anticipated, pushed off the ground with his leg and shook, forcing Angela to step off him before she lost her balance. He kicked her feet, jarring her one solidly placed foot, and she tumbled to the ground.

The Dalkhu sprinted toward the corner of the warehouse. By the time Angela was upright, he was already twenty feet from her and slowing to a jog. Then he stopped entirely and glanced back at her quizzically.

"You're her," he said. "You're the unlucky Anunnaki woman."

Angela winced as she began walking toward the Dalkhu, still gripping the brass knuckles in her fingers. "What do you mean?"

The Dalkhu shrugged. "I see you've still got a head about you. Haven't completely lost it yet. You're holding on very well, actually, but if answers are what you want, I suggest you take me someplace safe. I only seek asylum here."

Angela stopped a few feet away from him, just close enough that she could lurch forward and hit him quickly if she needed to. He knew enough about her to allude to what was happening, which was already much more than she had hoped to gain from the encounter. As odd as it was to speak with a Dalkhu not cloaked in flames, let alone trust him enough to not kill her, she needed to know what he knew.

"Asylum?"

He nodded.

Angela motioned for him to move. Maybe getting him to read the scroll would be easier than she thought.

The Dalkhu smirked and began to jog, and Angela followed. The sun revolved enough that it was less than a quarter until prismal time, which meant soon more people would be out on the streets. The only problem was that she wasn't sure where she should lead him. Obviously, not her house or anywhere she would normally have access to.

"We need to get somewhere inside," Angela said between steady breaths.

"I agree. Is there a name I may call you by?"

"I'm Angela." She pointed at a warehouse across the brass and steel platforms. It was almost like they were running across the top of a shimmering sea. "What about you?"

The Dalkhu gauged her expression and weighed something in his mind. "Shedim," he said.

This building was shorter and plagued with cracks in the foundation and up into the mortar between the stones. They passed a broken window, and the inside was stuffed with metal racking and dusty boxes. It looked abandoned, which wasn't surprising when she considered how far on the outskirts of the city they were, and that was enough justification for Angela to try to break in. They rounded the corner and a faint *rumble* started in her chest. The feeling progressed until she felt rather off-beat somehow, but she didn't have to puzzle over it for long; tiny fingers of flame began to peek through the cracks in the stone bricks and the seams of the metal plating beneath her. She jumped away from the fire spreading from the building, bit her lip, and steeled herself.

"You're going to have to get used to that," Shedim said in a matter-of-fact tone.

Angela scoffed as she stopped in front of a door half-covered in fire. "I believe otherwise." Even though he was seeing his own flames, he acted as though he was invulnerable to them. Sweat beaded on her forehead as she reached for the black iron handle as quickly as she could, yanked, then released it with a yelp.

She shook her hand furiously and asked, "How do you know about me?"

Shedim didn't answer for a moment as he considered something. "I was there," he finally said.

"What?"

"You know what I said. I played a part in what has happened to you."

A memory from the attack on Earth resurfaced. She took a step closer to Shedim. "You," Angela said, pointing a finger. "You were the one with the cup, weren't you?"

Shedim patted his right thigh. "And the one you shot."

Her lip curled. "You worlds-damned—" She swung without a thought, fist landing straight in his chest and forcing the air from his lungs. He hit the ground and lay there for a moment, wheezing as she considered hitting him again.

"I know it was a possession spell."

He raised his eyebrows, still huffing.

"I've seen a scroll. It said something about transferring one's soul and taking over another's body."

Still, he didn't speak.

Angela considered the possibility that she had read it

wrong, but she was growing tired of his silence either way, and she loomed over him with a closed fist. "It destroys the original soul. Am I close? How did you do it?"

"Two problems with your statements," Shedim said as his breath began to catch again. "Firstly, I had no part in the spell's ritual. Secondly, the effect wasn't a possession, even though that was the aim." He pushed himself to his knees. "Your soul isn't destroyed. I know exactly where it is, and if you hit me again, I will kill you."

Angela froze. She wanted to believe it, but she also didn't want to fall for a lie. "My soul is alive?"

Shedim rose to his feet. "My"—he paused—"*former* master has it. Your souls were only swapped. Now, if you would, kindly." He pointed at the building.

Angela wasn't sure what to say, so she simply turned and smashed the bottom of her boot into the door with a *thud*. It croaked in its frame, and on the second blow, it burst inward. Rows of metal shelving stuffed with a haphazard array of wooden crates lined the inside of the building. It was dingy and unlit inside, but only one of the sections of racking appeared aflame.

It would have to do, Angela deemed, and she jaunted through the threshold of fire. She waited for Shedim to enter the building behind her, then asked, "How do I get it back?"

The Dalkhu chuckled deeply and knocked his knuckles against one of the wooden crates. "Get what back? Your soul?"

"Obviously. Tell me how and I won't inform my superiors I've met you or tell them where you are."

He shook his head, a smile still lingering. "You don't understand. You *can't* get it back."

Angela pointed as she stepped forward. "*You* don't

understand. This is getting out of my control. It's ruining my life, and I know that you don't care about me, but I will break your knees if you don't help me cast that spell again."

He shrugged as he walked past her. "I don't doubt you would try, but listen, swapping souls with my master was an *accident*. Even if you were to recomplete the ritual I doubt it would have the same effect. I have no idea what went awry in the first place. To try and twist it to get a specific result—*this* mistake—is impossible."

"We'll see about that," Angela said. "Where is your master?"

Shedim chuckled. "Probably in the lower tunnels of Kur, or Earth, if you truly care to know. When I threatened to confess the crimes he had committed to his fellow councilmen, he went berserk and tried to kill me like he did his other pupil. Considering the spectacle he created the last time I was in Kur, I'd imagine that he's fled from the Council."

"Why would he flee his own Council?"

Shedim laughed loudly. "You don't have the slightest idea how things work, do you? It's a war spell. The Council forbade that spell—and others—centuries ago, knowing that the use of them would start an all-out war between Dingir and Kur. My former, Udug Hul, has no home now."

Angela rubbed her temples. "Why are you seeking asylum in Dingir, though? Wouldn't you be worse off here than on Earth?"

Shedim sighed. "I have betrayed a very dangerous *councilman*. Udug has more skill and cunning than anyone I've ever met. I can't hide on Earth because he'll likely find me there and I cannot return to Kur for that same reason. Until the Council catches him, I'm being hunted for exposing him, and what better place to hide than under the noses of his enemies?"

Angela nodded. "Good to know, I—"

"Here!"

Angela jumped. A man stood at the doorway, pointing at her. Flames of red and orange waved to her, unfurling from the spaces between leather padding and shrouding his entire silhouette. Beneath the fire, he was an Uri Gallu.

They sprinted farther into the warehouse, dodging the hissing steel spike of a tether gun as they rounded the corner of a row of shelves. They ran, turning again and again, but boot steps followed them no matter which direction they took through the maze.

"Enough," Shedim said. He stopped and gazed into her eyes for a long moment. "Good luck."

"Wait, what?" Angela asked.

Shedim closed his eyes, then vanished from sight.

Dammit!

The concussive burst of wind from his teleportation struck Angela, and she staggered back. Her eardrums screamed a high-pitched tone and she felt like she was going to throw up, but she steadied herself and focused. The shouting was louder now. The Uri Gallus were so close.

Heart racing in her chest, she reached out with her mind and touched the veil. With a flick of her wrist, she powered the shifter at her waist, formed her mental picture, and sharpened her mind. The device crackled with electricity and vibrated. The footsteps were closing in on her, and the last thing she felt was a breeze on her cheek before she lurched headfirst between the worlds and disappeared.

Everything in the warehouse grew quiet. The Uri Gallu who fired his gun and missed by only a few inches cursed.

People began chattering to one another about the presence of the second Dalkhu, their surprise that it was a woman, and how rare that was. They detested the knowledge that it would likely be some time before they had another chance to catch the flamed invaders.

The soldiers began to trickle out of the building with their heads down. But Michael, who stood on weary legs between the rows of metal and wooden crates, stared blankly at where the Dalkhu had been just a few moments ago.

Half to himself, half to the world that never seemed to listen, he asked, "Was that Angela?"

CHAPTER EIGHT

Michael paced the length of the hallway, then went into the kitchen, returned to the bedroom, and sat on the floor. His fingers found his curls and he rested his elbows on his legs. He couldn't wrap his head around it, couldn't make up his mind about what he thought he just saw. The woman, the *Dalkhu* woman, was standing right in front of him just long enough for him to catch the gist of her flame-cloaked outline. She was a bit on the short side and favored her left leg, and there were vague shapes of armor underneath all that fire.

Michael rose from the floor and marched toward the kitchen.

If there was just some way I could verify that it wasn't Angela…

He paused in the living room. The general outline of the Dalkhu, and Angela's admittedly odd behavior, clicked in Michael's mind. The scratches, the unusual amount of distance between them, and the constant pain that she appeared to be in.

What if there's a connection? Why hasn't she told me about it?

Michael yelled and kicked at the sofa, mad at himself for even being suspicious of her. His foot landed on the bench, knocking it over and sending the cushions to the floor. After a few moments of slow breathing, he released his fist and opened his eyes, then pulled the couch back upright.

Behind it, he stooped and picked up the cushions from the floor and placed them back where they belonged. Just when he thought he was finished, he heard a crinkle as he turned.

He picked up a torn piece of parchment from beneath his boot.

A scroll?

He settled himself on the couch and tried to read it, but the scroll was written in a crude dialect too old for him to understand much of. Occasionally, he could glimpse bits of information and fragments of sentences. When he read over it twice and he could learn no more from it, he took a deep breath.

It makes sense. I understand. And, Angela, I'm so sorry.

Michael curled himself on the bench's cushions and wept.

A part of him had wanted to point the blame at something for Angela's condition. Knowing that his wife hadn't simply lost her mind gave him a sense of saddened relief. She wasn't insane; she was *dead*, and as horrible as that was, it felt better to know that she wasn't in misery. As much as the dots appeared to connect, he knew that this spell and the signs she was showing wasn't something to make assumptions about, so he rerolled the scroll and tucked it into the pocket on his cuirass.

A PINE ROCKING CHAIR SAT ON THE OTHER SIDE OF THE room. The scent of tree nut, the body-forming squishiness of red cushions, and the itch of the brown blanket draped over her were the first things she noticed. Angela lay alone in the quiet room, unable to remember what happened or how she had gotten there.

A small desk in the corner held an inkwell with the quill still standing upright inside it. A map was pinned to the wall, and an open window let the cold breeze wisp through the silk curtains. Despite the room's small size, there were two massive bookshelves on both ends of the sofa she lay on. Curious, Angela sat herself upright and rose on wobbly, aching legs.

She teetered as she approached the desk and leaned on the wall for support, almost feeling woozy. A row of stacked papers three inches thick lined the floor next to the desk. There were four, and each stack was held down with a brass sphere to defend against the wind from the open window.

Angela bent at her knees and removed one of the paper-weights, and her eyes grew wide as she read the title page, "*Heaven's Burst*, written by L.A. Matta." Somehow, she had awoken in the study of one of her favorite authors, and in a moment's notice she was tearing through the novel's first hand-written paragraph.

Then, something stopped her. The pieces in front of her were probably unfinished and unedited. By reading them, she was not only doing herself a disservice, but the author as well. With companion pieces to some of her favorite series lying right in front of her, secrets and dreams in the form of words, she loathed her own ethics.

She knew well enough that given the appropriate amount of time the stories in front of her would be told the way they were intended to be told. Rather than jumping in and stealing an incomplete experience that the author would likely change in some way or another, it would be best to wait for them to be released properly. She sighed and began reassembling the stack how she had found it.

The books that lined the shelves varied wildly in terms of topic; most were encyclopedias, dictionaries, and old tales while a few were fictional stories that she recognized. It was such an odd selection, but the sheer number of books, being almost twice as many as Angela had acquired over the years, impressed her.

The doorknob to the study rattled and turned. Then the door swung open. A man entered, and they caught sight of one another and stopped what they were doing. Red-hot liquid of melted doorknob leaked between his fingers, and footprints of fire scorched the wooden floor behind him like brands. His eyes were a strange milky mixture of blue and red, twinkling under the light of the flames that his soul produced.

His eyelids shut, and Angela considered jumping through the open window, but his appearance began to change. A sheet of tranquility blanketed the chaos of burning flames, which slowly dwindled and gave way until she could make out features of a man's face. Angela's jaw dropped; it was Donny.

He opened his eyes again. "Ah," he said, holding his mug to his chest. "It's you. I almost sprung a leak. I was afraid you were someone else for a second there."

Angela stuttered as she tried to speak, then reached out to touch his arm, but he jerked away.

"Don't touch me. You'll break my concentration."

Angela crossed her arms. "Concentration of what?"

He tapped his sternum a few times. "Suppressing my soul to keep things calm between us. Don't worry, though: I haven't done anything to you, and even though it seems we're one 'n' the same, don't touch me. It'll still hurt."

Angela nodded slowly, and she had a hard time forming her thoughts into sentences. It now appeared that Donny was a man she knew very little about. Truly, she felt ashamed to believe he lived the simple life she assumed. He was an author behind closed doors, a working member of the Dubah, and someone else entirely.

A sudden rush of nausea bubbled in her gut. Angela held a hand over her mouth and felt her stomach clench tight enough to form a diamond out of coal. She hunched over and steeled herself, afraid to begin a fit of dry heaving.

"Come on," Donny said, stepping forward. "Sit down, please." He motioned to the couch.

For nearly five minutes, Angela sat completely motionless, her hand still locking her jaw shut. Donny set his steaming cup of what she guessed was tea on the end table next to the rocking chair and sat.

"Did you find what you were looking for?" he asked.

Angela could only nod.

Donny sighed. "I'm sorry."

Angela swallowed. "It's all right," she said, breathing slowly as her stomach settled. "How did you quell your soul's flame? How are you not like everyone else?"

Donny intertwined his fingers on his stomach. "I told you before: I learned a lot on Earth in those two years. This is simply the fruition of meditation, self-control, and suppressing my own soul's aura. Unfortunately, I can't change what you see out there." He motioned toward the window. "But you'll see me as I am, and I will see you." He smiled.

Angela allowed herself to relax on the couch and let her eyes wander about the room as she thought of something to say. There was a moment of silence when neither of them knew where to lead the conversation. Angela hated the awkwardness.

She pointed to the desk, a grin across her face. "L.A. Matta, huh?"

Donny's voice shook. "Yeah."

"Love your books."

He picked up his cup from the end table and brought it onto his lap. "Thank you," he said, but he wouldn't look at her.

"I've always thought you were an Etlu. Your descriptions are so vivid that I knew you had to have been to Earth."

Donny shrugged.

"Do you ever wish you could go back?"

"Sometimes, but all that is behind me. Too chaotic there."

Angela beamed. "That's what makes it great. Somehow it's still beautiful."

Donny kept his gaze on the floor as he took a sip from his cup, and there was another long moment of silence. She knew what was coming, but wasn't ready for it.

He scooted forward in his rocking chair and rested his elbows on his knees, cradling his cup in his hand. "Look, I know this is probably the safest you've felt in a while, but you can't stay here for long."

His words felt like a shot to the chest.

"It's just... I've finally got my own life calmed down. I can't do much for you, and the fact that you teleported into my home tells me you were on the run before you came here."

"I know," Angela admitted. "It's just…" She paused.

"Just what?"

"I can't let Michael see me anymore." Her jaw began to shudder. She frowned, and her eyes grew teary as she choked up.

"Angela," he said, getting on his knees and scooting closer. He kept just far enough away that they didn't touch each other. "Don't say that."

"It's true." Tears began to run down her lips. "I was chased, Donny. They didn't know it was me. They could have killed me, and I don't even know what to do."

Donny fumbled over his tongue and carefully handed Angela his tea, which she took with both hands and held in her lap. "Listen, it isn't over until you let it be, you hear?" He stretched and tugged the blanket on the end of the sofa over her shoulders. "Just because you don't know what to do next or where you're going doesn't mean there's nothing you can do about it."

With the blanket as a buffer, he began awkwardly rubbing the sides of her arms, and Angela began to feel embarrassed for crying. She wiped her face dry and took a deep breath.

"How did you know?" she asked, struggling to keep her voice steady.

"Know what?"

"How did you know that I had this… Dalkhu's soul inside me?"

Donny shook his head. "I didn't, and it horrifies me to hear that's what happened." He shrugged. "I could just tell that something was different about you that day. More of a hunch that some kind of spell had taken hold over you than anything. There weren't many other options I could think of that would explain how your whole attitude, your *life,* changed for you so quickly."

She took another deep breath and tried the tea. It wasn't great.

Donny raised an eyebrow. "How do you know that you have a Dalkhu's soul in you?"

Angela slowly pushed herself to her feet and faced the desk in the corner. "I found a scroll and a Dalkhu who said so."

"Oh."

"It's just... I don't know what to do. I have no knowledge of anything involving spells, and I doubt I could find anyone willing to show me."

"I used to know someone." Donny stepped around her and walked to his desk. He pulled the tacks from the corners of the map on the wall, placed it on the desk, and grabbed the pen from the inkwell. He scribbled on it for a minute, then held it up to her when he was finished.

His fingers circled the entire map. "This is a region northwest of Akkad." He pointed to a circle drawn in black ink. "Last I knew, and this was years ago, the man that helped me when I was stuck on Earth for two years lived north of this tiny seaside village. I can't promise he'll be there, but if you find him and tell him that I sent you there, I imagine that he'd help you, too."

Donny looked deeply at her. He had a sense of sincerity about him that Angela hadn't seen in a long while, even in Michael. "His name is Teshub."

Angela sighed and looked at the map again. "Thank you, Donny." She put her hand on the parchment. "But I can't leave Dingir."

Donny furrowed his brow. "Take it." He hastily folded the map and held it up to her. "Just take it anyway."

Angela could see his agitation. She took the map out of respect and tucked it neatly into the pocket on her cuirass.

"Like he did for me so long ago, he can help you learn to control that soul," Donny said.

"No," Angela said, shaking her head. "I don't want to control it. I want to be rid of it."

Donny sighed, and they gauged each other for a moment. There was an unspoken fondness between them. She could feel it, but all she could do was walk toward the door.

"Where are you going?" he asked, following her.

"I'm going to find that Dalkhu and make him talk. He took part in the spell that did this to me."

"What are you going to do if he doesn't help you?"

She shrugged and turned to look over her shoulder. "Worst case, I'm going to say goodbye to Michael."

Donny sighed and didn't say another word as he relaxed the part of his mind keeping his own soul's aspect at bay. Slowly, he grew alight with flame again, and she walked outside.

CHAPTER NINE

Michael hung his shifter on his belt and marched up the Ascendancy's steps. He barged through the main doors, turned left around the corner, found the office he was looking for, and knocked brazenly on the door.

"Come in," a muffled voice from the other side said.

He took one big breath before turning the latch and stepping inside the room and shutting the door behind him. Ja'noel sat between piles of papers on his messy desk. Kushiel stood over his shoulder.

"Ja'noel," Michael said, throwing a fist across his chest. "I need to speak with you."

"Can it wait?" he asked, leaning back in his chair. He looked exhausted. "I've got two dozen reports to sift through and compile into one summary, soldiers to question, and now there's two Dalkhu to find."

"It's—" Michael stuttered and felt a lump in his throat. "It's about Angela. I think something's happened to her that will explain everything."

The older men looked at him in silence for a moment,

thinking, until Kushiel said, "We have time to hear it." He glanced down at Ja'noel and stood upright, placing his hands at his waist. "I can be informed of these developments, too?"

Michael furrowed his brow. "I'd prefer to speak with my own Grand alone."

"Well, if it's a matter of safety, then I need to know, too."

Michael growled under his breath, then took a seat across the desk. His mind began to spin, and part of him felt like a traitor, even though he knew it was the right thing to do. "There's—" Michael stopped. He couldn't bring himself to speak it out loud. He reached into his pocket and placed the scroll on the desk. Ja'noel snatched it up immediately and began unfurling it.

"Where did you get this?" Ja'noel asked. "You know these are forbidden, for love's sake."

Michael buried his face in his palms and rubbed his eyes. "I found it in my home."

"How was it there?" Kushiel asked, scanning the scroll over Ja'noel's shoulder.

"I don't know, but it—" Michael choked, took a deep breath, and laid his hands back on his lap. "It explains so much."

He gave the Grands a moment of silence to read, and when they were finished, they looked to each other, then to Michael, silent and dumbfounded.

In a low tone, Kushiel asked, "You think she's been possessed by a Dalkhu?"

Michael nodded. A tear streaked down his cheek, and his knuckles turned white.

"But the scroll says, 'The caster of the spell projects his mind and soul to the victim, overpowering and destroying the original occupant's soul.' Does that mean—"

"Angela's dead," Michael said. His chest rose and fell as he sobbed. To think that someone from another world killed her and took her place at his side was terrifying, provoking, and infuriating. Did the moments they just shared together mean nothing? Realizing it wasn't Angela that he'd kissed that morning, he kicked the desk in front of him.

"Stop," Ja'noel commanded.

"Every last bit of her is dead!" Michael kicked it again, snapping the wooden backing. "Perverted!" He jumped to his feet, whipped the chair into the wall with one hand, and watched it shatter into pieces. He kicked the seat a third time, then stomped. Suddenly, the fire in his veins ceased, and he could stand it no longer.

He fell to his knees and cried.

In a moment, Kushiel walked to his side and placed a hand on his shoulder. "I am so sorry," he said. "If it helps, I want you to know that you don't have to do anything about this. You can go home, if you like."

Michael slapped his hand from his shoulder and stared at the broken chair in front of him blankly. The tears had slowed and dried. His breathing was even again, and it was simple to him now: his wife hadn't lost her mind; vile people too cowardly to fight directly had subjugated her. They stole his wife from him and killed her, and the mind and soul of the person who did it resided in Angela's body. "No. I'll bring the Dalkhu in. I'll get it to talk."

THE FIRST THING ON ANGELA'S MIND WAS FINDING SHEDIM,

the Dalkhu who told her that he had seen the ritual take place in person. She would capture him, stow him away in a hole somewhere, then begin gathering the components or whatever was needed to recreate the spell tucked underneath the couch at home. If it didn't work, as Shedim had said, she'd try again and again until things were the way they were supposed to be and she had her soul back.

The hallucinations of aether-flame were everywhere she went and around every person. Dingir had changed from a city of metal to a city of rolling fires. Occasionally, the flames reached higher than the buildings in the alleyways she traversed. Some seemed to follow her, and others herded her in directions she didn't want to go. But she kept to the quietest parts of the city and slowly made her way through block after block and searched for most of the day with no rest, determined to find Shedim.

The sun cast the shadows of two large apartment complexes over her. It was already reaching the spectral hour, and she began to question her methods. Soon, even the less traveled streets and alleys would be busy. She wasn't ready to end her search yet, but she needed to stay hidden. It didn't feel right to stop when she had just found something to go after. So from that alleyway in the outskirts of Dingir, she began to head toward her home.

Angela sprinted across streets, vaulted over fences, and hid behind generators and homes when people were near. Eventually, she reached the doorstep of her home without being seen and fumbled through her pockets until she found the key. As soon as she got through the door, she locked it behind her again.

In the bedroom, she scoured the closet and found a thick red scarf and grabbed rough leather gloves from the top of the dresser. In Michael's room, among the various metalworking tools and slabs of in-the-works knickknacks and toys, she found a pair of tinted goggles. A shabby green knit hat hanging by the door served to cover her forehead and hair. While she was there, she headed for the sofa and pulled the first cushion off, then quizzically removed the second. She lay on her stomach and looked underneath the couch. There was nothing there, and she wondered if she had moved the scroll and just couldn't remember. Part of her knew that she hadn't, and she didn't want to think about what could have happened to the parchment.

It wasn't in the closet or underneath the sink. It wasn't anywhere. More than likely, Michael had found it. The thought worried her, and all she could do was hope that Michael would dismiss it as her being nosy and looking for more reading material and more knowledge, but she knew it would be worse. She hadn't been particularly open with him, and there was nothing she could do about it now besides ask for forgiveness when it was all over. It would be some time before she saw Michael again, and being there in their house, alone, rummaging through their things and reminiscing on their lives thus far, brought bittersweet feelings. It wasn't the end, Angela knew. But that didn't make it any easier or make it hurt her any less.

She would fix it. All Angela needed was time and she would be back to explain everything to him. He would understand. Talking to him about it now would only complicate things between them, and it was better for him not to be involved. If she died trying to cast the spell, so be it, as long as she wasn't remembered as the woman turned Dalkhu. She wanted Michael to remember her as his wife, the Anunnaki.

She tidied the home, removing all traces that she had been there, and then double-checked her work again.

Without the scroll, things would be a lot trickier for her. Angela knew that she would have to rely on Shedim's memory of the spell or re-obtain the scroll or a copy of it.

No big deal, she thought as she looked at herself in the mirror. Most of her skin had now been covered with cloth, and only small portions of the corners around her eyes were visible. *I will get there one way or another.*

She unlocked the door, and a cool breeze blew into the house. A fog, or more accurately a cloud, had settled over her home. From the doorstep, she couldn't even see the metal fence that divided her property from the neighbor's, only mist. The moment the outside air touched her clothes, the moisture of the cloud clung to her. Sleeping on the streets would freeze her to the bone, and the reduced visibility would certainly make it harder to find Shedim, but she could not find the patience to stay.

Angela stepped down from the doorstep, locked her home behind her, and passed through the fog until she came to the street. After visualizing the roads in her head, she guessed which direction she wanted and began walking. After nearly five minutes of clinging to the side of the road, afraid to veer from her only visible marker, the cloud had still not thinned.

Must be a large one, she thought.

She heard the faint sound of footsteps closing in from ahead, and the fog began to flicker as it turned yellow and orange. Angela froze. The glow grew brighter and wider until she could see the faint silhouettes of two figures walking toward her. She dashed across the street as fast as her legs could carry her.

"Hey!" a man's voice cried, distorted and warbled.

Angela kept running.

"Did you see that?" a second voice asked.

"Who's there?" the first asked aloud.

Angela's heavy boots were too loud out in the open, and she narrowly avoided ramming headfirst into a building that broke through the fog at the last second. She jolted to the side, spinning around the corner and nearly twisting her ankle.

"Stop!" a voice called from the mist. The heavy clomp of a soldier's boots persisted behind her as she ran.

They can hear my footsteps, but it's not like I can stop running!

The narrow alleyway split off into three directions, and none of the paths looked familiar. She wasn't sure which direction to head, and there were no dumpsters or doors for her to hide behind. They would chase her until the fog cleared or she ran out of it and was seen anyway. But an iron manhole cover sat in the center of the intersection, and a thought sparked.

Under the city. Of course!

Angela rushed to it, jammed two fingers into the small opening around the outer edge, and lifted the heavy lid to the side. She dropped her legs inside the hole. Her feet found the ladder and she climbed down. When her head was clear, she tugged the cover back into place and paused to listen.

A few minutes passed on that ladder without so much as the sound of a footstep permeating the layers of metal above her. Beneath her feet, tufts of white fluff seemed to flow like a river of cotton. Astoundingly, the cloud was large enough to be beneath the city as well. She smiled, thinking the sight rather unique and new, and began her descent into it.

Angela placed her feet on grated metal. Railings, covered with thin layers of ice and snow-like crystals, ran up to the middle of her waist. Wind, unhindered by buildings, flexed and bounced off the catwalk beneath her. The only thing between her and an endless fall into the blue sky below was thin metal and bolts that could shear at any moment. The thought made her uneasy.

Even as the fog cleared, she found that she could only see so far. Pipes and bundles of cables hung loosely from the platforms and seemed to be affixed to something only when they had to be. Regardless, she moved forward, constantly keeping her head on the move and trying and catch new angles between the mess of things beneath the city. The catwalk led her to a T-intersection, and she turned left.

As time went on, she came to realize that the catwalks and intersections were nothing other than a maze. There were no signs, either written or landmarks, to point her in any vague direction. The sky was only shades of blue, and the sun was not low enough to show her which way she was facing or give her a way to measure time.

All Angela could do was wander the hanging corridors, blustered by the harsh wind that tore through her moist clothing, in the hopes of eventually finding someplace to take refuge. A black tank nearly twenty feet deep hung just an arm's reach from the catwalk railing. Angela held out a hand to touch it; it was warm. A faint sound like bubbling emanated from it, and then the smell of burning garbage flooded her nostrils.

Trash boiler, she thought, disgusted.

Angela plugged her nose and left, and in the distance, something large and pointy hung from beneath the city. She navigated through the turns and twists of the catwalks and saw that its color wasn't the usual gray iron or glossy brass of Dingir. The downward spike was made of jagged rock, and she realized that she was headed for the central mass of Dingir just beneath the Ascendancy.

When she walked on the metal platforms above, she had no idea of the immense size of the natural landmass. The rock had been hidden away by the platforms Dingir lived on, and support beams were anchored in the stone. It was almost as though the city was founded on a mountain that had been cut at the bottom, flipped upside down, and left to levitate in the sky.

"You're the first person I've seen in about six hours."

Angela turned. The hooded man tugged his robes tighter around his waist and leaned his back against a beam. Shedim shivered and said, "It's quite dull down here, to be honest." He pushed off the support beam and cursed. "Can't stay warm, and excitement, as bad as it may be for me, seems rather appetizing."

"Shedim, we need to talk," Angela said.

He looked at her quizzically and shrugged. "Then speak, but let us get out of the wind, at a minimum." He turned and started walking, his sandals slapping against the grated floor with faint twangs. Angela followed him.

"Where?" she asked when she reached his side.

"There's a few storage rooms closer to the rock. The groaning noises they make are quite eerie, but I feel the warmth is worth the risk of falling." Shedim glanced at her from under his hood. Only his nose and one eye were visible. "What do you wish to talk about?"

Angela removed the goggles from her face, and she rubbed the rings around her eyes gently. "I'm afraid you won't care for me any more than what little you probably do, but I demand that you help me recast the spell your master did."

Shedim laughed and stopped in place. "I told you it can't be done. Why do you not believe this?"

Angela caught a bit of nervousness in his laugh, and it only strengthened her conviction. "You don't understand. I have no one else to turn to. If the spell was done before, we can do it a second time. I can't keep living like this."

Shedim shook his head. "You'd have to be trained, and I'd be risking my own life. As much as I enjoy your company down here, if this is what you came to talk with me about, then I have to request that you go away." He shooed her with his wrists and walked past her.

Angela didn't want it to come to this, but she said, "I'll make you help me if I have to."

He spun around and marched up to her. "Is that a threat?" His breath smelled like sour milk.

Angela glared as sternly and uncompromisingly as she could, and she held it there until he got it.

He bore his teeth. "You irritate me. For the last time, I cannot help you."

"I don't believe that," Angela said.

"You would be the one that has to cast the spell, Angela, and that requires that you have complete control over your mind and the soul inside you. It would take *years* of training. You'd have better luck forcing Udug to cast it than doing it yourself."

As they stared into each other's eyes, Angela weaved her fingers through the brass knuckles at her waist and gripped them tightly.

"I think you underestimate my strength and desire, Shedim. Besides, I have you here, right now."

His lip curled. "You really are a good example of how ignorant your people are, aren't you? Get out of my sight."

Shedim closed his eyes, and he stood motionless for a

few seconds before Angela realized what he was doing. She swung upward as quickly as possible and pressed the button on her shifter at the same time. A deafening boom pounded against her chest, and she hung between the veils for what felt like an hour. But in reality, she reappeared a fraction of a second later, and Shedim opened his eyes.

The shifter at Angela's waist hummed loudly and cast a faint blue light through the viewport. Shedim cringed and pushed harder, and Angela disappeared from the catwalk a second time. Even in the frozen space between worlds, she pushed her left arm to swing and fought the stasis.

Shedim faltered and she reappeared right in front of him again. Her fist moved six inches closer to his chest before she disappeared. Angela reappeared a third time, and the arcs of electricity on her brass knuckles sparked only half a foot from Shedim's face. A cold sweat beaded on his forehead. His expression contorted in agony and rage as he concentrated on pushing her away, and she disappeared again.

The sounds of thunder beating on Angela's eardrums brought a constant ringing. But she knew she was on a winning streak. Every time she overpowered Shedim's push and broke back through the veil, she swung a little bit closer. It was only a matter of time before she made contact with him and he fell to the ground, spasming uncontrollably.

But a part of her worried that her batteries wouldn't last long enough. She had already used a good amount of charge from her flight earlier that morning, and even in the space between worlds, where time held no one or anything to its rules, she was still using energy to fight Shedim's push.

So like a catfish's feelers prodding along the bottom of

a river, Angela reached outward with her mind and followed the oblong torrent that was Shedim's mind, then grabbed ahold of him as tightly as she could. She pushed the soul inside her, funneling its wicked energy and the shifter's remaining power to pull Shedim from the catwalk.

The crash of air against them echoed throughout the city and knocked the wind from their lungs. Shedim's jaw dropped. They were falling fifty feet above the Ascendancy, and Angela smiled. The ornamental brass spikes on the Ascendancy's roof grew closer. Shedim whipped his arms and legs, trying to control his spin, but no matter how he flailed, he couldn't stop himself.

Angela shut down her shifter, grabbed the controller at her back, and yanked it free. With the press of a button, the pack on her back erupted open, and she nearly strained her neck at the full stopping power of the wings' force. After a moment, she regained her orientation, and when she did, she heard screaming. At first, she thought it was Shedim, who lay on the edge of the Ascendancy's angled roof, but it was the cry of a woman on the street below. She pointed and shouted, and within seconds a group of spectators had formed in the streets.

Quickly! Angela thought, and she twisted herself into a dive.

With another thrust of her wings, she landed on the rooftop where Shedim clutched his leg. He moaned in agony and tore scraps from his robe, revealing the wound. The rooftop's brass spike protruded three feet through his calf.

"Could have been your lung," Angela said.

Shedim spat at her. "You have no idea what I am going to do to you."

Gusts of air too strong to be natural wind blew Angela's

hair aside. Uri Gallus with hellfire wings rose and hovered near the edge of the rooftop with tether guns ready to fire.

"Get on your stomach!" they shouted.

Shedim clamped his jaw and breathed through gritted teeth. He howled as he pulled his leg free of the brass spike, tearing the muscle on the back of his leg. Blood spilled down the roof and trickled onto the grass below.

Angela dropped next to him, cringing at the sight of him ripping his own leg free. He screamed and pressed on the wound as Angela held his back upright, horrified at all the blood.

Shedim glanced at the Uri Gallus above them, then twisted to Angela. He grimaced. "Sorry, but I can't let them take me." He wrapped his hand around hers, squeezed down on her thumb, and shoved the sparking brass knuckles onto her leg. Lightning coursed through her, and she dropped with a limp numbness. The brass knuckles fell from her hands and skittered down the red clay shingles.

Seconds before prongs from the tether guns hit him, Shedim rolled and disappeared from the rooftop. The blast blew Angela's hair back. Everything spun around her, and just as she began to feel her fingers move again, a sharp pain tore into her lower back. Every synapsis in her brain fired as the spike embedded itself under her skin and shocked her. She screamed and shook until the current stopped, and she was too tired to force herself upright again.

Gloved hands grabbed her forearms and yanked her wrists behind her. Iron manacles held them there. She was tugged to the edge of the roof, and a boot pushed her over. The tether gun's cable wrapped around her midsection like a snake as she fell, and the ground came to meet her quickly. Her paralyzed lungs burned for air, and she lay there on the lawn and watched the Uri Gallus rush next to her. Under the flames of their souls, their skin was cracked and dry.

They've got me.

The soldiers unbuckled her belt and pulled it out from under her. They unsnapped the pauldrons from her shoulders and the cuirass from her torso. Every shake made the spike cut deeper into her back, but she didn't fight them. She accepted it as they undressed her down to her cotton underclothes right there in front of the crowd on the street. Angela wondered if anyone recognized her through the fires they saw on her, and she felt embarrassed being stripped of everything she'd worked so hard to attain.

Is this how I'm going to be remembered?

Another wave of electricity surged into her. All of her muscles tensed, and she stiffened like a board. They attached a heavy band to her left ankle with a lock and key. It hummed faintly. The device, powered by its own internal battery, was an anchor meant for Dalkhu prisoners. There was no fleeing now.

Angela looked at the crowd, which was bathed in flame like the Uri Gallus and the city beyond. Rolling waves of flame swept over the distant buildings, and she almost laughed. In such a short amount of time, her heaven had become a lot like how she'd imagined hell. Gripping her by the arms, they hoisted her up and dragged her around the Ascendancy and into the double doors of the building.

They went through the corridors of the left wing, past Ja'noel's office, and down a flight of stairs behind a closed door she'd never been through. The walls were rough-cut sheets of metal bolted to supporting frames, and the yellow bulbs that lined the hallway at the bottom flickered occasionally. Angela was pulled past empty cell after empty cell until her captors threw her into a suitable one. The prong was tugged from her back, and the bleeding hole it created was left unpatched. The iron door slammed shut against the prison bars with a *clang*, and she was left there in the dark cold.

Being imprisoned by the people she swore to protect was bittersweet. She had wondered if things would lead to this for quite some time and imagined she'd be treated like any other Dalkhu that had ever been caught in Dingir: interrogated and then given a pair of broken legs before being sent to Kur to ensure that she'd never try to come back. Standard procedure.

Angela chuckled.

The Dalkhu are in for a surprise when I show up. Especially being a woman. I wonder if they'll just assume I was one of them my entire life, or maybe the Council will investigate me, too, and discover that I was the victim of Udug's spell. Maybe they'll help me reverse it.

Angela sighed. Broken legs would be a heavy price to pay.

Her cot's wooden frame seemed to give her splinters every time she touched it. The mattress was straw wrapped in unpleasantly rough burlap, but the dusty cotton blanket was thicker than she imagined it would be. She tossed and turned for at least an afternoon, maybe the whole night, as her mind drowned in a sea of thoughts.

That is, until stomping echoed from down the hallway. The sound grew louder, and then she saw a shadow on the wall before the man himself appeared. It was Michael. Angela was sure of it, even though his figure was cloaked in flame. He was wearing his armor, and he leaned ever so slightly to the side. His right hand was crunched into a fist.

Angela placed her feet on the ground and stared at her toes for a moment.

Where to begin?

"Do you have any idea what you've done?" Michael asked in a low tone.

"I haven't done anything," Angela said for lack of anything better to say.

"Haven't done anything," Michael mocked. He put his hands behind his back and began to pace. "You are bold, even now. What you've done to this city is a blow that will be remembered for ages, certainly." He stopped walking long enough to glare at her. "But it's over. On behalf of my superiors, I am to offer you a deal. Tell me how you did it and you will be returned to your people."

My people?

Angela swallowed. "You... You found the scroll, didn't you?"

He nodded.

Her hands began to tremble as she realized that her husband now believed that the woman in front of him was someone else entirely. She stood and said, "I know what you're thinking right now, and I have to tell you that I'm sorry that I didn't tell you about this sooner."

His fingers wrapped around the metal bars in front of him. Molten iron oozed down and formed a puddle on the floor. She couldn't tell if he was glaring at her or not.

"I thought I could handle this by myself," Angela admitted, "and I didn't want you to see me like this." She felt stupid for finally vocalizing how she felt. "What happened to me on my last mission on Earth, the Dalkhu running around outside, the spell on the scroll, it's all connected. I understand what you must be feeling right now, but you have to believe me when I tell you this: the spell didn't work. I'm still me." Angela began to reach for her chest, then remembered she was still in handcuffs.

"If you're Angela, then why do you look the way you do?" His hand slipped to his side again. "If you're Angela, then why did you run away?" He began to pace the cell again. "If you're Angela, why were you with a Dalkhu?" His hands clenched into fists, and he pounded the cell without recoil. "If you're Angela, then why the fuck did you keep me in the dark?"

"Michael," she said, "my soul's still out there." She wanted to reach out and take his hand.

Michael pressed his nose through the bars. His lip curled. "Stop trying to save yourself. Too much points to your guilt. You violated my wife on a level I cannot tolerate. You intruded into her life and my home. To think I even slept next to you is horrifying." Michael shoved himself away from the bars. "You've started a war between you and me. Despite what my superiors intend to do, I will kill you before you leave this place."

Michael turned and walked down the dim hall.

Half of her didn't believe he really meant what he had said. The other half was nervous.

CHAPTER TEN

Time dragged on in Angela's cell. With no need for food, she'd often go for as many as twelve hours without seeing an Uri Gallu walk down the hall to check that she was still in there. Conversation became something she craved. She wanted to know what was taking so long for Ja'noel and Kushiel to make their way down and speak with her. Her wrists were still bound together. She had attempted to slide her hands through already, but her skin was sore and raw.

Shit, I'd even take the company of an interrogative torture session. It'd at least keep my mind off these walls.

She plopped onto the cot and rested until her mind began to dance the line between consciousness and sleep. Thoughts trickled and filtered through the spaces of her mind until she was on the precipice of actually falling asleep. The bed vibrated and she thought nothing of it. Something settled on her cheeks, and the thought of spiders sparked her alive again. She jolted upright and brushed at her face in a frenzy.

There were wisps of white fog in her cell. A thicker

wave tumbled down the hallway just outside. She wondered if a door had been left open and a cloud had snuck into the Ascendancy and managed to settle all the way down there. The cot shook again, and the floor and walls rumbled as the nuts and bolts that held them vibrated. A second later, the sound of thunder reverberated from down the hall. Dust shook from the cracks between the metal sheets of the cell's ceiling. Another boom tore into Angela's eardrums; it was louder that time, and the prison bars set into the floor rattled violently.

Whatever is going on is huge. I have to get topside.

She pulled her arms apart until the skin on her wrists tore under the pressure of the manacles. She wrenched and flexed every muscle she could until it felt like she was about to pull her own shoulder from its socket, but after five minutes, she was exhausted.

Footsteps raced down the hall. An approaching person lit the hallway like torchlight, and when he came into view, Angela stood upright, beaming from ear to ear.

"Donny! What in the world are you doing here?"

His breathing was heavy, his head swiveling down both hallways, and he held up a finger. "Gimme a second."

He held his breath for a moment, then released it slowly. The flames of his Anunnaki soul dwindled, and she saw him for who he was. He smiled, jingling a ring of keys in his hand.

"That's better," he said.

Donny twisted the key in the cell door until it made a clacking sound. Then he pushed the door open and said, "Wouldn't want to see you any other way."

Angela approached him, intent on giving him the biggest hug he'd probably ever received, but she stopped awkwardly. His nails were caked with brown dirt, and patches of what appeared to be soot had rubbed onto his face and clothes.

"First," Donny said, "I want you to know that I've only ever put my life on the line for one other person, so you'd best be grateful for this." He motioned his pointer finger in a circle, and Angela nodded and spun around. Donny flipped through a couple of keys after scrutinizing the lot of them, then gingerly inserted the smallest key into the manacles secured around Angela's wrists.

"Ouch!" Angela winced when the feeling of a hot brand singed her wrist.

Donny jerked his hand back and stuck his finger in his mouth. "Sawwy," he said. "I furgot, no touchy."

He wagged his finger in the air and went back at it. With a click, the lock was released and Angela shook the cuffs from her wrists, letting them fall to the floor. It felt so good to be free. Donny poked his head out of the cell. Angela picked up the ring of keys and found the one for the anchor at her ankle, inserted it, and removed the anchor as well.

"All right," Donny said, walking back to her. "We have to get you out of here."

Angela stood upright. "Well, obviously."

Donny shook his head. "No, out of Dingir, Angela. You're not safe here, and I don't care what you say or think because by life's wrath I will make you go."

Angela was taken aback.

Donny waved his arms dramatically. "Oh don't give me that look, Angela. Listen, I know you don't want to leave Michael. I know you want him to understand, but for people with no grasp of spells or souls, you've just got to let them believe what they want. There's no point in risking your own life trying to explain everything. In the end, *show* him he's wrong, but for now, you've got to let him go."

Hearing it hurt, but Angela knew he was right. Michael had seemed convinced that she wasn't Angela, and there was nothing she could do to change that until it was over with.

Angela nodded. "You're right."

He grinned and glanced at the watch on his wrist. "Of course, I'm—oh, we need to go." He spun around and began walking out of the cell.

"What's the matter?" Angela asked, catching up to him.

"Well, we have roughly fifty seconds before another explosion rips a hole in the armory."

"You set charges in the Ascendancy? That's what all the noise is?"

"Don't worry. The first one went off in the attic and blew a hole in the roof three minutes before the second one did."

Angela relaxed. "Well, that would give everyone plenty of time to evacuate."

"I placed the bombs for distraction more than destruction, and all for you." Donny glanced at her with a smile. "Like I said, you should feel pretty special."

"Oh, I do."

They jogged down the hallway. The shaking of the explosions had rumbled a few of the metal sheets loose from the wall, exposing jagged rocks and support beams. Even the panels on the floor teetered and flexed in certain places as they ran across them. When they began their ascent of the stairs, Angela's legs quivered under her weight and from the sickly fatigue she could never seem to shake. Their feet clacked against the metal risers, and she was grateful when they found the door at the top.

She slowly turned the handle and pushed the door open a crack to peer out into the immense amount of smoke that filled the hallway. The smell stung her nose as it blew into the stairwell.

"How long has it been?" Angela asked.

"Uh," he said, looking to his watch. Then the sound of another explosion reached their ears, followed by the crash of tumbling stone. The ground shook more violently than the last time, and Donny nearly tumbled backward down the stairs. "About that long," he said.

"Time to move, then."

Looking at Donny, Angela almost felt as though they had been brought to that point in their lives by outside forces. Not by some mystical, otherworldly power at work, but by the people around them forcing their hands. It was only a hunch, but a man like Donny didn't just help a now-rogue soldier because he felt like it. He'd been in her shoes once before, on the run from people trying to kill him. She could see it in his eyes. His facial expressions, mucked by the dirt and smoke, were calm. He was relaxed in the wreckage of the explosions.

Deep down, she asked herself if she was going about her problem the right way. Angela didn't want to leave Michael, but she knew that he wasn't seeing clearly, and it was too late to change that. It was her fault, and she felt awful about it, but getting her soul back was more important than her desire to stay close to him. Hopefully, that could be repaired.

I was the one born with my soul, and I deserve to have it back.

She took a deep breath, pushed the door open, and stepped into the smoke with fire in her chest and a heart that still beat. If running from the person she loved most was the price she had to pay, so be it. There were no limits and no barriers that would hold her back. This was about her, and at the end of it all, Michael would either be there for her or not.

Angela led Donny to the right to avoid the main entrance and slip down the back hallway to the Etlu wing where the armory was. Keeping her fingers on the wall was the best way to navigate through the haze, but the sounds of yelling startled her. Donny had done some serious damage, she knew, and even though seeing the Ascendancy falling apart filled her with regret, she tried to focus on reaching the armory.

They turned down the little-used back corridor and passed half of the storage rooms before the burning in Angela's lungs became unbearable and she had to take a breath. The taste of the smoke gagged her and didn't help the itching sensation in her lungs. She coughed, and just when she thought the fit was over, it started right back up again a moment later.

"Damn smoke," Angela croaked, then paused to cough into her forearm.

She picked up the pace. Chunks of stone and charred splinters of wood became larger and grew more frequent as they neared the edge of the Etlu wing. Not long after that, a glimmer of brass underneath rubble and dust caught her eye. Angela heaved stones, picked up the plaque, and read the word "armory" on the bronze plate. Nearly half of the hallway flooring had been busted; a giant crater had opened in the far wall, and just inches from her toes was a hole in the floor.

"Donny," Angela said quietly.

"What?" he asked, catching up to her side.

"Don't you think this was a bit excessive?" She motioned to the hole in front of them.

He lifted a finger to his lips and thought. "Yeah, it *is* a bit bigger than I expected."

Angela shrugged. "It is what it is. Let's not brew on it and hope for the best."

She crouched and tried to peer down into the hole. The door to the armory was completely missing, Angela judged, and the only light in the area came from a window ten yards away. Down below, nothing was illuminated, but she was certain she was looking into the basement level of the armory, which, she remembered, was larger than the room above it.

She covered her mouth with her hand and let loose a cough, which led to another. They were harder than the last, and Angela felt light-headed.

There are crates down below, Angela remembered. *Stacks upon stacks of them.*

Best-case scenario, she would land on one of them only five or six feet below. It was worth a shot. Her coughing subsided, and she turned to Donny. His mouth went agape, and he pointed to her face.

"What?" Angela asked.

"You've got a bit of blood, there."

She wiped at her mouth with her hand, and sure enough, ruby-colored blood was smeared across her palm.

"Damn smoke," she cursed.

"You feel all right?" Donny asked.

Angela wiped the blood on her cuirass and said, "Yeah, I'm fine," and shifted her weight to her toes. With a slight spring of her ankles, she hopped down into the hole.

She smashed into the top of a crate, the wood splintering under her weight and her feet sinking inside the box.

The stack began to shift from her forward momentum, and with outstretched arms she tried to retain her balance. A yelp escaped her when her shoulder slammed into the wall, but she was grateful that she landed mostly on her feet.

"You all right?" Donny yelled from above.

Angela looked up at his hazy outline. He was still crouching on the edge of the hole. "Yeah, come down here."

Donny shifted his weight. "Uh, how far down do you think it is?"

Angela pondered it for a moment. "Probably nine or ten feet. Just come on, Donny."

"I think I'll just wait up here. Keep guard, yeah?"

Angela shrugged, not that Donny could clearly see her do it. "Fine, just be careful."

"You too," Donny said.

Angela searched the basement, using one hand to guide her along the wall until her fingers found a light switch that didn't do anything when she flicked it. When her foot ran into a bookshelf, and after she cursed in the dark, she searched its shelves and found a hard tube on the second shelf to the top. With the press of a button, a yellow light emanated from the flashlight.

With the light's aid she scoured the room on a broad spectrum, looking for any sign that her armor was tucked away somewhere. To her surprise, a cuirass lay neatly across a flat workbench in the center of the room. The light glimmered off the fresh coat of beeswax on it and all the other pieces of equipment next to it. Batteries, tether gun, clamp—all of it was polished and cleaned. She imagined her gear was probably pending to be refitted and given to someone else, but most importantly, the folded map that Donny had given her lay atop the cuirass.

Angela began stuffing herself into the greaves, cuirass, bracers, and pauldrons as quickly as she could. She secured the straps on the sides so it held her snugly, then began strapping the battery packs to her ankles, belt, and shoulders. The wires fit the channels and hooks of hardened leather well. All led to the front pocket of her belt.

Angela had never felt so rushed to get geared, and she never realized just how many straps and buckles there were to her outfit. The shifter, tether gun, a few shocking anklets like the one she had just rid herself of, and the brass knuckles all hooked on loops at her belt. Finally, she attached the bear trap—like a clamp to the hooks and snaps on her right shoulder.

The ornate box of rosewood still rested on the same table. She unclasped the latch and lifted the hinged lid. The red velvet inside was the same as it was before, but two of the leather bags were missing since she had last looked inside. Angela reached in and took out one of the bags, leaving three in the box. Pulling the drawstring and peering inside with her light, she saw the crystals glimmering and glowing at the bottom of the bag.

There was a multitude of colors, but most were green and red. In fact, she could only spot one blue crystal, which was curious to her at first, but then she realized that blue crystals saw the most use, so it would make sense that there were fewer of them in the armory. She closed the lid, pulled a green crystal from the bag, and placed it inside her shifter. A sigh escaped her when she hung it at her waist again.

I guess I say goodbye now.

When she reached the wall of crates, she looked up to see Donny's silhouette standing tall in the smoke above her.

"All right," she said as she began to climb the wall of crates. "You need to get out of here. I'm going to head to

Earth. I don't know what I'll do when I get there, but thank you for everything."

When she reached the top and glanced back up at Donny, hoping he would extend a hand and pull her up, the outline of someone else moved behind him. The stranger was aflame. As words of caution formed on her tongue, a silver blade protruded from Donny's stomach. He tumbled to the floor, clutching his wound while the murderer stood behind him. The shrouded figure stepped over her friend and looked down at Angela, and she yelled at the top of her lungs.

"Michael!" Angela cried. "He didn't do anything!"

Michael's eyes glowed red through the smoke. He wiped the bloody knife on his greaves and said, "We can't do this dance forever, demon." He pointed the knife at Donny. "That man was missing for almost two years, and I know you Dalkhu got ahold of him during that time. Forced him to spy on us. And now you try this." Michael motioned to Angela. "Subterfuge. New tactics, I applaud you, but they are failed efforts."

Angela fought to hold back tears. Donny was the only one who helped her, maybe because he knew more about souls than anyone else, but nonetheless, he helped Angela what little he could. Now, he had even betrayed his own people by blowing holes in the Ascendancy, simply because he believed her.

"I will not let you keep hold on my wife's body," Michael said, crouching low and readying himself to spring. "You taint everything that she was!" He jumped from the ledge. The blade shimmered in his hand above his head.

A small part of Angela knew that it would come to this, but she hadn't wanted to believe her intuition. Her left hand rose to protect herself while her right hand dropped to her waistline and gripped the shifter that hung there. She pressed the button. Michael bore down on her as the shifter began humming its song and rumbled in her palm. He stabbed the blade downward, and Angela held up her arm to block him. She had moved quickly, but the machine needed more time. Their wrists touched, and they vanished from the armory.

They stared straight into each other's eyes in the space between worlds, never looking away. The hate, disdain, and the pain on his face haunted her. Frozen in time, he held his knife overhead. His eyes burned red and tendrils of fire formed over his cracked skin. Even though the sight of him like that filled her with a sorrow, she thought about trying to stay there. Michael wouldn't be able to kill her between the veils, and they'd be together forever, but she knew it couldn't last.

The birds, cawing and singing their tunes, were disturbed by the thunder among their lush green trees. They squawked and rose like colored clouds from the treetops. The insects along the vines and bark didn't notice much and continued their busy work. The beast on the forest floor jumped in fright, but it did not run from the noise. The large black cat was far too curious about the subsequent sound of breaking branches and Angela's yelling.

She wrapped her hands around her head, using her fore-arms to guard her face as she crashed through the trees. Through the space between her arms, she saw the leaves and limbs whiz past her. Sharp sticks scraped and cut her as she fell. Then a large branch caught her in the thigh and sent her into an uncontrollable spin. Flipping forward as she fell, she fought to retain her wits. A grunt escaped her lungs with each impact. Finally, she stopped on the forest floor.

Angela lay in pain, clutching the muddy ground beneath her. The air in her lungs didn't want to move, and a feeling rose in her gut. She pushed herself onto her elbows, then vomited acid onto a patch of brush next to her and rolled onto her back, exasperated. Bushes, hanging vines, tall grass, and trees—all speckled with dashes of vibrantly colored flowers—surrounded her. A loud thud came from nearby: Michael had reached the ground.

Angela forced her lungs to function, and once her breaths became easier, she wobbled to her feet. The mud soaked her boots up to the ankles. She called out for him, but only the cawing of birds, the chirps of insects, and the croaks of frogs answered her. Searching in a small perimeter, she peered as far out into the green flora as she could. As she rounded a large mahogany tree, she found him lying on his side, half covered in the tall grass.

"Michael," Angela said. "Get up."

No movement, no noise. She treaded through the weeds and made her way toward him, wanting to make sure he was alive. As she parted the grass between them, he rolled. His brow furrowed, a scream shot from his lips and the dagger flashed at Angela's face. The tip of the blade stung her neck and skewed up her temple as she threw herself backward. Stumbling through the muck, Michael dove on top of her.

Angela caught him with her forearms. The knife was pointed at her eye, and she fought to hold him above her, groaning and pushing, but with his weight and strength she struggled to keep him at bay.

"What are you going to do?" Angela asked through

clamped teeth. "Huh? What are you going to do when I get back?"

Michael didn't answer. He pushed down harder, leveraging the weight of his upper body against her. Time was running out. She brought her knees up to her stomach and lifted Michael from the ground, launching him into a roll over her. She reached for the shifter on his belt and pressed the button. They broke contact, and he disappeared in a blast of air before his back landed on the ground.

Angela lay there until the cold of the mud began to seep into her armor and soak her skin. Her muscles were stiff and sore, her skin bruised, her veins overcome with a feeling of sickness, and now blood dripped from her neck. Under the gentle press of her finger, she could tell it wasn't a severe wound, but the blade had been sharp. As long as she was careful to keep it as clean as possible, her body would close it naturally without bandages. When a small feeling of vigor returned to her limbs, she stood and began to think of what to do next.

It was great that she hadn't arrived on Earth over a vast expanse of water or a deep canyon, rushing herself as she did, but the forest around her drew no memories. The trees were much thicker and taller than any she'd seen before. It was hotter than she was used to and nearly humid enough that she could drink the air. The unfamiliarity of it all frightened her. Earth was no small place, she knew.

An urge, quiet and humble, grew inside her. Something told her to walk, not just into the distance but in a certain direction, like a premonition was telling her where to head. It confused her. The only thing that Angela could infer was that either something off in the distance was calling for her or something inside her was urging her forward.

The desire disturbed her. It was humble, yet it grew to the point where it seemed like a natural part of her primal desire to survive. It made no logical sense, yet she found it a hard thing to decline. It didn't feel the same as the intuition that had saved her life countless times before. It wasn't a fear of danger, she deduced, and it wasn't even a surge of wanderlust. It was a feeling of familiarity, like the feeling of being *home*. It was the same feeling she had felt when the Dalkhu in the crowd provoked her after her speech. That was the day she first saw Dingir through the eyes of a Dalkhu.

It was him. The man in the cloak that day—that was Udug. The man with my soul.

It suddenly made sense. The feeling inside her burned and craved that she move where it told her to go. Demanded it. The soul inside her, Udug's soul, wanted to go home, and that meant Udug was on Earth. She was feeling a connection between the soul and its proper host. Her own soul was somewhere in the distance, beckoning her. A nervous feeling close to panic grew over Angela. If she knew that Udug was on the Adrift, he would certainly be able to tell where she was as well.

With shaking hands, she examined her belt and shut the shifter off, almost forgetting that it was still draining power from the batteries. Electricity was now very valuable. Running out would trap her on Earth or, worse yet, leave her unable to anchor herself if the time came.

Glimpses of bright blue sky glowed through the trees, the light sparkling in the dewdrop moisture of a recent rainfall. The blue, even being hardly visible, tempted Angela to break loose and fly once again. It had been such a long time, it seemed, since she had felt the wind surround her and experienced the adrenal rush that swooping between the rocks of narrow canyons and the lush green foliage of a forest gave her.

Oh did she want to break from the ground and see the beauty that Earth possessed. Unlike on Dingir, here the world would grow dark. It was called night, and she could see the stars again. Angela, now more than ever, wanted to see an ocean's expanse and the foamy lapping of waves on jutting seaside boulders. Every corner of this massive, lost world called out to her. Escape and live simply. No more fighting, just peace.

She slipped her fingers into the pocket on the front of her cuirass, retrieved the crumpled map that Donny had given her, and unfolded it carefully. It was vague in its detailing of settlements and landmarks, but with it she could accurately guess what parts of the world the lines on it represented. This particular map encompassed a much larger area of land with multiple human nations and cities. In Dingir, it was considered the central region of Earth.

Angela went through the steps in her mind, trying to identify where she might be on it, and concluded that she wasn't even anywhere on that map. The kinds of trees and the wildlife suggested that she was somewhere south of the region the map showed. Yet she could be dead wrong and be somewhere north of it, too.

She could either wander until she found a recognizable landmark or a human to speak with. Neither sounded ideal. Roaming about the largest world in existence would waste untold amounts of time. Finding a human that spoke her language could be just as challenging, not to mention her lack of more fitting garb or a cloak to cover her equipment.

Angela sighed in bewilderment; any direction could lead to death or success. If finding the man Donny had wanted her to meet was her goal, it would assuredly take her a very long time of trial and error. She simply didn't recognize this place and had no clear direction to travel. It was impossible, she realized, and part of her was glad.

Her eyes drifted down to the map in her hands, and her heart sank as she came to a terrible realization: she could die here on the reckless and chaotic Earth while a soul other than her own lived inside her.

Will I carry on with this Dalku's soul to the waylines or fade away?

The clairvoyance that urged her to set off into the distance grew in strength, and she folded the map neatly and tucked it inside her pocket again. She didn't know how she was going to do it or if she was even prepared enough to try, but she decided then and there that she was going to find Udug and make him fix everything he'd done to her.

"Sorry, Donny," Angela said, and she took the first step toward the unknown.

CHAPTER ELEVEN

"Your mind and soul are your greatest weapons," Udug shouted. He paced in front of his youngest students as his words echoed throughout the large chamber. His gaze drifted over each child lined in front of him. They met his gaze, covered with sweat and stinking of fear, and Udug would have it no other way.

"This is what separates us from the Anunnaki. They rely on machines because they refuse to acknowledge how important and basic the soul is to both of our kind. They have long since cast out the old truths and have ever since been our enemies."

Udug paused for a moment when he saw a robed figure enter the room on the edge of his sight, but he ignored the visitor.

"Nourish your mind and soul through constant meditation and reading. Exercise your mind's reach and your ability to command the energy of your soul, but do not forget your body."

He stopped for a moment to gauge the children. Most had already developed bruises from the day's training regimen, and a few had large scrapes and crusted blood. The boys remained silent and patient, waiting for Udug to continue, which pleased him.

"What is our purpose?" he asked.

"To defend our people and bring forth an age of unity!" the boys shouted together.

Udug nodded. "There is no greater mission. Out of the seven known worlds, four hold the primary elements: water, flame, air, and stone separated by a veil as weak as linen, and every linen has space between its fibers. Kur, Earth, and Dingir were all made from fractures and leaks."

Udug spun around and began another pass in front of the boys. "With time, you will learn to use your mind to puncture, warp, and force yourself through the veils. Only some of you will make it, but those of you that succeed with me will have the option of taking your training further and learning the old spells. Perhaps you'll take the same path as Shedim and become a teacher someday." Udug pointed across the room to his robed pupil standing near the entrance.

A few of the boys had begun to fidget, and Udug sighed, feeling a bit distraught by their young minds and short attention spans. They didn't understand the seriousness of it all.

"Dismissed," Udug finally said.

The children dispersed from their line formation and rushed to the base of pillars that ran along both sides of the room. They gathered their mats and body padding, stuffing them into burlap sacks and whispering to each other as they went. When the patter of little sandaled feet swept past Udug and went silent in the tunnel outside, he turned to face his oldest pupil.

Shedim was leaning against one of the pillars, arms

crossed, when Udug approached him. Shedim lowered his hood to his shoulders and asked, "Are you sure this is the right way to do this?"

Udug clenched his teeth and exhaled slowly through his nostrils for a moment, then took another step closer and whispered, "Do you doubt me, the plan, or yourself?"

"All of it, I suppose," Shedim said. "I just wonder if it's worth it, considering how so much is out of our control and the certainty that there will be repercussions for what you've done."

Udug rested a hand on his pupil's shoulder. Their eyes met. "This will spark the beginning of a war. Not the petty skirmishes we deal with now, but a definite, *finalizing* war. We can end this, Shedim. We have the ability to make great strides. All it takes is one more risk."

"Are we to break everything? I remember the oaths we made to protect our own. If we expose ourselves for the laws we have shattered and your plan doesn't work how you predict, we're as good as dead."

Udug's hand slipped to his waist. He sighed. "By the time you reach my age, you'll be a master of the soul, too. Spells won't intimidate you. You'll teach, and you'll love it. And after some time, Shedim, you will begin to realize that every single day is the same as the day before because the Council will not act in a manner that will end this eternal conflict.

"They will not break away from the traditions formed by those before them. They pass laws that inhibit our own desires for fear of malpractice. A great sacrifice for the many that saves only a few. They are delusional. Some of them believe the Anchor can still be restored without all of the knowledge in our grasp. The other councilmen do not want it to happen, anyways, but they will play along if we show we have the strength to crush Dingir."

He sighed. "When one of the students you have raised since boyhood returns to you with holes through his shoulder and a missing leg, you will know the grief I feel."

Tears formed in Udug's eyes.

"The Anunnaki send them back broken and damned to live paralyzed, useless lives. It would be better if they were killed outright. We send our own soldiers on pointless missions that don't accomplish anything. We set our children up for failure, Shedim. It has to change."

Udug shifted his weight and sniffled, looking away for a moment while Shedim stood there coldly. The pupil had thought about his relationship with Udug a lot lately. Part of his consciousness told him that there was a reason Anzu sought to turn Udug into the Council after the possession incantation had gone awry, but another part of his mind understood Udug's pain and reasoning.

Shedim could still walk away or run away if it came to it. He didn't have to risk his own life for his master's actions, and in some senses, that would be stupid of him.

"How long have we been together, Lamid Piristi?" Shedim asked.

"It has been four years since your commencement as my replacement," Udug said. He chuckled. "And much longer since you began training under me."

"Centuries…" Shedim muttered.

Udug nodded.

"With all of the years between us and the effect your teachings have had upon me, how they have changed my life, what makes you think that I would move against you now?"

Udug's eyes glimmered as a faint smile appeared on his timeworn face.

"You are right," Shedim said. "I don't know what it is like, but that doesn't mean that I cannot sympathize. I am afraid of what the future hides from us, but you are the only councilman I have met that is not complacent. The only one that does not want to simply maintain the status of our people but upheave it. In the pursuit to restore the Anchor, the end justifies our actions. Your fervor is contagious." Shedim rested a hand on Udug's shoulder. "And because of it, I will follow you to the end."

Udug smiled widely, droplets forming in the corner of his eyes again. He grabbed Shedim by the shoulders and pulled him close. He spoke into Shedim's ear: "You will be a part of the greatest Anchor-shard heist of our people. Our upheaval of Dingir and Kur will spur the end into motion."

ANGELA MADE HER WAY THROUGH THE JUNGLE WITH difficulty. The vegetation, thick and unavoidable in some parts, nicked wire-thin cuts on her cheeks and hands. Salty sweat burned in every tiny slice and flooded her sight from time to time. A shower or some rain would be great.

The trees gradually grew more spaced out, and she paused for a few hours to break in the cool breeze and dry her irritated skin. The land was flatter, and before too long she resumed her walk and found that her speed on foot increased on the even terrain. Even though she had no idea how far she had to travel to find Udug—or exactly where she was headed—the soul inside her pushed onward.

Angela oftentimes wondered why she was following such a vague compulsion, and she contemplated pulling

Donny's map back out of her pocket time and time again. But she couldn't bring herself to abandon her search; Udug was on Earth, and maybe he wanted the same thing she did. That night, she slept with her back on the dirt and with the stars as her company.

The ground changed, and the air changed along with it. In the jungle, the air was thick with moisture that clung to her, but by the end of the second day, she had reached a much drier atmosphere. Only small, dying shrubs and tufts of long grass covered the dry, cracked earth. Even the creeks and small rivers she crossed had the tan color of soiled water. It was easier for her to track the time there. The days on Earth lasted a few hours longer than those on Dingir, but even though the extra time tired her for the first week, she still found the presence of warm sunlight enjoyable.

Angela traveled on, making her way toward Udug with every passing day, but she became distraught when she stepped onto the shore of the largest river she had ever seen. It was too wide for her to cross, as she couldn't justify using electricity that might save her life later, and with the weight of her gear, it would be foolish for her to swim it. Angela, recognizing the impossibility of it, regretfully changed course and turned to follow the river until she hopefully found a place to cross.

Two days later, she spotted something in the distance by the riverside. Over the tops of green shrubs, she could see buildings and small ships with furled sails near the river's edge.

It was a large town, by Angela's judgment, especially for humans. The green along the riverside continued to the edge of the town, where men were cultivating the land with hand tools and tamed animals. There were tall-shafted reeds and shorter plants of grain. The men in the fields wore next to nothing, only cloths draped about their most sensitive areas, while other people she saw around the outskirts of the town wore colored robes.

The biggest and most impressive aspect of this particular human settlement was the massive structures they had built off to the left. During her time serving in a camp nestled in a desert canyon, Angela had heard that humans from another land created massive shapes of stacked limestone blocks to serve as tombs for their deceased leaders. Angela knew, based on both the rumors and the sight of the angled edifices pointing upward into the sky, that these were those same pyramid tombs. From this distance, she couldn't make out the individual blocks, but she was certain that they must have been giant. Their sheer size, and the fact that humans had achieved such architectural feats, impressed her.

She sat on a small boulder, rested her chin on her palm, and thought for a while. The soul inside her told her she needed to cross the river, but that meant that she would have to deal with humans. That was an idea she didn't like in the slightest.

Humans were always very group-oriented, and in some places, they would try killing anyone they didn't recognize. They were volatile beings, but at this point, they were also what Angela needed. So with little other choice, she watched the sun fall toward the horizon, and at the first touch of darkness, she began walking toward the town.

The thought of a warm bed teased her mind, and with little self-convincing, she began to feel as though she deserved one good night's sleep. The ground had been rough on her back, and the cold settling into her bones every night was growing rather tiring. It had been over a week since she last slept on a bed, and even the horrible cot in that cell on Dingir would have been welcome. She'd have taken it with her, if she could have.

As Angela reached the precipice of the town, it became easier to see the finer details of the town. The houses were made of mud and straw bricks, and even though most of the people had retired for the night, some still stood atop the flat roofs of buildings, their faces illuminated by their torches. Angela could see the glimmer of swords at their waists and knew that they were watchmen. They moved from side to side, keeping an eye on their precious city, and Angela slipped between the gaps of their wavering eyes. They were too spread out and too few, she deemed.

She found a burlap sack hanging off a wooden stand and retreated to an alleyway, then stripped off her gear and hid it inside the bag as carefully as she could without dinging metal against metal. Down to nothing other than her boots and the white linen cloth she wore under her armor, she stretched and felt the freedom to move in ways she hadn't in over a week.

The sack was incredibly heavy. The weight of her equipment was supposed to be spread around the body, not throw into a lump over her shoulder. It was difficult to walk with a straight back, but the cost was worth it. A woman in full leather armor and glossy brass objects at her waist would probably draw the attention of thieves and guards alike.

Angela walked about the town a while longer, eying everything about it and enjoying her anonymity. To her surprise, the tops of all the homes were flat. Some even held cloth canopies and tables with chairs on top of them, signs that the living area of the homes here extended beyond the mud-brick shelter. She thought it was a curious thing at first, then admitted that if she lived on Earth, she would want to see the night sky from the roof of her own home, too.

There was another building, much larger and of better stone construction, that sat between her and the fields before the riverfront. While it wasn't quite the size of one of the warehouses back in Dingir, it was another impressive piece of architecture. Torchlights lit small windows on the ground level and the second level. The main door was propped open with a single stone to allow fresh night air in, and Angela saw a man standing behind a counter when she peered inside. He was a weary man; his beard was largely untrimmed and frizzy, and he continued to constantly rub his eyes with the backs of his hands. He beckoned her inside.

Angela took a deep breath and entered the building. Even though she didn't have the slightest idea what the writing outside had read, she did feel somewhat certain that this was the kind of place she was looking for. It felt similar to the establishments others had lodged at in human settlements. All Angela hoped to do was pay for a bed.

There were a few tables scattered about the front room, and a small clutch of embers still smoked in a circle pit of sandstone. Cups sat on the ground next to the chairs surrounding it, and she wondered how the inside of the place didn't smell worse, considering its lack of a chimney.

The man had sunken eyes underneath a mop of unkempt black hair. His hands fiddled about a cloth and cup, cleaning them with some watery solution in an urn atop the wooden counter he stood at. Even as his eyes watched Angela, he continued working diligently.

She placed the burlap sack at her feet and cleared her throat. "Hello. Is this a place where I can rent a bed?"

The man half-turned his head like a dog, raising a single eyebrow at her. Angela wondered if it was the way she was dressed, or maybe it wasn't the right kind of place.

"If not, can you point me toward a business that does?" Angela asked, suddenly nervous that she was speaking with a human.

The man placed his palms on the counter and studied her, squinting. He finally broke the awkward glare a moment later, exposing black teeth as he said, "Eh, Sumer?"

Before Angela could dissect the phonetics of his speech, the man bent and retrieved a clay mug from underneath the countertop. Angela screamed inside. She should have known that these people would speak a different dialect.

Why can't humans be like Anunnaki and Dalkhu? Stick to one language. Can't imagine how many problems it causes.

The man filled the brown cup with liquid from a separate jug and scooted it across the countertop toward her. Angela, not knowing the customs of these people—because for some reason they all had to be different from each other in that regard, too—took the glass in her hands out of fear of being disrespectful and brought it to her lips.

The drink was surprisingly sweet, but like the tea that Donny had always raved about, it contained a slight bitterness that soured her tongue. The initial taste was good, Angela admitted, and she would have probably enjoyed it more if it weren't for the surprising chunks of soggy bread that floated into her mouth and gagged her.

Angela placed her hand over her mouth as she coughed, then thanked the man, but he didn't seem to pay her any mind and continued cleaning the other cups that had been piled to one side of the countertop.

Angela had forgotten entirely that subsets of humanity spoke differently from one another. Her training sessions from years ago assuredly taught this one, but at that time she had been more concerned with getting out of Dingir and seeing Earth for the first time. She had declined the opportunity on the basis that she would restrict herself solely to the central region of Earth. Now Angela regretted not taking the time to pick up an extra language.

Angela sipped and mulled there for a short time until the man returned and refilled her cup without her motioning for him to do so. She thought little of it, figuring it would be easier to continue drinking the slush than trying to tell the man she didn't want any more. As nasty as it was, she didn't want to stop.

There was alcohol in the drink. A slight tingling sensation gripped her legs and fingertips, and she felt loose and wiggly like she imagined a flopping fish on a deck would feel.

Except I can breathe, she thought, smiling in her own amusement and placing the cup back down.

"You know," Angela said, "this is a pleasant place."

The man, yet again, didn't add anything to the conversation. He kept his hands busy and his eyes on her as she drank. Part of the whole situation bugged her. She wanted to hear the man speak again. Even if she couldn't understand it, she would at least feel like she had some company.

"This place you work, the drink you've given me, you've probably worked quite hard, I imagine." Angela tapped her fingers against the sides of the cup. "I've worked a lot as well, but not in the same field as yours."

The man leaned against the wall behind him, staring at

her indifferently. Angela bent forward over the countertop, realizing the good bit of fun she could have with a man who didn't understand a single thing she said.

"I was a warrior, if you would call it that. Hard to believe, I know, considering most of you don't operate in the ways that we do." Angela straightened, took another slurp, and wiped her lips with her forearm. "I'm a woman who did her duty well and served my people, as I'm sure you do in your own sort of way. I'm sure I would spend most of my years drinking, too, if my life was as short as yours. But let's be honest with one another." Angela drained the rest of the cup and placed it on the counter, and she suddenly felt sullen. "It really sucks. It's been such a long time since I've felt this way. Now, I know that he's not dead or anything, but that's how it feels." She pondered it for a moment, questioning her statement for accuracy, then nodded. "It feels like he's dead."

Angela was quiet for a moment, staring dully at her own hands. When the man went to refill her drink, Angela placed her fingers over the top of the cup, stopping him. She sighed long and slow, and the man put the urn back underneath the counter.

"It doesn't matter what I feel like, though, does it?" Angela asked. "What matters is that I show him he's wrong. It's the only chance I've got, and I can't hide from what I have to do." She acknowledged her need to move forward and keep her chin up. The last week in the wilderness had been tough on her, and she finally admitted that what she was going through was the hardest thing she'd ever experienced. It was okay to feel sad about it.

Angela sighed, then half smiled at the man on the other side of the counter. She brought her palms together next to her cheek, tilting her head as she did. To her surprise, the man nodded, took her glass, and added it to the slowly dwindling mass of dirty ones. He retrieved a small candle on a shoddy wooden holder with a handle, lit it, and handed it to her. Stepping out from behind the bar, he motioned toward a hallway off to the side of the large entrance room, then insinuated a turn to the left with a flick of his wrist.

He spoke in his own language again, and Angela couldn't make heads or tails of it beyond the gesture. She just picked up the sack at her feet and the candle and headed toward the door. Behind it was a long stretch of hall that ran along the outer edge of the building. The windows were left open here, too, and black lamps hung evenly spaced down the hall. Doors of boarded lumber lined the hallway, and the first door on the left, just as the man had tried to convey, was wide open. The room was more like a closet packed with furniture. The bed was a wooden frame stuffed with straw and topped off with a woven reed sheet and a rough linen blanket. Angela groaned when she saw the headrest sitting atop the bed.

A square wooden box with a few hasty carvings and flat cushions? No thank you.

Angela placed her candle on the nightstand and dropped her sack, then picked up the wooden headrest and set it on the ground. After closing the door, she fell onto the bed and squirmed and rolled, gauging the comfort of it. A few times she swore she could feel the prick of straw poking her through the reed sheet, but she never could find them. She blew out the candle, let darkness fill the room, and waited until she fell asleep.

ANGELA LURCHED UPRIGHT WHEN THERE WAS A KNOCK ON

the door. Squinting, she stretched, fumbled to her feet with outstretched arms, walked to the door, and lifted the small wooden bar that held it shut. The man from the night before stood in the hallway. He half smiled and tried to speak slowly, and Angela, in her grogginess, shook her head.

"I can't understand," she said, annoyed and half asleep. She nearly turned and plopped back onto the bed, but morning sunlight shined through the window behind him. With great sadness, Angela sighed, held up a finger to try and tell him it would only be a minute longer, and shut the door.

She sorted through everything she had in her burlap bag at her feet, weighing the value of each thing until she decided on something that she could part with. Certainly, the brass metal of her equipment would be valuable to any human, but it was worth even more to her. She couldn't justify parting with any of her armor, or much of anything, until she came to her belt and found something the man might be able to sell.

Angela picked up the headrest and placed it back on the bed, straightened the blanket, and took the remnants of last night's candle before throwing her things over her shoulder and heading back to the front. The keeper sat behind the countertop without a single glass to wash, and he eyed her as she approached. She placed the glowing blue crystal on the counter and watched the man's eyes widen as he snatched it up. He eyed it with scrutiny, then motioned to her and back to the crystal again. He shook his hands ecstatically and beamed with a smile. Angela swore he was going to leap over the bar and tackle her with a hug. Seeing his joy warmed her.

"Thank you," Angela said. "I am grateful for your

service and lack of questions. I hope that will be worth something to you."

It's not like it's worth much to me anymore. I won't head back to Dingir anytime soon...

She stepped out into the sun-soaked street, where humpbacked animals pulled carts and wagons. Crowds bustled past her. Most wore light robes or simple clothes. Some wore rolled-up hats, and others wore masks of soft cloth over their faces. Even amidst all the people, she stood in solitude, undisturbed by glares or any ill-will. It felt good to be able to stand in front of humans without any of them coming at her, and she thought it curious as to why humans didn't see her cloaked in the flame of her soul's energy.

Angela could disappear. Neither the Dalkhu nor the Anunnaki would ever be able to find her if she chose to hide. She remembered hearing about people who had gone rogue before; distant coworkers and Dalkhu rogues traveled the Earth as well. She could integrate into human society, too, and live a quiet life on some discreet island or in some hidden valley. When the humans she lived beside noticed that her body did not age at the same rate as theirs and they grew suspicious of her, she could simply move somewhere else and start the cycle all over again.

In some ways, having a life she could simply reset whenever she needed to would be beneficial, but it would also have its curses. Angela would make friends, no doubt, and watch them grow old while she stayed in nearly complete stasis. Eventually, they would die naturally or by disease or sword, and Angela would be alone again. The idea of attachment to a human didn't sound as appealing when she thought of it like that, but she couldn't decide if their fragility made their existence pitiful or beautiful.

Every step they took in their lives meant something and had more importance, more passion.

Certainly, humans being unable to perceive souls and their nature must have had to do with their lack of them. They had the same physical shape as the Anunnaki and Dalkhu, but they never seemed bothered or affected by things of the soul. Their faiths told them that there was something more to the worlds, but they could not perceive the truth.

Angela closed her eyes, shrugging the thought from her mind. She listened to the squeaking wheels of wooden carts rolling past her, the puffs and snorts of the animals pulling them, and the shouting kids in the distance. Slowly, she tuned it all out and listened only to the soul inside her. It stirred and warmed up like a pot over fire. Her skin felt frozen compared to the blaze that Udug's soul contained. It was filled with its own sense of dignified anger and confusion, and as she searched and felt what it was trying to say, she noticed its subtle cry for movement. It pointed toward the other side of the river, and she began to walk.

The fields near the river turned out to be mostly rice with only small patches of tall shafts of reeds jutting from the muddy soil. Rough-cut planks were laid on the ground to ease the movement of wheelbarrows and carts across the soggy ground. There was a small dock at the end of the greenest patch of land she'd seen in days.

Men along the shores tended to small dinghies and nets, paying her approach no mind. It wasn't until she stepped foot on the dock that one man turned to see her. He was of the same ethnicity as the man behind the counter; his skin was a deep tan color, and he wore a short black beard, but his eyes were a striking blue. She walked up to the man and he rose to his feet and said something she couldn't understand.

It was pointless to try and ask her question with words. Instead, she pointed to the other side of the river, and he glanced across the water, then curiously back at her. With a rough exchange of gestures, Angela felt confident that she had conveyed that she wanted to cross the river when the man nodded and shouted down the river. Another person sitting in one of the smaller sail-less boats fifty feet away called back. He was sitting with a net across his lap. Dressed in a black robe and a woven reed hat, he flailed his arm above his head.

The bearded man motioned her away with a flick of his wrist and began to seat himself again, leaving Angela to walk the muddy riverside closer to the boat. The boatman rowed his craft to the shore with a one-handed paddle, and when the bow touched land, he waved for her to enter.

Angela had never been on a boat before, but she quickly stepped on. The boat shifted under her feet and pushed back out into the water, forcing her to spread her legs apart. She launched herself into the gliding boat before it floated away, and the contents of her burlap bag clanked and clashed as she tumbled headfirst onto the boat.

"Sorry!" Angela exclaimed, pushing herself upright. People all along the river laughed.

The boat rocked as Angela got herself seated as quickly as she could. She pulled the sack off the man's netting and onto her lap. The rower laughed haughtily as he spoke. His tan skin was wrinkled and leathery, the stubble on his chin was gray, and his lack of teeth was disconcerting. Angela just wished she could tell if the smell was coming from the few dozen fish beneath his seat or his mouth, but she couldn't help but smile at the old man's pleasant laugh. She probably did look like a fool.

The man calmed and began to row, and they slid out into the steady-flowing river. The man, watching her as he rowed, tried to start a conversation with her, but all Angela could do was shake her head and motion to her ears. He frowned, then briefly shrugged. They had nearly traversed three-fourths of the waterway when she noticed that the man was staring at her sack when she wasn't looking. When Angela caught his gaze, she pointed to it.

He must want some form of payment as well, Angela thought begrudgingly. *I don't know what I have to spare. I can't give out crystals to everyone, but I don't have anything else I can really spare.*

Angela sighed and began to untie the bag. A gust of wind, coupled with her own miss-care, blew a portion of the sack open to reveal the brass-plated clamp she attached to her pauldrons—and brass looked a good bit like gold. The man's eyes were wider than the river, and she could almost see foam at the corners of his cracked lips. Certainly, any metal that well refined and polished was worth a lot on Earth. The man pointed at the bag and said something again.

"Listen," Angela said, covering her equipment, "I don't understand what you're saying and you cannot have that."

The old man's brow furrowed, and he glared at her for a moment, trying to gauge her. He stopped rowing, rested his arms in his lap, and then began to yell and wave his arms about. The fishermen on the other side of the river yelled back to the old man, and he returned their calls with some other gibberish Angela couldn't understand. Then the old man began to row them back toward the town.

"No," Angela said, reaching out to the man, pleading.

"Don't. I have to go that way." She pointed past the man's shoulder, but it didn't matter. He glared at her intensely, then spat out more words.

"Give me the oar," Angela said, and she lurched forward to wrench it from him. He swatted her across the face. Stunned that such an old man had struck her, Angela paused for only a moment, then swore and reached for the oar a second time.

She grabbed him by the wrist and said, "Don't make me hurt you!"

He groaned and cracked the oar into the back of her head.

Angela reeled back and shielded herself with her hands. She rubbed the tender skin for a moment, fumbling to find words, then realized it was pointless to try. She just couldn't believe the gaffer struck her upside the head with the oar.

Shouting came from behind her, and Angela twisted to see that four other boats were gliding toward them. With two men on each, Angela knew that it wouldn't end well if they reached her. The old man continued to row, and this time, Angela wasn't in the mood. She got on her knees and stretched out to the man. This time she grabbed the oar by its handle and tugged.

"Let go!" she yelled, twisting the oar at an awkward angle. The man grumbled, then let go of the oar with one hand and balled a fist. Again, she was appalled.

"Haraamiya!" he yelled once more as he swung. Angela blocked it with her forearm easily enough—his thin arms and weak wrists couldn't beat a drum—then aimed for an area on his body where she wouldn't risk severely injuring him. She punched his gut. His head rolled back and he moaned, and Angela began to row as hard as she could.

The man clutched his stomach as he glared at her, and they crossed the rest of the river. When the watercraft reached the shore, Angela tossed the oar into the water, threw her bag over her shoulder, then bolted for dry land, kicking the boat out from under her. The soil on that side of the river was unfarmed, and shrubs and long grass grew wildly. After trudging through the mud and up the incline, she looked back from the top of the shoreline. The old man had retrieved the oar from the river and held it above his head as he shouted at her. The other, younger fishermen were ten feet behind him and rapidly approaching.

Angela shrugged and ran. The hill dropped down a few dozen feet, then rose again as the ground stiffened under feet. She kicked up dirt and dust as the scenery changed back into lifeless and dull yellows and browns. An hour passed before she looked behind herself again. The men were nowhere in sight, and she slowed to a shaky walk and found a place to sit behind an outcrop of stones and craggy earth.

Why did that man suddenly get so volatile? Angela wondered. *He must have thought I was a thief. It would be a rare thing to see a woman with a bag of something that looks like gold...*

When she was rested and her breath returned to normal, she began covering her mud-stained clothes with her greaves, cuirass, and then pauldrons and gear. Once fully armed, she looked into the distance, over the never-ending yellow and brown hills of dry earth. She worried that the walk would be long and dreary, swearing to herself that if it took her a month she'd lose her mind, toss aside her policy of electricity conservation, and try to fly the rest of the way.

The days passed, testing Angela's endurance as she

strode through the countryside. Earth's sun, brighter and hotter than Dingir's, wore her down much more than she thought it would have. It didn't matter that there were no glistening streets of alchemically produced gold to reflect light into her eyes; it was simply bright enough to force her to constantly squint. And the mirages. She had forgotten about mirages. Angela swore on multiple occasions that she saw a flowing pool of water in the distance, only to find cracked, dry dirt when she got there.

Dying plant life gradually gave way to sparse specs of green. While the earth had eased up on her, the sun had not. Angela pushed herself through the discomfort and realized on the second day that it would be much better for her to travel at night, even though it would be difficult to adjust her sleeping pattern quickly. That night, she stayed up as late as she could, walking until her legs wobbled underneath her. Then, when the time felt right, she lay in between a patch of brush out in the open wastes and slept.

The morning sunlight woke her, and she rolled over and buried her face into her arms and her nose into the dirt, trying to keep the sun off her face. Even though the soul in her beckoned for her to get up and move, she managed to find another hour or two of sleep. When she awoke for the second time that day, she carefully glanced up at the sun, holding her hand just over it, and gauged how far along in the day it was. Angela figured it was late morning, still not afternoon like she would have liked, but late enough that traveling into the cool evening would certainly be that much easier. So she started up again, slowly at first, and then gradually picked up speed as the afternoon passed.

Night fell over her faster than she imagined it would, and still feeling a spring in her leg, she continued onward. Not until the second hour of darkness did she begin to feel a bit nervous. There were sounds that she knew came from animals in bushes and between rocks, the creaking of branches, but her mind wouldn't listen to logic: it demanded that unidentified sounds without visible sources be treated as dangerous threats.

How could she react to something she couldn't see? Her chest pounded as the night went on, pushing her to walk faster as she considered that the animals, or whatever was making the sounds around her, had looked down on her as she slept the night before. She tried brushing the thoughts from her mind, knowing her fear was getting a grip on her, but in her defense, she'd say that darkness was something she very rarely experienced in Dingir.

A flicker of light in the distance caught her eye. At first, she saw the light reflected, glowing off of shrubs and rock. Then a torch broke over the top of the hill and into her field of vision, but when a pair of shoulders and a torso became visible, Angela froze.

At first, as habit would have it, she instinctively believed she was looking at a Dalkhu, but then she realized that she was the Dalkhu now. The figure just a few hundred yards away, then, was an Anunnaki. She broke into a sprint, trying to keep as many shrubs and boulders as possible between her and the flaming figure in the distance. She glanced back occasionally as she ran toward the outer edge of a thin forest. It didn't appear that she'd been spotted yet, and she meant to keep it that way.

Her head spun as she ran. Too much time had passed with her out in the open. There was no way she'd make it before she was seen. A second light appeared over a hill to her left. Then a third directly behind her as she closed the gap between her and the trees. Sticking to the low side of a hill, she tried to keep herself hidden, but out in the open, there was nothing she could do. The Etlu to her left appeared to be walking, quite lazily, in the same direction as her while the others were headed straight at her.

What are they doing out here? Is there a camp nearby?

Angela heard shouting behind her; she'd been spotted. The Anunnaki moved up and down the hills of the dead land in a sprint, bobbing in the distance. Angela cursed. It wouldn't be long before the others around her heard the first's yelling and joined in and came at her from three sides.

The trees were sparse for another fifty yards before they began to provide her with any real cover, and by that time the others had begun shouting at her as well. Maybe it wasn't such a good idea to travel at night; she stuck out in the darkness.

A flowing creek brought Angela to a dead stop, and she nearly tripped over her own feet and crashed into the eroded bed five feet below. To her relief, she even heard the creek's trickling water over the sound of her breathing and running; she could barely see the drop-off in the earth in the darkness. Taking a few steps backward, then pushing herself into another sprint, she bounded over it, clearing the ten-foot gap. Angela tumbled, rolled, and resumed her run.

The trees began to thin out again as she left the creek behind her, and the voices grew more muffled. There was more dirt, rocks, and sand stretched out ahead of her, and it looked like she was going to leave the woods. Then two more flaming figures appeared in front of her, their glowing silhouettes becoming more visible with each stride. Angela was surrounded.

MICHAEL AND KUSHIEL WALKED ALONGSIDE ONE ANOTHER as they approached the timber. Reports of a Dalkhu mingling with a human settlement brought them to that lifeless region, and they knew there was truth to the report when the sound of the other Etlus yelling reached their ears. The previous day, they had spread themselves out over twenty square miles of land with their shifters. Their instructions were to walk toward one another for four hours, then break for two and continue again. Kushiel had assumed that they would run into each other emptyhanded, but it seemed as though that was not the case.

"It's not the one we're after," he said.

Michael turned his head. "What makes you sure?"

"Whoever possessed Angela was obviously an expert, probably a high-ranking Dalkhu. They wouldn't be so stupid and walk into a trap like this." Kushiel pointed into the trees fifty feet away from them. The wind howled between them. "It would teleport the moment it saw anything that was a possible threat."

"I'm not sure about that. Last I saw it, it used a shifter to get to Earth. It's become incapable of traveling through the veils with its own strength, I think. Something about taking over Angela's body has disrupted its own abilities." Michael gripped the tether gun's handle and pulled it from its holster, then rerouted the power cable to the base of it with a snap. "Even if it isn't the imposter, we'll still teach it to think twice before crossing Dingir."

Kushiel paused. "What do you mean? As far as we're aware, this one hasn't done anything."

Michael laughed. "They all do something, eventually."

"Now, hold on, Michael." Kushiel touched his icy shoulder, pulling him to stop. "I've met Dalkhu of the Council before, set up peace agreements, and settled on land ownership, and just like us, they have rogue counter-parts as well. Zealots who sully their own name. As far as we're aware, only one of them has wronged you, so we can't go around starting a bigger fight than we can handle."

"Peace agreements? Do you mean the ones that dissolve within a month when a Dalkhu weaponizes the veil and rips an Etlu apart?" Michael shook his head, grinning at the old man's stupidity. "They don't change, Kushiel." Michael spun around and began walking again. "So, we have to."

Kushiel watched Michael enter the timber, stooping low through shrubs and scanning for threats. He sighed and grabbed the gun at his side, too, thinking about what Michael said. There was truth to it, he knew. If the Council hadn't given the order for Angela's possession and it really was a rogue Dalkhu, there was little they could demand other than the specific individual who cast the spell.

Now that he thought about it, the Dalkhu really were the same as they had been back when he was first voted in as the Grand Etlu—grubby-fingered and lurking in the shadows, always taking scrap from the bodies of his soldiers. Still, that wasn't enough justification for Kushiel to comfortably allow what was likely going to happen.

Michael had threatened he would reveal Kushiel's secret if he wasn't permitted to come along for the hunt, so he'd already broken one of his own rules by letting an untrained Uri Gallu come to Earth.

Kushiel sighed and followed, thinking about how Angela and Michael were the only two who knew what had happened all those years ago. Now that Angela had been horrifically destroyed, he thought about how much better it would be if Michael were dead, too. No more weight on his shoulders.

ANGELA WHIPPED HERSELF AROUND AND BOLTED BACK behind the tree line, nearly twisting her ankle in the process. Her eyes bounced around the forest, searching for anywhere to hide. The crunch of rocks and the snap of twigs under her feet worried her as the shouting grew louder. They were in the forest with her now, and the only thing she could think to do was turn on her shifter and warp the heck out of here, but that would only hurt her in the long run.

Shifters required a rather large amount of energy to function, and she'd already used it once. At that point, if the batteries gave her half an hour of combat, she'd be impressed.

Angela shook her head. There was no way she'd fight so hard just to find Udug and not be able to defend herself if it came to it. She needed all of the power in her batteries. Picking up her pace, she jumped over toppled logs and scoured the woods for something to hide behind. The creek snuck up on her again, although this time it didn't surprise her as much.

"There's a crick!" someone shouted.

Angela's gut wrenched into a nervous knot. One of the Etlus had already found the water, and that meant they were right down the stream from her. All it would take was a turn and quick jaunt through the trees and she'd be found. She bit her tongue, trying not to curse out loud as she squinted in the darkness. There was nothing—no rotting tree big enough to crawl into, and hiding inside a bush seemed stupid.

Then she saw it just up the creek: a leaning tree had tipped over the water. The dirt was eroded enough to reveal its mass of mud-crusted roots clinging to solid ground as best as it could. She ran toward it and jumped down into the creek bed. Her palms scraped against the shoulder-high drop-off as she collided with it, and she was lucky the water along the edge was only high enough to touch her ankles.

Angela heaved herself shoulder-first into the mess of scratching roots. Their thick entanglement snagged on every one of her hairs as she tried to shove herself into them. They caught on her weapons and threatened to steal them from her. The roots were stiff and pushed against her from all directions, and she imagined them as spider webs holding her above a twenty-foot drop.

"Did you find anything?" a voice called out. It was more distant than the last and an entirely different tone. Angela almost recognized it.

"Not yet, sir," the familiar Etlu said, his voice much louder now.

"Are you sure you saw one?"

"I swear it! I saw a damned torch-head!"

There was laughter all around her. At least four or six people's worth, but she couldn't be certain.

"Well, continue your search. It'll be morning soon enough."

Kushiel, Angela realized. *He's here?* She felt bitterness swell up in her. It wasn't enough that she was shunned and that Michael had tried to kill her; apparently, she needed to be hunted wherever she went, too.

Angela brewed for an hour as the soldiers searched above her. Luckily, they never got close to her, and she came to feel more worried about the rest of the tree falling on top of her than being found. Hung up in the muck and the roots, Angela eventually passed out.

The blasts of teleportation woke her before she even realized she'd fallen asleep. She counted eight in total, and after five minutes of silence she began to push her way out of her hole. Her boots were completely soaked, and she imagined her toes looked like swollen grapes about to burst. The roots clung to and pulled her hair until she used her knife to cut handfuls off at a time. Freed of the tree, she clawed her way up the drop-off and was happy to see the orange sun break over the horizon and to feel its warmth on her cheeks.

She sat on a log and drained the brown water from her boots and rung out her socks, but she didn't bother wiping the mud off her greaves and cuirass. She stretched under the sunlight a moment longer and listened to the waking birds, then headed for Udug once again.

As she walked, her mind continued to analyze what had happened to her and how everything had changed. She wondered if Dingir would even let her return if she did get her soul back. The whole predicament probably scarred her reputation, and she'd probably always be on the receiving end of glares.

But it doesn't matter, Angela told herself. *I have to do it. I have to get my soul back.*

Two more thankfully uneventful days passed. The landscape continued to show signs that she was making progress. The brush that did grow was greener than what she'd seen before, and the air seemed more humid. Even the clairvoyance that drew her in the right direction had grown stronger and more persistent.

On the third day, long stretches of sandy beach surrounded a massive body of water, and she could smell the salt in the air. There were rotting fish, shells, and white birds along the shore.

On the fourth morning, Angela awoke feeling invigo-
rated even though her body had developed cramps and
screamed at her to stop walking. She ignored it all and
trudged on through the day, completely oblivious of nearly
everything until a large brown mass along the horizon
turned into clutches of homes. At least a dozen ships with
enough vertical space to house a second deck floated in the
water just off the beach. On land, a train of wagons
departed the city. It was a paradise compared to many of
the other places Angela had seen. She couldn't help but
smile and secretly hope to find something sweet to sip.

A jittery sensation came over her as, there in the open,
she undressed down to her white cotton pants and long-
sleeve shirt. The ocean breeze cutting through the cloth felt
wonderful and cooled her skin. Extra care went into
keeping as many wires attached between batteries and tools
as possible as she stuffed everything into her bag. With the
sack over her shoulder, Angela walked toward the city in
the distance.

The houses, most constructed of sandstone slabs
slathered with mortar and some made of wood, looked to
be of the same style as the homes in Dingir. The dirt roads
were almost as hard as bricks, compacted by the weight of
wagons and baked under the sun. The people, wearing linen
skirts and tan-colored robes, were oblivious to her. Beards
were popular among men, and the women wore shawls of
various colors and with embroidered designs. Wooden
stands lined the street in the center of town, which was full
of boisterous commotion. The city was a mixed variety of
people, and some of them spoke her language. At least she
could ask a question if she needed help.

She walked through the square on long strides and had
no intention of drawing out her stay or spending another

night in a human settlement. There were places that she had to be, a person to find, and she felt no need to stop there. The market shrunk behind her and the buildings reduced to single-level dwellings as she neared the outer edge of the town again. The yelling of tradesmen had faded under the noise of the salty breeze in her ears. She sighed and realized that she had been so enthralled with the sight of such a lively place that she hadn't been paying attention to the direction she was supposed to be going.

The soul inside her was now pointing directly behind her. The pull had shifted. She turned to face the city again, uncertain that what she thought she felt was true, but the feeling didn't go away. The compulsion *demanded* that she head back into town.

She dropped to her knees, laughing and crying from joy and fear at the same time. All the damned walking was over with; she'd found him—Udug was in that town.

CHAPTER TWELVE

Angela could hardly believe it. She hadn't seen anyone that looked odd or inhuman in any way. No lurking pedestrians in alleyways and no Dalkhu or Anunnaki, as far as she was aware. Yet she sensed a small vibration inside her as she traveled back into town.

The soul inaudibly hummed as though it was unable to point her any closer to Udug. Not that she would want to when not wearing her armor, but she couldn't rely on his soul to bring her to his exact location. As disappointing as that was, she didn't let it bother her. Nothing other than its clairvoyance had brought her this far in the first place.

The thought of stumbling into Udug unprepared worried her. She needed to be at the ready at all times, but waltzing around the town in full armor wasn't a passable idea, either. Being accused of robbery again, getting mugged, or being spotted by an Anunnaki or Dalkhu traveling through town were more reasons to be careful.

It was all the justification Angela needed. She'd have to be cautious, but nothing would stop her now that she'd come so close to finding the man who ruined everything for her—she swore it. So upon passing through the markets again, she spotted a line of well-crafted robes at a stand.

A man, dressed in a light purple robe much like the ones that hung behind him, was bartering with a woman. Angela approached the stand, eyeing the multitude of colors and styles in front of her. Theft crossed her mind, but she didn't want to go down that path if she didn't have to. If she were caught, she'd have to run, and there was no way she was going to leave the city willingly.

With a flick of the wrist, the man motioned the other woman away from his stand, shaking his head as though the deal between him and her was off. He turned his attention to Angela. His eyes glinted hues of green in the sunlight, and he said something to her.

"I'm sorry," Angela said. "I don't understand you."

The man smiled in a professional way, not a genuine glad-to-see-you kind of way. "Not a problem," the man said. "But you will 'ave to forgive me. Akkadian not my native tongue, see?"

Angela nodded, surprised at the man's bilingualism. While his words were heavy with an accent, she could understand him well enough.

"What interests you?" the man asked.

Angela pointed to the row of robes. "The ivory one. And the gray one."

The man nodded and plucked the two robes off the stand next to him. He showcased them as best as he could with one hand holding each color, and Angela admitted they both looked excellently made. While the gray one was more lackluster, its fabric felt much stronger. The ivory had dainty embroidery of a yellow flower coming up from the bottom, which Angela found a disheartening touch.

Still, she tried them both on. Mostly, she was looking for a robe that was a bit too big for her: she needed that extra room to allow her gear to rest somewhat unnoticeably underneath it. Bothered by the stupid flower on the ivory one, she ended up taking more interest in the gray one.

"What would I owe you?" Angela asked as she pulled her arms out of the gray robe.

The man placed a finger on his lips and tapped, humming as he thought. Angela rolled her eyes; he knew exactly what he wanted for it, but of course the man had to say it like it was a steal when it was really quite overpriced.

"I'd be willing for a single silver rin-guh or coin," the man said.

Angela cringed. "I don't have any silver. Anything else?"

Then she felt a tug at her waist. A boy with brown eyes and long hair dirtied by either dandruff or sand looked up at her. There were smudges of dirt on his cheeks, and he was missing a front tooth. He removed his hands from her waist and held them open to her.

Angela frowned and guessed the boy was somewhere between six or seven, and begging for money at that age was not a good sign for his future. She barely had the means to take care of herself, so she motioned the boy away, but she felt sorry for him.

The man watched the boy leave, then looked back at Angela, shrugging. "You wouldn't happen to have a coppa mirror or any-ting of value in that bag? Some-ting dat I could trade myself?"

Angela moaned in disapproval, quietly enough that the human couldn't hear her. After a quick glance over her shoulders, she stepped to the side of the stand and began rummaging through her bag. She sorted through it as discreetly as she could, trying to keep her equipment hidden from prying eyes, and closed it back up again. Holding her last red crystal to the man, she said, "What will this do?"

The man's eyes grew wide, and he reached out to grab it. Angela pulled away. He ran his fingers through his hair, suddenly looking exasperated by the sight of the crystal. "I can—" he stammered.

"The robe and something to cover my face and hands," Angela demanded.

His head cocked to the side. "Very well. I am impressed by your skill of... trade. Being a man of honor, I believe that the crystal is worth far too much for my wares. I will give you a few pieces of silver to go with you garbs, lest I feel guilty of robbing you. Very well, yes?" He held out his hand, and she gave him the crystal.

"Thank you," Angela said weakly. She had no desire to part with another crystal, but at least it was a red one. Those were of lesser value compared to the greens she had.

Within an hour, the man had set Angela up with the hoodless gray robe, a matching veil, a pair of pigskin gloves that were surprisingly soft, and three silver rings. The rings were small, thin, and unsuitable for wearing; none of them would fit on any of her fingers, but they appeared to be pure silver. After the transaction was complete, both Angela and the man nodded to one another, and Angela left to find a place to change clothes.

The city's streets had calmed as the shouting of busy people gave way to quiet murmurs. It was after midday, and the sun had already begun its descent. Ships anchored just off the docks had left, and a few she didn't recognize had shown up. As the city was winding down, Angela was gearing up.

She found an unoccupied home a few blocks off the main drag. Its single-story roof and a corner of the wall had crumbled to piles of sandstone both inside and outside the home. Whoever had owned the home hadn't left anything inside it, and it smelled more like the rock it was made of than any living quarters she'd ever been in.

Angela emptied her bag inside and dressed, covering herself and all of her equipment with the clothes she purchased. Looking down at her frame as best as she could, she realized that the clamp on her right shoulder was too large to hide. With regret, she stowed it away and tucked the sack underneath the rubble in the corner. Without the bulky trap, she looked acceptable enough, although a mirror would have aided her immensely.

A ladder led to the roof, and despite how unsound the construction was, Angela climbed it. Under the stare of the sun, and probably those of a few people somewhere below her, she sat cross-legged and looked out over the town. The soul inside her still hummed its excited song, and she took it as a sign that Udug was still in the area. She simply needed to wait for him to slip up and make himself seen.

Night came faster than Angela had anticipated; her mind was too busy thinking and watching for Udug to realize the time. She slept curled into a ball on the roof, not wanting to venture too far away from her post. The sun rose again on the other side of the city, and Angela watched the people awake and smelled the morning work of a bakery. She eyed crewmen working to load a boat with crates before setting off. Horse-drawn wagons came and left the market square, and she began to feel that she was getting nowhere.

Angela knew full well that Udug should have been rather easy to spot, considering his Anunnaki—*her* soul—

was inside him. He'd be aflame just as the Etlus were the day before, a product of the differences of the energies inside them, yet she hadn't seen a single flicker at any point.

He must be hiding.

Angela spent most of the afternoon watching the market. Feeling rather dull, her mind craved entertainment, and without her realizing it, she started watching a boy. It was the same child as the day before, the brown-haired boy who had tugged on her clothes and begged with open hands. He roamed around the main drag, begging travelers and merchants, and Angela felt disheartened again.

Does he not have parents? Who would leave their child so unaccompanied?

The boy turned away from a stand, clutching something to his chest, and began to run away. Even at her distance, Angela could tell that the boy seemed desperate to get away, and she wondered if he had stolen something. Needing something to do and feeling curious, Angela leapt to the ground below her.

She weaved through the homes between her and the square and stepped onto the busy dirt road. The boy dashed down a side road, through the rolling wheels of a cart and busy passersby. Angela wondered what gave the boy such a spur of energy and followed him. With a quick stride, she crossed the street and entered a narrow alleyway between buildings.

As she walked, she tried to find him through the restricting view of the veil over her face. There was a gasp to her side, and she found the boy hiding amidst a pile of discarded baskets of woven reed. He looked at her with wide eyes, clutching a piece of paper to his chest.

She kneeled and pulled the veil off her head. "Hello."

The boy looked confused for a moment, then relaxed when he recognized her.

"What have you got?" Angela asked, motioning to the paper.

He glanced down at his hands, then back up at her.

"Can you speak?"

The boy nodded. "Paper."

"I see that. Did you steal it?"

"No!" the boy blurted. "I'm not a stealer!"

"Well, where are your parents?"

The boy looked at his paper again. He shrugged.

"Are you all right?" Angela asked. "Do you have a home?"

He nodded, and she wasn't sure which question he was answering.

"If you need anything, you can say so," Angela said. "I'll be in that old home with a broken roof for a while, if you know where it is."

The boy nodded again, and his quietness somewhat annoyed her. He only had to say yes or no, and Angela would do her best to help in whatever way was possible. She was in need of something to do until she found Udug, anyway, and helping the boy would be a good way to burn time.

But the boy remained quiet, cautious, and thoughtful and seemed untrusting of her. When it seemed he would not speak, and her patience expired, she rose and said, "Have a good day."

As she turned to walk away, a small voice finally spoke behind her. "I need a customer!"

Angela spun around. "A customer?"

The boy stepped out from behind the mound of discarded baskets. In one hand he had the parchment, and in the other an inkwell. He looked up to Angela and came closer to her.

"I want to be a scribe," the boy said. "But I need customers."

"You know how to write?" Angela asked.

"Yeah. My father taught me a little, and I can do it."

Angela crossed her arms. "Well, that's good. I've been needing a letter written for a few days now."

His eyes glowed and his smile stretched from ear to ear. "Okay! I can do it for you."

He plopped onto his stomach right there on the ground, placed the parchment and inkwell in front of him, then rolled to the side and pulled a stick out of one of his pockets. It was a tiny, bent thing that had been whittled to a point on one end. The boy untied the string holding the inkwell shut and removed the lid, then liberally dipped his stick into it. He looked up at Angela. "What do you want it to say?"

Angela bit her lip, trying to think of anything. She began to pace the alleyway in front of the lying boy until the first thing came to her.

"Dear Michael," Angela started.

"How do you spell Michael?"

Angela held back a chuckle and told him. He scribbled as she pronounced each letter.

"How are you?" Angela said. "It's been a long time since we've spoken, and I'm happy to say that I'm getting very close to completing my quest. After that, I'll be home to see you. Until then, please do not forget to water my tree. Last I saw, it looked rather sad and mistreated."

The boy looked up from his scribbles. "What does that mean?"

"Mistreated?"

The boy nodded.

"It means to be handled without care or with cruelty."

The boy raised an eyebrow. "Okay," he said, returning to his paper.

She helped him spell it and told him, "Finish it with the words 'Sincerely, Angela.'"

Angela watched him scribble the last of it. When finished, he pushed himself to his knees, shook the stick to dry it before stuffing it back into his pocket, then handed Angela the paper. She scrutinized his handwriting. While there were misspellings and a few places where his stick had pierced the parchment, it was all there. He had managed to convey the idea, although she knew that the boy needed more practice and someone to guide him.

"Thank you very much," Angela said, smiling.

She dove her fingers into the pocket on her cuirass and held out a single silver ring to the boy. He took it gleefully.

"Thank you!" he said. "If you ever need anything else written, let me know and I'll do it for you."

Angela smiled. "I will do that. Until then, I hope you find many more customers." She bowed and left the boy where she had found him.

The street was just as busy as it was before. People weaved their way around one another, and shouting filled her ears. She felt good about hiring the boy and hoped the best for him as she crossed the street, but something red stood out in the corner of her eye, and she stopped. A man in a dull blue Simla and with a hunch in his back stood near a stand. He reached out and picked up a necklace from a stand and drew it closer to his hooded head. His hand was on fire.

Angela could feel the soul inside her spark to life, vibrating at the other's presence, and she began to march toward the figure. She closed half the distance between them, eyes locked onto the figure through the space between the fabric of her veil. Across the street, a second man turned and began walking toward the first, and Angela caught a glimpse of his face. He was shrouded in fire, too.

Angela spun around immediately. Neither of them could have been Udug. As far as she was aware, he was acting alone, and that explained how careless the man was in covering his skin and the unusual blue attire. She doubted he would have changed out of his customary black robe that Dalkhu councilmen usually wore, but for that moment, she wanted to believe she'd found him. They were Etlus, and she'd nearly walked right up to them.

She rushed down the street, turning off the main road at the first chance she could to break the line of sight with them. Her heart hammered in her chest, and even only jogging made her wheeze. Within a minute, the tickle in her chest elevated to burning, and she began to cough as thick mucus seemed to fill her lungs.

She had to stop, lean against the building next to her, lift the veil up the bridge of her nose, and hack between her wheezing. A small red pool of blood, mucus, and spit gathered at her feet. Her legs felt weak. That was the second time she coughed blood, which was too frequent to be a fluke. Something serious was ailing her, and she wondered if she had gotten sick or if the wound in her stomach had become infected.

Something came between her elbow and her side, hooking her by the arm and tugging her forward.

"With me," a rough voice said.

Letting the cloth fall over her mouth again, she swallowed. A man with gloved hands had grabbed her by the arm and pulled her forward. It took her a few steps to realize that he was dressed in a black robe. His hood was up, his face concealed by a clay mask with circles around the eyes and sharp lines along the jaw—the kind of mask humans wore when inflicted with lesions and boils. Small oval slits allowed him to see and breathe, but his eyes sparked, and she saw a flame birthing outward from somewhere deep inside them.

Angela felt like her heart stopped. "It's you."

The man's head swung about like a top, constantly looking to the sides and behind them. He paid what she had said no mind, and they walked another twenty steps. It was him, here, taking her by the arm and dragging her forward. Angela clenched her fist.

"I know who you are," she said. Angela wrenched her arm from his grip, stopping mid-stride and glaring into the man's eyes. He straightened his crooked back, pausing to look at her. Her hand had already reached into the folds of her robe and clasped the gun at her waist.

"Say your name," Angela demanded. "Say it!"

The eyes looked at her, his head tilted to the side. A raspy voice spoke from behind the mask: "I am Udug."

Angela's hand jerked out of her robe like the snap of a bowstring as she pulled the trigger. The tether gun sizzled and fired, ejecting the steel spike and a cloud of scalding steam with it. When it cleared, dust puffed behind him; she missed. Obscenities rolled off her tongue and she began to reach for the brass knuckles with her left hand while pressing the retraction button on the gun. As she fumbled through her robe, the winch inside the gun whirred, pulling the cable and spike back inside. Angela couldn't tell, but she was certain that Udug was amused. He lurched and grabbed her arm again, then pulled her closer and shook.

"Stop this," he said. "I'm trying to save your life."

Angela was appalled, disgusted at the thought of being saved by the man who put her in that situation to begin with. "Let go of me," she demanded.

"You don't understand. There is more than Anunnaki in this city."

The dreaded clashing sound of teleportation reverberated down the street.

A councilman was standing just fifty yards away. Humans screamed and tripped over one another as they ran from the cloaked figure. A scar damaged the skin where his eyebrow should have been. His auburn eyes glared from under his hood, and long brown hair spilled out over his chest. Not another second passed as more appeared. One by one, they arrived and lowered their hoods. Seeing the facial features of Dalkhu men was something Angela was not used to.

A majority were well aged, and all were men. A quarter of them had piercings in their lips, ears, and eyebrows, and fewer yet had tribal tattoos on their hands, necks, and faces. They walked toward her, relaxed and calm, and moved with meticulous, practiced strides. Each foot landed before the other with calculation and a sense of strength that said they deserved to show their faces in the open. They walked like hunters, and Angela had never seen ten of them together in one place before.

"Come, Anunnaki," Udug said. He pulled on her arm again. "They will kill us both if we do not flee."

Angela turned, brow furrowed. "Why would they kill me?" She pulled back her fist, ready to strike him.

His voice grumbled beneath his mask. "You're as tainted as I am, and they do not want war with your people. They seek to clean the slate."

Angela scoffed. "I didn't do anything in this. You're the one who cast the spell."

Udug's head tilted to the side for a moment as he contemplated it, and his eyes seemed to spark to life. "You've spoken with Shedim, then?"

Angela nodded. "He told me you—"

A heavy voice from down the street interrupted him. "Udug Hul." The man had a beard that covered his chest in a mess of gray and brown. Wrinkles ran across his forehead, his eyes drooped heavier than those of the others, and he stood in the center of the councilmen. "For defacing our traditions and code, for the murder of councilman Ninurta and your pupil Anzu, and for bridging the elements as recklessly as you did, we, the remaining ten of the Council, hereby demand you give yourself up. Stop running from your mistakes and we ensure you a quick death."

Udug tipped his head up as he laughed, then took a step closer. "Ruchin, is it not obvious that I no longer abide by Council law? I have done nothing for far too long." He spun and grabbed Angela's arm again, but she had expected that to happen. She could feel Udug's aura fill the air with vibrations as he pushed them into the veil, and she slammed the button on her shifter. In a matter of moments, she could hear him grumble and could feel the veil flex around them as he pushed harder and harder.

His eyes blazed and he shook her when he realized that her shifter was anchoring them there. "What *are* you doing?" he asked.

Angela smiled. Part of her didn't care if she died right there. At least he'd die, too. The councilmen just down the road knew what she'd done immediately. In the blink of an eye, they disappeared, only to reappear around them in a rough circle, blocking them from running anywhere. Udug grabbed his mask and pulled it off, knocking down his hood in the process. His lip curled and the sparks that bounced off his tongue stung Angela's cheeks as he said, "You are a fool." He released her, and with a great thrust of his mind, he pierced the veil, carved a circle around them, and bridged a hole between two worlds.

The ground beneath her feet trembled. Mounds of dirt formed and clouds of sand flew into the air. Rough walls of jagged stone erupted around them and crashed together above her head. She rubbed at her eyes, trying to clear the grit from them as the rock crushed together around her. By the time she was able to open her eyes again, walls of stone had encapsulated her and Udug in their cool shade. He had formed a prison by conjuring the rock from another dimension. A small breeze funneled in through an opening above. The stones around them stilled and the rumbling stopped.

Angela tried to take a step away from Udug, but her head clunked against the rock. "What are you doing?" she asked. "What are you gaining out of this?"

Fire sprouted from his mouth and spread across his face. He scowled and said, "I'm buying us time since you won't."

"I have no qualm with them, just you! All of this is your fault and you are going to help me get back my soul."

Udug shook his head. "You've no idea how incredibly difficult that would be."

"But it's obviously possible. Why else would you protect me from the Council? You want your soul back just as much as I do."

His voice was deep and cracked like the sound of a ship's hull breaking on rocky shores. "There are bigger things at play, much more pressing matters at this moment than returning things to the way they were."

Angela pulled back her fist as far as the confines of their small stone prison would allow. "You'll do it. Immediately."

He rose like a flaming giant and loomed over her. "Do you not know the basics of a soul's foundation? Are you so arrogant, like the rest of your people, that you cast out old truths for the sake of a peaceful mind and have discarded the knowledge available to you? What do you think happens when you rip a soul from the body it's aligned to? We're doomed! We are destined to die from this. Surely you've noticed: these changes are already destroying our bodies! I have no idea what would happen if I attempted to do the same thing twice, let alone how."

Angela let her fist fall to her side. Ever since they met on the rooftop in Dingir, she hadn't felt right. Sickness and fatigue had been constant. She nearly vomited on Donny's floor and actually did when she first arrived on Earth. She had coughed up blood twice: once in the smoke of the Ascendancy and the second time just minutes ago. The Dalkhu's soul was killing her.

"All the more reason to fix it," Angela muttered.

Udug shook his head. "Not now," he said sternly. "I have to make sure we survive *this* first, since you're too stupid to realize it."

"But you will do it?" Angela asked.

Udug looked at her, and even through the flames of his soul she could see the solemnness of his expression. "I may try. But I make no promises, and there is something I must take care of first."

"What's tha—"

Udug shushed her with an open hand. "Do you hear that?"

Angela slowed her breathing and listened. Ever so

faintly, a conversation was taking place just outside their stone shelter.

THE BEARDED COUNCILMAN STRAIGHTENED HIS BACK. "YOU defile the elemental barriers again, Udug," he mumbled. Ruchin had been inspecting the stone walls, trying to guess the amount of force it would take to crush the box. While he suspected there was enough room for one more person inside and he could try to teleport into the space, he knew that would likely get him killed. It hadn't sounded like the traitor and the tool had teleported out of there yet, so he figured it was just a matter of time.

Why did you not teleport away, Udug? Why have you allowed us to trail you so closely, and what are you waiting for now?

A hand touched his shoulder, and Ruchin turned to face his peer. A younger man with wooden piercings that looked like black-painted toothpicks in both eyebrows pointed down the street. Ruchin grumbled when he saw it; twenty-eight Etlus marched closer in the formation of a thick wedge. With their shimmering brass contraptions, all were cloaked in a spectacle of flame and sunlight. This was certainly the largest group of Anunnaki he had ever seen in person.

With a command, he signaled the other councilmen to form a tight line. Within moments they were in order, and they began to walk closer. Both parties stopped in the middle of the street a mere twenty feet from each other. A moment passed when no one said anything, and there were only glares until he broke the silence.

"What brings such a large force before us?" Ruchin

asked the Etlus, speaking loudly. "This matter with our councilman is ours to reprehend."

An Anunnaki stepped forward, and something about his figure reminded Ruchin of someone he had met long ago.

"How long has it been since we last attempted court?" the burning man asked.

Ruchin recognized his voice and looked down in thought for a moment, then said, "Decades, Kushiel."

Kushiel nodded. "I agree. It has been a"—he paused —"*relatively* peaceful time, yes?"

"It has."

"Then am I correct to assume, considering your statement thus far, that the Council does not claim to have ordered the spell that has devastated us?"

"We have no part in it. One of our councilmen has broken many of the laws set by our forefathers, but you did not answer my question. What brings you here in such numbers?"

"To fix your mistake. The woman whom your councilman has corrupted is ours," Kushiel said. "You can't have her."

The street was quiet except for the breeze. Ruchin shifted his weight and stroked his beard in thought. "Very well. Perhaps, for one time, we will work together and cleanse the mistakes Udug has made, so long as the woman dies before us."

"Agreed," Kushiel said. "I'm glad we understand each other."

Ruchin bowed slightly, "I feel the sa—"

Shouting erupted from behind him. Humans brandishing spears charged down the street. They wore nothing but skirts and simple leather bands across their chests. One of the men wielded a curved blade. His ears were pierced with gold earrings, and gemmed necklaces draped around his neck. They shouted like a war party and ran like a pack of wolves, kicking up dust as they sprinted. Ruchin groaned; humans were an annoyance.

With a few seconds of concentration, he reached out with his mind and took hold of the one that looked like the leader. With a push from his soul, he shoved the man through the veil from a distance of almost thirty feet. To make a better example of him, he only held the man in the fire for a fraction of a second and removed him. The movement was so quick that it appeared as though he had instantaneously burst into flame.

Ruchin smirked. It wasn't just a message to the humans to back away and stay out of higher beings' dealings; it told the Anunnaki that they weren't dealing with the average Dalkhu. Every one of the councilmen played a part in maintaining the Dalkhu's law and order for a reason. They had trained their bodies, minds, and souls for centuries. They were faster, they knew what a battle was like, and they were lethal.

By the time the man returned from his trip to the elemental plane, his skin had already charred and bubbled beyond his kind's ability to heal. In a world that contained the very essence of flame, death came quickly. The man screamed in agony as globs of molten necklace oozed down his chest. He toppled onto the ground, flailing and moaning until the street was finally quiet again.

The other humans stopped, their heads spinning as they tried to comprehend what black magic they had just witnessed. Ruchin chuckled, and he wondered if they thought it was the power of a devil or a god that had smitten their friend. He was neither, and it wasn't magic. Just simple projection. He watched them turn and run, leaving the stench of their comrade's burning carcass in the air.

Michael stepped to Kushiel's side and asked, "Are we going to do anything?"

Kushiel shook his head. "Not today."

Michael sighed, and Ruchin relished knowing they did not have the upper hand here.

The councilman said, "Let us also agree to keep our distances from one another. Your concern is in there." He motioned to the stone capsule. "We will take the far side, closest to the sea. Know that if they attempt to warp away we will not hesitate to go after them. If your devices cannot keep pace, we will leave you behind without a second thought, and you may lose your demands to see the woman dead."

"We understand," Kushiel said. "But you don't need to worry. We are not sluggish."

He fought the urge to scoff at his bluff. No Anunnaki could operate that unnatural device as quickly as a Dalkhu could command his soul. The councilmen turned and walked to the side of the street while the Etlus settled themselves across from them.

Together, they encircled the stone prison—except for Michael, who walked to it. He scrutinized it for weaknesses, just as Ruchin had earlier, and figured that if they sent someone back to Dingir for explosives they could take care of the problem with little delay. But even Michael wanted more than that; he wanted to see the aberration of his wife before it died. Speak with it. Curse it. Then kill it.

He placed a hand on the stone and said, "even I have come for you," and walked away.

CHAPTER THIRTEEN

Angela froze when she heard Michael speak. His presence—his actions—were like giant skeletal hands that reached out and gripped her by the heart. He squeezed the life out of her and filled her with grief and pain. Maybe it wouldn't have come that far if she hadn't tried to solve the problem on her own.

She thought herself a fool. She had betrayed his trust by keeping her sickness from him for too long, and now he'd come to his own conclusions. She had needed him the whole time, but with him set in his ways and as stubborn as he was, Angela knew she couldn't convince him that she was still herself.

He didn't understand that she was still *mostly* in her own body, just because she didn't ask for help when she needed it. Then again, Angela admitted that if she was going to die, she'd rather die by Michael's hands. At least then he would have a chance to put his heart at rest and live a happy life.

It was done: her fate decided, wrapped with a bow, and handed back to her. The only thing she could do was move forward, without him, and hope that in the end she would regain her soul and they would leave all of it behind them.

The worst of it was that Angela knew he was there to kill her. If he had come to Earth, he would have had to at least have some basic training over the past few days to learn what creatures to avoid, the plant life that caused rashes, and the policies on human contact. No one would go through all that for no reason.

A tear rolled down her cheek and touched the corner of her lip. She wiped at it in the darkness of the stone prison, glancing at Udug briefly to see if he noticed. He was sitting cross-legged, eyes closed in meditation. He'd calmed his soul and the fires she saw around him so she could see him for who he truly was: a hunched old man with gray and brown hair. Wrinkles were prominent on his forehead, and patches of scruffy beard grew along his jawline. She'd seen glimpses of his yellow eyes.

The talking outside had ceased a few hours ago, and time inside the box had been slow and silent. Angela hadn't spoken to Udug since their last conversation, and now he was busy trying to think of a way to escape their fate. Angela had turned off her shifter over an hour ago to conserve her batteries, but now it all seemed pointless. A life with Michael chasing her wasn't worth living, and Angela didn't want to run anymore.

"It's been too long," Udug whispered, breaking the silence abruptly. "I imagine it won't be long before your warriors begin blasting the rock away."

Angela, too weary to speak with him, kept her thoughts to herself.

Udug opened his eyes and tilted his head to the side. "Nothing to say, fire?"

Angela laughed. "Plenty to say. I just won't waste my breath on you."

"Good."

Angela ground her teeth. "What did you have to gain out of this? I mean, why did you do it? I don't understand."

"There was never anything in it for me, personally," Udug said, straightening his legs and arching his back. "I attempted the spell for the good of my people. Certainly, you can understand that notion. Don't take my actions to heart. You were just the unlucky Anunnaki that showed up in the human settlement that day. It's just war. Sure, I undermined my own Council and tried to find a way to learn Dingir from the inside out, and it might cost me my life, but I would do it again in my next life."

"All of this just to—"

A muffled boom shook the stone shelter, surrounding her with the sound of gnashing rocks. Tilting her head upward, she looked through the hole as if it would help her hear what was happening outside.

"Someone just left," Angela guessed. "Probably to grab those explosives you talked about. Maybe we should go. Sorry for keeping you here. I was angry, but maybe we can work together to escape your people and see about returning things to normal, yeah?"

An unnerving and menacing grin stretched across Udug's face. He shook his head and stood as he lost his concentration and the fire began to sprout from his nostrils and eyes again. "No, someone else has *come*."

He reached out and grabbed her by the elbow faster than she could slap his hand away, then pushed them into the veil's timeless expanse. The tingling feeling like frost had settled on her skin, and the journey that felt like forever was over instantly. Angela's ears rang, and she squinted in the sun's light as her eyes adjusted. They stood in the middle of the road, only a few feet from the blocky stone prison that looked much larger from the outside.

The size of the Etlu force was an astounding show of might. They were serious about getting ahold of her and using her as an example to the Dalkhu. The flames of their souls, so close together in formation, grew five feet over their heads, and Angela recognized a few of them: Michael, Kushiel, and a few others she had worked with before. Someone behind her cleared his throat, and Angela turned.

Councilmen put their weight on their knees and rose to their feet. The sight of them perplexed Angela; they carried some strength that she had never seen before. They were proud Dalkhu, whereas others were shifty.

"I've done it, Master," a voice said.

It was hard for Angela to hear over the ringing in her ears, but she found that it came from atop the roof of a home only a few feet away. Shedim stood up there, looking down at her and smiling, his shoulders back and pride gleaming across his face.

"What are you doing here?" Angela asked.

"Very good," Udug said.

Fresh cuts riddled Shedim's face and forearms. His chest was exposed where his robes had been slashed open. A section around his feet was frayed. He'd torn a piece off and used it as a compress on his leg where he'd been impaled on the Ascendancy's roof. There was a single blood-crusted mark the size of a dime just below his exposed shoulder, evidence that he was shot with a tether gun. Shedim reached into his robe and retrieved a leather bag from an inner pocket and shook it with a smile. The bag sounded as though it was filled with pebbles.

"Shedim!" Angela shouted up at him, demanding his attention.

"I see you there, Angela," he said, glaring down at her. "Be quiet."

Her eyes narrowed.

Kushiel took a few steps closer, the flames of his soul flickering in the wind. He pointed at Shedim and threw his palms in the air, confused. "He was as good as ours! What the hell, Ja'noel!"

Shedim leapt from the roof and cringed when he tried to absorb all of the impact on his good leg. He stumbled to a kneel, but in a moment, he rose and brushed past Angela.

"Certainly, this is not all of them," Shedim said. He smiled and handed the bag to Udug, who clutched it tightly in his bony hands. "Even so, I believe this will give us a drastic advantage in the war. One that will change the tides between Dingir and Kur."

Ruchin stormed to them with a reddening face, his beard swaying. "There is, and will never be, a war like that. Watch your tongues. To speak of it so openly will incite conflict. There *is* and there *will be* no war."

Udug held up a hand and said, "You are wrong, old friend." He untied the leather bag and retrieved a handful of shards that glowed with pulsing lights of green, blue, and red. "With such a portion of crystal shards, the means by which the Anunnaki travel between worlds, we finally have the upper hand." He began to pour the crystals back into the bag. "I have drawn the Anunnaki from their floating city and replaced them with a single thief. I have also drawn you, Councilmen." He tied the bag shut again and held it out, letting it hang from his palm.

Shedim wasn't running from Udug and seeking asylum in Dingir for fear of his life. He was a part of his master's plan to strike a blow at Dingir. That bag has to have hundreds of them.

Angela's ears pounded as Ruchin snatched the sack from Udug's hands and teleported to the other councilmen's sides. They frantically huddled around him, begging to look inside the bag.

"I give you the first blow of victory," Udug said. "With the momentum of it, may our dreams of unity no longer be a second purpose of our existence but our primary. Will you fight with me to restore the crystal shards of the Anchor and unify the worlds?"

"Unify the worlds?" Angela asked.

Udug stared down the bridge of his nose. "The crystals are more than just stones. They are the shattered remains of the Anchor. A crystal with the energy to hold the dimensions together, as it did for the Nephilim before us."

Angela's fist clenched. "Are you insane? Do you understand what joining all the worlds together would do? Two objects can't exist in the same place, and you'd be forcing them back together. If it is true, think of the destruction! You'd die, too."

Udug sneered and slapped Angela across the cheek. She held her skin softly as Udug stepped closer and said, "I will not accept criticism from you. Do you think I am daft? That I wouldn't know what restoring the Anchor entails? For nearly a thousand years I've watched pupils, brothers, and comrades suffer by your people's hands. So yes, I want to see this through more than anything I've ever felt before."

Ruchin clasped the bag shut and looked to Udug. As he thought in silence, he gnashed his teeth until he finally said, "Your means are absolutely preposterous, Udug. You defile too many laws we've passed for our own protection and to avoid angering the Anunnaki to the point where they hunt us like we are wild animals." He lifted his chin and sighed. "But it has been many years since I have felt that repairing our worlds was possible. Fellow councilmen, do we absolve Udug for the laws he has broken? Do we move forward and begin the reconstruction of the Anchor? What do you say?"

There was a moment of silence, and all eyes rested on those councilmen. Even though Angela felt strongly, she knew what the consensus would be. She still hoped that they would condemn Udug. The minds of the Dalkhu Council were weighed down by the seriousness of their decision, but one by one, each said yes.

And the decision was war.

Heavy boots stomped the ground in unison behind her. With a curled lip and fire jutting from his maw, Kushiel screamed, "Engage, Etlus! No forbearance! Kill them all!"

The front row of warriors broke into a bull rush. They brandished brass knuckles and knives, drawing them from their waists with trained precision. The second line's packs burst open and their wings unfolded with loud hissings and cranks as they shot into the air with a single powerful stroke. Their machines squealed in their effort, and on the third thrust, they angled to dive toward Angela and the Council.

Spikes and the cables of tether guns zipped through the air, past Angela, and kicked up sand where they missed their mark. Ruchin and several other councilmen screamed and clutched their chests as they were shocked. Shedim twitched and toppled to the ground at Angela's feet. With Dalkhu bearing down on her from the left and the Etlus from the right, she activated the wings on her back. In a moment they sprung free, jolting her body with the power they contained. She kicked Shedim's side while she still had the time, then launched herself free from the ground.

Angela furled the machine's right wing almost immediately, rolling herself to avoid one of the Etlu's tether bolts. Slamming her fingers down on the controller, she straightened, then looked past her feet. Three soldiers broke off the V-shaped formation and began to follow her upward. She cursed, and by pressing two buttons simultaneously, she surged forward over the yellow stone buildings.

Udug gripped the cable with his gloved hands and pulled the prong from Shedim's body. The boy's convulsions ceased, and he pulled his pupil to his feet and braced against him as he found his footing. The blood that poured from Shedim's nose looked like melted iron underneath the blaze of his soul. With great care not to touch his skin, Udug rushed him back behind the other councilmen. They formed a line between them and the advancing Anunnaki when Shedim murmured, "That's the third time I've been electrocuted."

Udug smiled, then turned Shedim by his shoulders to face him and said, "Go home. You've done a service to your people that will be remembered forever. In all my years of teaching, no other student could do as you have done. You bested the maws of death."

Shedim grinned at his master, proud to have received the acknowledgment.

"I will accompany you in the Kissum when this is over with," Udug said.

"I am honored, Lamid Piristi," Shedim said.

When he felt that Shedim could stand on his own, he

slowly removed his supporting hand and stepped back. His pupil closed his eyes and, after ten seconds of unsteady concentration, disappeared in an abrupt bang that blew his robes back.

Udug sighed and took a moment.

After all the years of watching his pupils return to him in suffering and feeling the pain and anger that came with it, he'd done it. While possessing an Anunnaki and learning their city from the inside out was his original plan, this one worked out just fine, he admitted. He had predicted the future with such accuracy it almost scared him.

He knew that Angela would be cast out and run from her own people if she had survived the spell. Those who chased after her would leave Dingir horribly undefended while he angered his own Council so that they would chase him. Angela would search for him on Earth while Shedim ransacked Dingir as best as he could. Eventually, all of them would gather here for the first large-scale battle in centuries.

Not only had he dealt a heavy blow, but he had rallied his Council into action by leading them here and showing them what could be accomplished.

Udug smiled to himself. *It worked.*

WITH DAGGERS DRAWN, THE COUNCILMEN CLASHED WITH the Etlus and their shocking weapons. Despite the overwhelming number of Anunnaki soldiers, they had difficulty landing blows on the councilmen. Before their fists landed or their blades cut, the Dalkhu would warp a mere foot away in any direction. The constant buffering bursts of air disoriented the Etlus and drove fear into their minds—they were up against targets they could barely keep track of. If it wasn't for the hard leather armor that the soldiers wore, the quick slashes of the councilmen's daggers would have killed them already.

"They will tire!" Kushiel yelled from behind the lines. He paced back and forth, analyzing every one of his soldiers as they fought to encircle and kill the Dalkhu. "Stay fast and wait for them to slip!"

Through the line of clashing brass, cloak, and flame, Kushiel could see Ruchin standing alone. His eyes fluttered as he reached upward with his mind and took hold of one of the Anunnaki flying above. With each push of the energy in his soul, Ruchin projected another Anunnaki into the other worlds, and one by one, those in formation in the sky died.

Some of the Etlus burst into flames and spiraled down to the ground as they screamed, hitting themselves in an attempt to put out the fire burrowing into their skin. Others were thrown into the dimension of air, and they appeared to explode in splatters of blood and limbs under the force of unimaginable torrents of wind. With splats, bloody chunks of their bodies and burning figures crashed into homes, carts, and stands and began to litter the area around the battle.

Kushiel grieved his dead soldiers. He'd seen something like this once before a long time ago. It was a typical Dalkhu tactic to keep a majority of the enemy force busy with hand-to-hand combat while one or more other Dalkhu stayed back and slowly picked apart the front line. He'd lost good soldiers that time, too, but swore that he would change his own tactics now.

"Shifters on!" Kushiel ordered. "I don't care what you have to disconnect, but shifters turn on!"

Michael stood only a few feet from him, his head tilted

upward, watching Angela soar above as three Etlu chased her. His fists were clenched and his eyes were as hard as steel. Kushiel knew that Michael was enraged like he'd never been before, and he couldn't hold that against him, but he was getting harder to control. He waved a hand in front of him to get his attention and said, "Ruchin will pick us apart one by one if we let him. I'm going on assault while he's preoccupied."

Michael only nodded in silence, then turned his attention back to the sky.

"If I die, Rig is in command," Kushiel said. He jabbed a finger into Michael's cuirass, and that got his attention better. "If he tells you to retreat, you do so. Understood?"

Michael ground his teeth. "Understood, but I'm breaking off from the group. I'm going after her."

Kushiel sighed and placed a hand on his shoulder. "Have speed and find peace for the both of us, then."

Michael was hesitant but nodded as his wings sprang outward. He wouldn't do anything for Kushiel after what he did all those years ago, but it didn't hurt to ask. With a few short sweeps of his wings, Michael rose into the air without a word.

Kushiel's right hand found the gun at his waist as he set his sights on Ruchin across the battlefield. His breathing picked up as he rushed into the front line. A dagger lashed out at him as he launched past the councilmen in a dive, hit the ground, and rolled. As he came to his knees, he raised his gun and fired. The wind carried the gun's steam back at him, stinging his cheeks and forehead and forcing him to cover his eyes. When it cleared, Ruchin was clutching the spike embedded in his side as he shook on the ground. The killing had stopped for a moment.

Kushiel walked to the old man still lying on his back

and moaning in agony. The flames that rose from his body heated the air around him, warping and distorting it into shifting mirages. Wondering who would lead the Dalkhu after Ruchin, he brandished his dagger from the back of his belt. The councilman's horrified expression reflected on the golden hilt of the blade.

"This is it," Kushiel said as he crouched and held the knife over the councilman. The heat was almost unbearable. "May the one who takes your place be wiser than you."

A gust of wind rammed into Kushiel with tremendous force, knocking him off the ground. The dagger and his gun flew from his hands as the air was forced from his lungs. His back crashed into a stone wall, jerking his head and neck in a sudden stop. The blast of teleportation had never hit him that hard before. He gasped once, then hunched over as his consciousness left him.

Udug stood twenty paces back, eyes closed as he concentrated on mending the area of the veil he had cut open. In a few moments, he sealed the breach where the constant rush of air originated and relaxed. He kneeled over Ruchin, careful not to get too close.

"I-I can't do this," Ruchin said. His breathing was labored, and Udug knew it was true. "Seems I cannot take a hit like I could when I was your age."

"I do not hold it against you," Udug said. "You take the Anchor's shards with you. Keep them safe."

Ruchin patted his robe and nodded. Then he frowned. "I am still not fond of your methods. You know better than to bring the elements forth from their dimensions. What if it tears out of control and can't be closed? And the Nephilim spell you've used… You have stooped so low."

Udug scoffed. "Do not chastise me for the means that I use when they give you results you have never seen. Now is the time we take chances."

Ruchin stared at him in thought, but when the words didn't come, he only shook his head and disappeared with the booming sound of thunder.

Udug laughed to himself. He knew Ruchin hated him, and it brought him great pleasure. A long time had passed since he first began to feel that the Council needed to change its ways, and now he had proven that the laws they abided by only complicated their path to victory and reforming the Anchor. Nothing could be off limits if the Dalkhu wanted to win.

ANGELA DOVE DOWNWARD, CASTING HERSELF BETWEEN A row of buildings. They whizzed past her, eerily close to the ends of her wings at times, but she was glad there weren't as many humans out. She hugged the ground as close as she dared, blowing clouds of dust into the air with each thrust of her mechanical wings. Looking over her shoulder, she caught glimpses of the Etlus' flaming silhouettes against the sunlight. They hadn't given up the chase, and Angela knew that if they switched places, she wouldn't, either.

The probes from their tether guns plinked the ground all around her, and she weaved what little she could in the street but knew that it wouldn't save her forever.

In a brash move, she angled her wings back and forced herself upright with a single stroke. The sudden thrust in the opposite direction brought her to a near stop, and the pressure of the straps pulling on her torso caused her to involuntarily groan. The pack shifted slightly on her back, but Angela paid it no mind. By angling herself and thrusting once more, she jetted sideways, turning sharply through a large archway.

Angela thought she was entering a large building, but she realized that the roofless structure was an open courtyard surrounded by walls of yellow stones decorated with pillars and arches at opposite ends. It was a temple with carved pictograms and colored writings along the walls and floors, and it was crowded with humans. As Angela tore above them, they wailed, ducked, and ran. She bent her knees, narrowly avoiding hitting heads with her feet.

The three Etlus gained on her, diving closer at incredible speed. She could just make out their tether guns and swerved before they fired, but one of the spikes pierced the linen of her right wing. The projectile continued onward and lodged into the skull of a woman below her. She collapsed onto the floor, dropping the child in her arms.

With both ends of the cable anchored and with Angela's forward momentum, the electrical cord tore a line through her wing, fraying and letting air slip through at every flap. The lack of force threw her into a spin, and the wing's metal frame began to beat against the humans below her as she passed.

A row of three arched gateways sat at the approaching end of the temple courtyard. To stop her descent, she slammed a button on the cabled controller and flapped the right wing. While she did level out, the force of the single wing was not enough to maintain altitude. She held her arms over her head as she began to bludgeon people and skip across them like a rock thrown over water. Mashing the controls did little to stem her as the stone pillars grew closer. There was nothing she could do about it.

Angela heard the metal frame of her right wing crunch and buckle backward on impact. It shed bolts and nuts and fractured into three separate pieces. Bracing herself, she was thrown into a spiral over the street outside the temple. In that moment of suspension in the air, through the space between her arms, she saw Michael barreling toward her, his brow furrowed.

He slammed into her with his shoulder, crushing her side and filling her ears with the sound of clashing metal as their wings collided. Angela could taste blood as she skidded across the dirt and sand. Once she stopped, she lay still, clutching her side and catching her breath. Her lip was torn open and bleeding and the pain in her ribs was more than just a bruise.

The wind carried the cloud of dust from the street. The air cleared, and she cursed and struggled to her feet. Fragments of metal lay scattered outside the temple, and the people who had been inside ran in the opposite direction now, leaving her and Michael in silence. He stood, his flames rising as he did.

The sound of clomping boots drew her attention behind her. The three other Etlus who had been chasing her were now on the ground and running at her, their daggers drawn and knuckles bared. They moved toward her without cranking their wings into their packs, flames growing hotter. But they stopped, and after a moment of hesitation, they nodded and returned their weapons to their waists.

Michael held a hand up, ordering them to stop where they were. His eyes burned like hot coals. She felt like they were a pack of wolves and she was his prey, and Angela almost smiled. Dying by Michael's hands would at least give him peace.

He held his chin up, fire spreading over his skin and veins of magma tunneling beneath the surface. "Here we are again. If there's any respect for law and order in you, rogue, you'll lay down your weapons and accept it. You have no right to use our people's weapons."

Angela shook her head and rattled her mind, trying to think of some way she could talk Michael out of it. Just one sentence that would make him pause long enough to really think about it. "I can't," she said. "And I'll only say this once: I am not the Dalkhu you think I am. It's me, Angela." She brought her hands to her chest. "I'm in here, Michael. You've just got to believe me."

His lip curled. "You are not her! I am not a fool. I've seen the scroll!" With quick hands he unbuckled the broken wings from his back and flung the pack to the side. "I know about the possession. I know what you did to her!" One hand reached for the silver dagger he stabbed Donny with; the other hand wrung fingers through brass knuckles. He pointed the blade at her. "You have violated everything that we had, and I will kill you for it!"

He crossed the distance between them and slashed at her throat, then followed with a swing of his brass knuckles. Angela stumbled backward and bent in awkward stances, weaving as a torrent of attacks came at her. Michael shifted his weight and worked his feet skillfully, his curved dagger flashing. He reached out to grab her, but Angela jaunted forward under his arm and swung for where his cuirass met his greaves, slammed the brass knuckles into his hip, and zapped him.

He stumbled and groaned. Angela retreated a few steps to catch her breath. She unstrapped her pack, shed herself of the extra weight, and removed the robe over her armor, knowing that he'd use them both against her. Facing her with hands held in front of him, he sliced for her midsection, swooping the dagger as far out as he could reach. It grazed against her cuirass but did little damage, and Michael began to stumble forward as he overextended himself. She bashed her fist against the underside of his chin with metal, staggering him to the ground. He rolled onto his back and spat blood, then wiped it from his lips.

"Very impressive," Michael said, his teeth glimmering red. "It seems I've underestimated you." He grunted as he rose to his feet again. She knew she shouldn't have been surprised; Michael never was one to give up.

"What are you going to do when all of this is over?" Angela asked.

He chuckled and began to circle her. "That's not your concern."

Angela shook her head. "No, I want you to answer me. What are you going to do when I come back? When your *wife* comes back?"

"Stop playing games with me." He lunged forward, thrusting the dagger into the air. "You're not my wife!"

Angela leaned forward and stepped back at the same time, bending herself over the jab at her midsection. His hand grabbed the back of her head and clutched her by the hair, and suddenly his knee came up at her and smashed into her face. Angela gasped and stepped back, clutching the bridge of her nose and trying to keep from drowning in her own blood. She'd never been hit in the nose before, and the agony astounded her. For a second, she paid more attention to her pain than to Michael, and he knew it. He surged forward again, sweeping his legs at her feet and knocking her onto her back.

Angela groaned as a streak of pain ripped through her back. Michael loomed over, quickly coming down with the dagger to finish her. She rolled, avoiding it, and pushed herself to her feet as quickly as she could, but he was swinging at her again. The tip of his blade nicked her chin as she regained her balance. She leaned backward and kicked out with her leg, striking him in the side. The impact staggered him, but he was quick to keep himself from losing his balance.

Angela shook the fog from her mind and collected her breath. Michael spat more blood, glaring at her as he raised his hands once more. She could see the rage in his eyes and sense it every time he swung at her. He had no self-control and lashed out at her without precision. That was his biggest weakness. She needed to remain calm. It didn't matter if she was going to die or if she would escape; the fight would end and things would get better for both of them.

Bursting forward, Angela sidestepped Michael's swing. She grabbed at his pauldron and ripped the clamp from his shoulder. Dropping to one knee, she rerouted the power from her shifter to the clamp and slammed the device onto his leg. It engaged with a sharp clank as the vice snapped down. Then the drill began to whirl. Pure horror streaked across Michael's face as he realized what was happening. He lobbed his knuckles at her head, knocking her back in another dizzying attack.

Michael bent over and fidgeted with panicked fingers as he tried to disengage the device. The pitch of the drill fell an octave lower as it burrowed deeper and began to tear muscle. He screamed and clawed at it, trying to wrench the bear trap open. The panic in his cries was too much for her. Angela wrenched the cable free, disengaging it, and pulled it back to her and reattached it to her shifter. Both watched the blood running down his leg for a moment.

Michael spat and cursed. The Etlus shuffled anxiously behind her, but he held up a hand again, staying them, then straightened himself and began to limp toward her. He bore his teeth and groaned as he inched closer, leaving behind a trail of blood.

"I've won, Michael," Angela said, panting. "What if I'm right about all this? Just let me go. I'll come back to you."

Michael staggered forward, sweat glistening on his skin. "I don't believe you. Too much evidence to the contrary, Dalkhu. The soul-flame, your connections with the traitor Donny who freed you, being seen with the other Dalkhu who stole how many crystals… There are too many contradictions." He almost fell over in pain, then dropped his knife onto the sand and unholstered his gun. "My wife never returned from her mission that day." Michael raised the gun.

What can I do?

A blast of wind blew Michael off the ground and into the air. He skidded underneath the temple's gateway arch and came, wincing, to a stop. The ground began to rumble, and a pillar of cragged rock erupted from the dirt, kicking up clouds of dust. Michael was lifted into the air until he crashed into the stone archway above him. Bone and metal *crunched*. He gasped but couldn't scream as blood and saliva dripped from his bottom lip.

"Michael!" Angela screamed. She ran to the base of the pillar.

Another portal through the veil emitted a torrent of fire, igniting the Etlus behind her in a quick blaze. Their faces were charred before they hit the ground, and within moments, their screams quieted to whimpers. The flames faded and Angela was alone with Michael.

He was pinned face-down, his head drooping and his breaths short. She grasped at the rocky obelisk, trying to find a place that would support her weight. She climbed five feet before she lost her grip and fell. More blood dripped at Angela's feet, and she knew he was dying. She cursed and began to cry.

"What do I have to say, huh?" Angela yelled. "What do I have to say to make you believe me, Michael?"

Michael coughed and said, "I want to believe," and his eyes closed.

He was quiet then, and Angela didn't bother trying to speak to him. Didn't call out to him to hold on. The flames of his soul slowly withered as it left him, and she shrunk to the ground with her back to the pillar. The drips of blood continued, and she stared past them, out across the street and beyond the buildings on the other side. A gentle breeze had picked up, and the sunlight was warm on her cheeks. The crying had stopped. There was still pain, but there was also numbness.

Disbelief and outrage mixed into a confusing cocktail inside her. Michael was gone. There was no getting him back, no returning to him with her own soul after a hard fight for the soul that was hers all along. There would be no reward. Without a treasure to take home to him, what was the point of going on? What was the point of fighting any longer when the person she fought to be with again was dead?

The street was quiet now that the blasts of teleportation had slowed, but Angela just couldn't convince herself to get up off the ground and keep moving. She knew that the Etlus, if any of them were left, would begin searching the area for stragglers and survivors soon. The little fear she had of death before was now completely gone. Running would only prolong her struggle, but killing the man who killed Michael, the cloaked bastard who stood atop the building across the streets, would make the pain worth it.

Angela clutched the brass at her side with white-knuckled rage, gritting her teeth as she stood. Her head and nose hurt, her back and side screamed in agony, but there he was. His mere presence egged her on, enraged her like she'd never been before. It wasn't just a desire to kill: it was a desire to beat him to a mess of pulpy liquid and to torture him until he wept her a beautiful song. She wanted him to beg for his life and swore that Udug would pay.

Angela pressed the button on her shifter and disappeared. She was standing directly in front of Udug, arm raised, before the thundering boom reached his ears. His eyes bulged in surprise before her knuckles connected with his jaw. A jolt of compressed lightning coursed into him, and his muscles seized. The flames of his soul singed her exposed fingers, but she didn't pull away. Udug stiffened and moaned as he fell onto his back, landing softly on the thatch roof.

Udug gasped. "That is always an experience most unpleasurable."

Angela loomed over him until he pushed himself up on his hands, then punched him again. The skin on his cheek broke open and blood dribbled down his jaw and onto his robe. He seized on the ground for a moment, and when he regained control of his body a second time, he lay there with a furrowed brow before he moved.

"Why? Why did you kill him?" Angela asked, her fist poised to strike him again.

Udug's infernal eyes stared bleakly into hers. "He was

going to kill you, either today or tomorrow. He's made it very apparent that he wanted you dead, and if you hadn't changed his mind already, you wouldn't be able to later. There was no alternative."

Angela stiffened. "You didn't give him a *chance* to change his mind. Didn't give me a *second* to prove to him I'm not possessed. You robbed him of that decision."

Udug shrugged. "Look at it however you wish. I only did the best for the both of us, in case I want that soul back someday." He pointed at her.

"Souls be damned. You killed Michael."

Angela's lip curled. She swung at him again, but he was faster. A crushing weight slammed against her chest, blew her hair, and sent her flying from the rooftop. For the second time that day Angela crashed into the ground on her back. The pain shocked her, coursing through her entire body with every pulse of her heart, and she could only watch Udug's blurry form jump from the roof and stand over her.

"Look around yourself, Angela," Udug said. "Existence isn't meant to be like this. Out of the seven known worlds, there are only three habitable dimensions. The elements rest in worlds of their own, leaking into the others and making up the physical matter that we breathe, see, and touch. It's unnatural. Disgusting. And humans embody this perversion. Soulless, lost people that couldn't work together if their lives depended on it."

Angela tried to relax the spasming muscles along her spine. She needed to get up.

Udug shrugged. "Our disagreement doesn't matter. Everything is already in motion. Soon, the reconstruction of the Anchor will commence, and in time, perhaps after years of more work, it will begin to rejoin the dimensions."

"You're wrong," Angela said through heavy breaths. "This world, all worlds, may be imperfect, but each houses people with their own lives. Their own way of life. You can't do this. If what you say is true, you will kill everything, even yourselves."

"I know that," Udug said indifferently. He began to pace around her with his eyes cast on the ground, unworried that Angela would get up and strike him again. "Certainly, the reunion will be cataclysmic, but the survivors will have a chance to continue on in a world that is pure. I can only hope to be one of them."

Angela spoke through gritted teeth. "Think of the buildings, the rock, and all matter. The people! Seven things cannot exist in one place, and to force it all together will destroy so much."

"Can you imagine the beauty, though, Angela?" Udug asked, bending closer to her face. The smell of his hot breath rolling over her face was putrid. "Earth is assuredly the most complete world that we know, and it is already full of sights of beauty. Imagine what the new world will smell like, what creatures will be there. I have to say, you Anunnaki have done an excellent job collecting the shards of the Anchor for the last millennia. You've made it much easier for us." Udug stood. "It's just like your people to hide yourselves from truth, and do you even know why? Why do you shield yourselves with machinations and sneak about the world, policing us with instruments of pain and torture? You are afraid of us and what we can do. *We* are weapons, and for that reason, we need none."

Angela shook her head.

"You see, Angela," Udug said, looking into the distance. "We aren't meant to live like this. Neither Anunnaki nor Dalkhu. We are all the same, and only segregation and births on opposite ends of existence have made us different from each other." He bent and fumbled with her belt. Angela tried to slap his hand away, but he overpowered her, unafraid to touch her skin. With gritted teeth, he took the leather bag of crystals at her waist and yanked her shifter free. "The worlds won't be the only thing that will be united. The children we birth will be whole and untethered to a specific dimension. No longer subject to the prejudices of the soul-flame, they will be powerful. They will be as the Nephilim of the world before these ones."

He smiled devilishly, then struck her in the sternum to shove the air out of her lungs again. "Don't go anywhere, Angela," he said, rising to his feet. "You've been instrumental in all of this by drawing the Etlu from their heavenly city. Thank you for that."

As Angela worked to regain her breath, Udug closed his eyes and disappeared. The shockwave pounded her chest, somehow snapping her lungs back into action. She pushed herself onto her hands and knees and looked around. "I will get what's mine," Angela swore. "I won't let you do this."

CHAPTER FOURTEEN

Kushiel gazed over the bodies of his men and women. Even though Ruchin had left somewhat early in the fight, his lost soldiers had been reduced to burnt corpses and collections of detached limbs. He knelt over a woman whose face remained contorted in pain postmortem. The blood had ceased flowing from the cut across her neck some time ago. He'd recovered after the battle had already ended when one of his underlings shook him awake, and to see such a mess shook him in his core.

"Sir," a voice said from behind.

Kushiel stood, twisting himself to face his second in command. "What's the count?" he asked.

"Nineteen of ours and six of their councilmen, sir," Rig said. He rubbed his thick muscled arms through the leather, partially to massage the discomfort out of them and partially to fidget the discomfort of the situation away. "We did lose a few shifters and crystal handbags, too."

Kushiel grumbled. Almost a third of the Etlu force now

lay dead around him. All in one fight. And the lost crystals. Unacceptable.

"What about Michael?" Kushiel asked.

"We found him," Rig said. He pointed down the street. "Check the temple. I've already sent for explosives, sir."

"Explosives?"

Rig nodded. "You'll see."

Kushiel wiped the sand from the crannies of his eyes and stepped away from the woman's corpse. "Rally everyone and start taking the dead home. After that, begin a search for any stragglers."

"Yes, sir," Rig said, somber.

He walked at a fast pace, his mind eager with anticipation—so much that Rig's shouting behind him did not register in his mind. Shortly, though, he realized his daydreaming and focused again. A few unharmed Dalkhu had warped away near the end of the battle while others had suffered grievous injuries and simply ran. They were too badly hurt to concentrate and teleport, a downfall of their "natural" method of transportation. They would still be a threat, but much less lethal.

Three more charred corpses lay on the street in front of the temple. Kushiel couldn't tell who they were through their bubbled flesh, but none had the same lanky figure as Michael. He sidestepped the downed soldiers, spotting screws and broken brass frames, then the two discarded wing packs on the ground.

The pillar of stone erupting from the puckered ground caught his attention, and his eyes followed it upward as he turned to face it. Certainly, the pillar itself was a product of Dalkhu mischief and a sight very rarely seen, but Kushiel sighed when he saw Michael's arms and legs hanging limply above. He called his name, but Michael didn't move, and after the second attempt, Kushiel actually felt a little sorry for him. The boy didn't deserve to die this way. He understood Michael's anger and unwillingness to follow simple orders, and Kushiel even shared some of his pain.

He unholstered the tether gun from his waist, raised it to eye level, and looked down the sightless barrel, pointing it at Michael.

"I'm sorry. I'll admit that I've been waiting a long time to be rid of you, albeit not like this. You won't be holding anything over my head any longer, and I won't live under your constant pressure." Kushiel breathed out slowly, steadying himself and closing one eye. "I promise that I'll see to your last wishes and that Angela is remembered untarnished. Goodbye."

The gun fired, and the spike impacted Michael's skull, filling the air with a *crack*. Michael's limbs twitched wildly under the torrent of electricity, and when he was certain Michael was dead, he grabbed the cable and yanked the prong free of his head. The prong thudded on the ground, and Kushiel recoiled the cable inside the gun. Fresh blood drained onto the ground.

He wasn't worried about being caught; the explosive devices used to bust the stone pillar would probably damage his corpse, and no one would suspect he'd been the one who shot him. Relief washed over him. The years of blackmail were over. Now the biggest of his concerns was cleaning the carcasses of his dead warriors. After that, he would meet with Ja'noel and discuss what in the blazes had happened on Dingir to allow Shedim to steal so many crystals. He suspected Ja'noel would blame him for taking so many soldiers out of Dingir, but it needed to be done.

Kushiel replaced the tether gun to his waist and stared up at Michael for a few minutes until Rig arrived. He stood at his side for a moment. "I'm leaving you in charge," Kushiel said. "I need to head to Dingir and speak to Ja'noel, and I think I'll get it over with now."

Rig nodded.

"Watch over everyone. Keep in groups of at least two," Kushiel said. "If you find the woman, send someone for me immediately."

"Yes, sir," Rig said, saluting.

With that, Kushiel was only a press of a button away from returning home.

NAMTAR CLUTCHED THE STRETCH OF CLOTH IN HIS LEFT hand, pinned the other end between his teeth, and pulled his limp arm upward. He groaned, pain shooting through his arm as it bent and jiggled unnaturally at the elbow. It took him a frustrating amount of time to tie the knot with only his mouth and one free hand, but he slunk back against the mud and brick wall with a sigh of relief.

Great walls of fire, Namtar thought. *You've done it again. Just wait until you make it back to the Council and show those old men you do have what it takes. No more will they talk behind your back and belittle you!*

He smiled to himself.

Today you've proven that they made the right decision making you a councilman. Certainly, when you return, you will put their hearts at ease and quash any fears that they may have had about you. Yeah. Damn, Namtar. You survived.

Without warning, fatigue fell over him and sealed his heavy eyelids shut. The invigorating feeling of stasis snuck up on him, and he succumbed to a nap. It wasn't until he felt a nudge on his leg that he began to wake. When he became aware that someone, or something, was touching him and moving his leg about, his eyes sprang open.

Namtar convulsed and screamed at the first sight of her kneeling over him. Despite their souls being of the same alignment, seeing a person in Anunnaki armor startled him. Instantly, his mind raced and he began to push himself into the veil. Anywhere would be better than there, he knew, but a shock rippled through him and he stayed there on the floor of the human hovel. A small red light blinked on the anklet attached to his leg.

As she drew her knife and brought it close to his face, Namtar kicked his legs at her. Angela, however, was unfazed by his blows, and she pressed the blade of her curved skinning knife to his throat and he stilled himself, whimpering.

"Keep it down or I'll finish you right now," she said.

Namtar's heart beat wildly. The knife nicked his neck when he gulped. "What do you want?" he asked softly.

The corner of Angela's mouth lifted into half a smile. "I imagine it won't be long until you'll be well enough to go home?"

Namtar's eyes narrowed as curiosity struck him. "That's right," he said. "I ask again, what do you want from me?"

Angela removed the knife from his neck but kept it in her hand. "First, stand up." She grabbed him by his good arm and began pulling him up from the dirt floor. Namtar winced and pulled away, slipping his arm free.

"I'll raise myself, thank you."

The councilman rose in a deliberately slow and cautious manner and stared at Angela for a moment. Even though she was a fairly attractive woman, he couldn't help but feel disgusted by her presence. She was an alien parading around with something that wasn't hers. While Udug's actions had produced strong results, Namtar himself did not particularly relish the actions he had taken. It wasn't natural to swap souls with another being, and a part of him hadn't wanted to cast a vote to absolve the councilman. But for fear of being the only one to say no and potentially being pushed even further from the other members from the Council, he had agreed.

"You are going to take me with you," Angela said.

"What?" Namtar couldn't help but laugh. "Are you serious?"

Angela scowled.

With a faintly incredulous smile, Namtar said, "You *are* serious!"

In a flash, Angela brought the knife back up to his throat. "I said keep it quiet. Both humans and Anunnaki are looking for the both of us."

Namtar raised his hand with an open palm. "Apologies, I just cannot take you genuinely. It seems like a bad plan on your part."

She pulled the blade back to her side, shaking her head at the Dalkhu's gall. "Do you have a home? Someplace private from the rest of your people?"

The councilman scoffed. "Of course. We aren't feces-dwelling pigs crammed in a pen, now are we? Please do not be a fool."

"I'm not a fool," Angela said, shoving him back against the wall. "I've never been to Kur, nor do I have the means to get there. I don't know where to break through the veil, and I know the surface of your world is dangerous."

"Ah, not completely devoid of knowledge, are you? Too bad. If you would have tried, you might have died."

Angela balled a fist and struck his cheekbone. He jerked back and squawked like a child, then began to comfort himself with his hand. "Fine," Namtar said. "Enough talk."

Angela bent, inserted a key into the anklet, and turned it, and the red light faded as the device shut down.

"We go now," Angela said as she stood upright.

Namtar opened and closed his jaw, stretching the muscles, then shook his head and said, "You'll never make friends like that. But if you insist..." He took a deep breath and held it in concentration for nearly a full minute before they disappeared from the dingy home with a loud clap. The sensation, a mixture of the heat of fire and the tingling of ice, overwhelmed her. They traveled, looking at one another with long, unblinking stares, and when they arrived in the Dalkhu world of Kur, the concussive blast echoed off the cavern walls.

A muffled pulse like a slowed heartbeat reverberated inside her. It was Udug's soul calling out and giving her urge to move again. Rather than the constant reverberation she had felt on Earth for the past few days when he had been close, his soul's directional pull now told Angela that he was farther away.

It was a safe assumption that Udug felt the same soul-pulling sensation as she did and he now knew that she had entered Kur, even though he had never said so on Earth.

Angela didn't know, and she likely never would. She wondered if he would seek her out if he was capable of tracking her. Part of her doubted it. Udug was probably busy with his Council, and he hadn't killed her the last time they tussled, so it wasn't likely he wanted her dead. His concerns were much larger than her now.

The chamber she stood in was relatively confined. The

floor was possibly once part of a cave, cut and polished smoothed just like the walls. The colors of the stones were hues of brown and black, and Angela was impressed by the craftsmanship. Bright red drapes hung over two arched doorways. A piece of dark furniture against one of the walls held scrolls in small square cubbies. Wooden rocking chairs were scattered around the room, and a table sat in the middle.

"Nam!" a woman's voice said from behind a curtain. "What have I told you about coming in the house like that? You about scared the life out of me."

A gaunt hand pulled the red drape aside. A thin woman with brown hair and a sharp jawline took a half step through the threshold, then paused when she spotted Angela. "Who is that?" the woman asked, pointing at Angela.

"Well, she's not a friend…" Namtar said.

Angela couldn't be mad at him for speaking the truth, but she still hushed him. "I'll speak for myself." She stepped closer to the woman. "My name is Angela. I'm sure that the gear I wear makes you suspicious of where I'm from, so I will tell you honestly. I am from Dingir. I was—*am*—an Anunnaki. I mean you, nor any of your family, any harm so long as you do as I say. I only seek Councilman Udug."

Namtar's eyes widened. "Ah. Now it makes sense. But good luck with that one."

Angela turned and drew her knife. Within the blink of an eye, it was firmly pressed against Namtar's throat again. "Do not belittle me. I have one mission and nothing more to lose."

He nodded cautiously. "I see. A single Anunnaki travels into the heart of darkness, seeking revenge on the man who wronged her. Daring, I say. Just know my wife knows nothing of combat, nor does she possess the ability to travel between worlds. I have no ill-intent against you, Angela, or plan to interfere with your desire for revenge. I have little belief in the myths of Nephilim or the others of the Council, only the power I can and have attained through the Council that ensures my family's best interests. As far as I am concerned, Udug brought your wrath upon himself. Rightly so. I only warn that if you injure my wife or son I will have a personal reason to speed up your death."

Angela stirred, staying her knife. A twist in her gut brought about feelings of guilt. She'd never met a Dalkhu who viewed love of family over their peoples' creed. He reminded her of Michael. He broke rules when doing what he thought was right, and she was somewhat disappointed in herself for stereotyping this councilman. But in her defense, the number of conversations she'd had with *any* Dalkhu was less than the number of fingers on one hand.

"That is all I can ask for—" Angela paused, trying to remember his name.

"Namtar," he said.

The sound of a single musical note filled the tunnels, then vibrated the chamber they stood in. It sounded distant, yet the cavernous walls amplified the note's long resonance. The councilman relaxed all but his eyes. He was wary of her, and she was happy to be under his skin at least that much. His unbridled tongue and sarcasm irritated her greatly.

"That is the Kissum's bell. It summons me for a Council meeting," Namtar said.

"Will all of the Council be present?"

Namtar shook his head. "No, I already know what you are thinking. Those of us that have returned from Earth will be there, but you will stay here until I return. I don't know what you plan to do, but your best bet will be to catch Udug in his chamber when things have calmed down."

"I don't understand. Why do this?" Angela asked. "I've watched you for the slightest movement toward the dagger in your robe, yet even after forcing my way into your home you don't move against me. Now you apparently guide me. Why?"

He pondered it for a moment. "To be honest, I truly have no palate for Udug, and I am somewhat curious to see how this will unfold. I don't believe we've seen the end of this. But the sooner you're gone, the better it is for me and my family's safety."

Angela looked away.

Namtar turned his eyes to his wife across the room. "Ardat, do us all a favor and find her a robe that will fit. I do not want anyone to get the idea we are 'harboring.'"

Ardat nodded, her bony cheeks moist with a nervous sweat, and motioned for Angela to follow her behind the red curtain and into the room beyond. Taking the fabric in her hand and stepping through, Angela glanced back at Namtar, who glared at her with a furrowed brow and uneasy eyes. An apology almost escaped her lips, but she stayed her tongue and slipped behind the drape.

A boy lay on his stomach across a bed draped with gray and brown blankets. There was dirt underneath his nails and smudged across his cheek. His eyes were locked onto a small stone saucer with raised borders. Small, detailed slabs of thinly cut rock had created a maze on the bowl's inner surface. By tipping it, the boy was trying to navigate a multicolored marble of yellow, gray, and white from one end of the maze to the other. The boy's concentration surprised Angela as he paid her no mind.

Ardat searched through the top drawer of a dresser, then moved down until she reached the third drawer and retrieved a gray robe with a dull yellow cord. It was much more fitting for blending in with the Dalkhu, but the woman's wrists shook when she handed them over.

"Thank you," Angela said.

Ardat bowed slightly and kept her eyes to the floor, then walked from the room in silence. She returned a moment later with a small bowl of water and a rag, which Angela dipped and used to wipe the blood from her hands and face. When she was finished, Ardat took the rag and bowl and placed them atop the dresser, then sat next to her son on the bed. She gently rubbed the boy's spine, keeping her eyes cast downward as Angela covered herself in the robe. Ardat's touch stirred the boy from his concentration, and he looked to Angela.

"Who's this, Ma?" the boy asked, sitting upright and holding onto her arm.

It took her a few moments to form the words. Finally, she said, "A visitor from a place far away." Ardat faked a smile.

The boy raised an eyebrow and tilted his shaved head to the side. "Lady, why're you dressed like that in our house?" He pointed at the exposed leather pauldrons as she dressed.

Ardat glared at Angela, and she knew why.

"I just finished a game not long ago," Angela said, pulling her hair free from the robe's folds and letting it flop onto her shoulder. "Your father was kind enough to offer me a few days' rest here and new garb for the journey home." The boy nodded, seemingly satisfied with her answer. "My name is Angela. What's yours?"

The boy kicked his legs off the edge of the bed. "I'm Neti. My mom's Ardat."

Angela nodded, smiling.

"What kind of game did you play? Are you good? Did you win?" Neti asked.

"Well—" Angela began, then stumbled over herself. "I didn't do half as good as I thought I should have, but—"

"That's enough," Ardat said, holding out a finger. She turned to her son. "No need to intrude on the woman. It isn't kind to remind her of her loss, and she'll be leaving soon anyhow. Why don't you go sit on your father's mat and practice your meditations like he's been telling you to?" She glared at Angela as the boy bounced off the bed and to the ground.

"Okay." He skittered to the corner of the room, pulled a brown mat from behind the dresser, and placed it on the floor next to the bed. It looked thin and uncomfortable; any padding it once had was clearly flattened years ago. The boy faced the wall, and unlike any form of meditation Angela had ever seen, he rocked back and forth on his bottom and fidgeted with his hands. She smiled and turned her attention back to her clothes.

The robe was quite a bit heavier than Angela had anticipated. Cotton added padding and cushion, and even the fibers used to craft the garment seemed thick. Under the scrutiny of her fingertips, she noted that it wasn't a very soft material, either. She fastened the red sash around her waist, letting it hang loose enough that she could reach her tools if she had to. There were pockets on the inside, and a set of adjustable loops staggered vertically around her midsection confused her. At first glance, she thought they were tie-offs for the sash, but they were meant to hold the scabbards of knives, Angela deemed. She fumbled with the sash before giving up and trying to tie it another way, then struggled with it more until Ardat rose from the bed, short-tempered, and took both ends from her.

"Here," Ardat said. "Tell me quietly, how is it that I can't see your soul's flame?"

"That's why I'm here," Angela said, watching the woman's hands work, "and it's a story I don't care to explain."

Ardat lifted an eyebrow. "Very well." With a snap of her wrists, she finished tying the knot and sat back on the bed.

Other than Neti's humming, it was awkward and silent for a time, so Angela walked out to examine the living area of their home. The chair in the main chamber was comfortable enough for Angela to sit and rest, and putting space between her and Ardat seemed like a good idea. She didn't feel the need to watch them that closely. They seemed calm, given their condition, and far warmer to Angela than she likely would have been to a Dalkhu in her home under the same conditions.

As hours passed, Angela fought through a fit of coughs that brought blood from her lungs. Eying the ruby splatters in her palms, she gauged that it wasn't a drastic amount. An ill sign nonetheless. It seemed ironic that a sickness could originate from inside the body, and she wished that her cure was easier to obtain.

What if Namtar turned me into the other councilmen and they're busy planning how to storm in and take me out?

Angela bit her lip nervously. Namtar hadn't given her that impression, especially considering he had left her with his family.

Ardat, her hands behind her back, appeared from the

bedroom. The woman paused and locked eyes with Angela, then came closer with small steps and a stern expression.

"Do you need something?" Angela asked.

Ardat paused before her, her brown eyes twinkling faintly. She raised the boy's stone bowl over her head and said, "Yes."

Nothing was worth the risk. Angela rose from her chair, ready to throw herself at Ardat with all her might, but the woman's thin arm brought the bowl down onto Angela's head faster than she expected. Angela stumbled back into the chair and shook the buzzing from her head.

"Run, Neti!" Ardat yelled.

The pale woman swung at her again, but Angela brought her arms up. The bracers on her forearms absorbed most of the impact; Ardat was weak, and Angela's blood pumped furiously enough she didn't feel anything. The pit-pat of Neti's sandaled feet entered the room, and even though she couldn't see him, Angela knew the boy was running for the door, and she kicked out with her leg.

A grunt escaped Ardat's throat, the beating paused, and Angela lunged forward. Her head and shoulder connected with the woman, blowing her back a few paces. Angela reached out and grabbed Ardat's thin wrist, then twisted it, bending the arm backward and holding her awkwardly. She unholstered her gun and pressed it to the woman's temple.

"Boy!" Angela shouted, spinning the woman around to face the child. Neti stopped in the threshold and looked back at his mother. "You will come back here right now, or I will see that your mother feels fire in her veins."

Ardat squirmed. Angela tightened. Neti stared, a look of nervous contemplation across his face as Angela's finger pulled the slack out of the trigger.

"Just go," Ardat said, whimpering. "Do as I said."

Angela wrenched the woman's arm upward, pinching more nerves in her shoulder.

"You have no right to be in this home or in Kur, Anunnaki," Ardat muttered through her teeth. The woman swung the bowl over her shoulder, clacking it against Angela's forehead and causing her to stagger and reach to protect her eyes. When Angela realized she had released Ardat, her lip curled and she swooped her arms around the woman's midsection and clasped onto her. She howled as she picked Ardat off the ground and threw her. The paper-thin Dalkhu grunted as she smacked into the wall and fell to the floor. Neti watched nervously, too afraid to move.

As the woman recovered to her feet, Angela grabbed her by the forehead and slammed her against the wall, then hit her across the cheek with a brazen fist.

"I have *every* right to be here!" Angela yelled. She hit the woman again, bouncing her head backward as it bobbled on her shoulders. Ardat's eyes fluttered and blood began to pour from her nose.

"My fight is more important than anything you've ever breathed for. I'll see this through to the end whether or not you, or anyone else, gets it."

She grabbed the moaning woman by her robes and shook her, pulling her close and looking into her weary eyes.

"No matter what it costs, even if the worlds are reunited and I die, I'll stalk Udug as a phantom until he ends his own life," Angela spat. "Curse that damned man for dragging me into his vendetta, and curse your damned people for creating him. I'll kill as many of you as it takes, and when I kill him, I'll laugh about it."

Angela shoved Ardat into the wall and she crumpled to the floor, holding herself like a coiling snake and clutching the back of her head where she bled the most. The woman's eyes closed. She spit red between slow breaths. When Angela was confident she would stay down, she turned to Neti.

He stood still and silent, the red drape covering everything but his head. Angela stood, catching the sight of the glimmering tears in his eyes, and pointed the barrel of the gun toward the bedroom. The boy stepped forward, shrunken and cautious like a hound that had just caught a beating. He glanced at his unconscious mother twice, then disappeared into the bedroom without a word.

Slowly, Angela calmed. The chaos was over with, and everything was under control again. The Council wouldn't storm the tunnels and kill her, and she still had a chance to get to Udug. All it would take was a simple explanation to Namtar once he'd returned. His wife couldn't handle the stress of her being in their home, and she meant to protect their child. Understandable, really, but still an action that justified her self-defense.

Enveloped in her thoughts, Angela paced about the chamber's living space for almost half an hour. Even though she knew everything was fine, she couldn't help but feel a creeping sensation of nervousness. She tried the rocking chair, but even that was too still for her anxiety, so she resumed pacing. Neti occasionally sobbed from the other room, and Angela couldn't bring herself to shush the boy.

Eventually, Angela knelt next to Ardat, who still lay on the ground, holding herself, and tapped her cheek lightly.

"Come on. Let's get you off the floor," Angela said, grabbing her by the wrist. As she lifted Ardat's arm, her hand hung limp and relaxed, and her head rolled loosely on her shoulder. She placed a finger against her neck, then frowned. Namtar's wife was dead.

The blunt trauma to Ardat's skull was too much for the woman to handle, and somewhere in her unconscious sleep, her heart stopped beating. Angela tried to find some way to rationalize her actions, her justification in the form of words, knowing she would need to defend herself. Even though Angela hadn't meant to kill Ardat and only struck her to ensure her own survival, she knew Namtar wouldn't care. Angela had killed his wife no matter how she tried to paint the picture. Now, the question was if Angela should wait for Namtar to return or flee before he did.

She grabbed Ardat by the wrists and dragged her into the bedroom. If anything, she would at least hide the woman. She propped her up against the wall and dresser. Neti lay on the bed, watching her with intensity.

"Let her sleep now, okay?" Angela said to the boy.

He nodded, eyes still shimmering under the candlelight.

Angela picked up the rag and bowl of water from the dresser and left the room, the red drape fluttering behind her. She mopped up the mess as best as she could, then leaned against the wall, exasperated and guilty.

That poor boy...

Angela shook her head. She had to move on—and quickly. Staying put was a stupid decision. She took two steps toward the doorway, expecting to make it outside unhindered, but paused when a faint sound reached her ears. It was a distant patting noise, and she realized that her chance to leave was already gone. The sound grew louder, and Angela had to remind herself to breathe. Jaunting across the room and leaning her back against the bedroom archway, she began picking at her nails in an attempt to act casual. Then Namtar entered the chamber.

Angela straightened, then cleared her throat. "Anything?"

Namtar shrugged. "There is always something, and you're not going to care for it." He looked at her cautiously until she motioned for him to continue. "Udug was there."

A glimmer of hope.

"So that's good for you, but there's something much bigger brewing."

"What's that?" Angela asked.

"There are some who are growing serious about trying to restore the Anchor. Udug seems to be convincing."

"Are you serious?" Angela asked.

Namtar nodded.

Angela scoffed and started pacing again.

"I've seen the crystals," Namtar said as he watched her. "There's a lot, and Udug has almost half the Council convinced it's worth trying. That will mean years more of research and trying, but they want more of your peoples' crystals. That is for certain."

Angela bit her lip and walked another round in silence, then said, "They—*you*—would gain the upper hand. Not only are the crystals some part of your Anchor ideology, but they're also how we travel between worlds. I imagine the scales have already tipped."

Namtar raised a hand. "Please, extremists and rogues hold those beliefs, not me. And perhaps you should take another, more critical look at your people and what they've done to you."

Angela scowled. "Whatever. This doesn't change much. I'll just have to move a bit faster."

Angela moved to pass Namtar, but he held out a hand and stopped her from walking through the door. "Angela," he said, softly. "I understand. Well, in all reality, I *don't*.

But I do empathize with you. I imagine losing your soul is something traumatic, and I feel bad that it's happened to you."

Angela nodded, breaking eye contact. "Are we back to normal? Me and you?"

His eyes searched her for a moment and he sighed. "Aye. This never happened, and let's hope we never see each other again. Good luck."

Angela took a deep breath as a lump formed in her throat. She knew what was coming next and looked away. "I'm sorry," she said, and she stepped into the tunnel outside. The exact second she was on the other side of the red drape and out of Namtar's view, Angela broke into a sprint. The breeze of her movement pulled at the robe around her and made it hard for her to keep the hood over her head. Tears pooled in her eyes when she heard the screams begin behind her.

CHAPTER FIFTEEN

ngela swore she was running down the tunnel Namtar had returned from, but the curves and dips spun her head and confused her. Udug's soul was like a compass that pointed straight, and the tunnels weaved. Occasionally, she passed entrances to chambers like Namtar's—carved archways draped with colored fabrics to serve as dividers and privacy screens—and Angela slipped past each one.

At the first three-way intersection, she admitted to herself that she was lost. The soul inside her told her to head straight into the stone, leaving Angela with a fifty percent chance of going down the correct tunnel. She looked for signs of dirt or scuff marks on the cavern floor, weighing her choice heavily.

But two tolls of the Kissum's bell told Angela which way to head. Namtar had said that it was a summoning bell, and it seemed like a better reason to choose a direction than dirt on a cavern floor, so she turned down the left tunnel. Within a minute, the last note faded, and she ran in silence.

Archways into homes grew frequent enough that

Angela couldn't risk running; the clomp of her boots was too loud for a place where sound traveled far. A figure some thirty yards in front of her entered the tunnel and began to walk away from her. This Dalkhu, dressed in a gray robe as well, walked down the tunnel with a light gait, and Angela felt even more certain she was headed in the right direction.

He disappeared from her sight behind the cavern's slope, but when she reached the point she had last seen him, the walls opened up above her, peaking at nearly three hundred feet. Stalactites larger than the trunks of old trees hung from the ceiling and speckles of some kind of vegetation cast faint glows of green and white. The plants hardly did much to illuminate the cavern, but it was enough for her to see its grand scale and fill her with the feeling she was looking at a starry sky filled with brown clouds.

The floor became a steep incline downward, and torch stands had been driven into the ground, lighting a set of chiseled steps. The stairs weaved side to side as they descended through cavernous outcrops and stalagmites, leading to the Dalkhu city below.

There were gray and brown houses packed together and more torches and lanterns to see them by. Several paths came in from other tunnels on the cavern's outer ridge and met in the middle, where a massive structure with five spires jutting upward on bulbous domes loomed over every other building. There was a single bell tower in the center, and rows of steps led up to a massive set of double doors.

The Kissum...

Angela could see the opposite side of the cave beyond the building. She thought the distance must have been at least fifteen hundred paces long and only slightly less in width. Dalkhu walked all along the edges of the massive chamber and on the paths below, heading toward the center.

Something bumped into the back of her arm, shoving it out of the way. A man with scruffy cheeks and a fresh black suture that seeped blood just below his eye moved past her and headed down the steps. Angela waited a few seconds, eased her mind by knotting her hair behind her head, and began down the steps behind him.

She kept her feet light as she tried to glide down the first two dozen steps, worried that she would get too close and he would hear a piece of her equipment jingle at her waist, but the Dalkhu never turned and the soul inside her continued to pull her toward the city—and Udug.

He has to know I'm here by now. He's a councilman. Highly in tune with the nature of souls and their energy. If my presence hasn't caught his attention by now, he is no great councilman by any means.

Angela's gut twisted and turned into a swelling knot of anxiety.

What if this is a trap and all these Dalkhu are gathering together to ensnare me? It would be a perfect ploy. Udug knows I'll come at him again and again. Or at least he should. Angela bit her lip.

Maybe Udug doesn't even care that I'm here. He thinks I can't—won't—do anything to him, so maybe he's not even concerned.

Angela smiled. It didn't matter if it was a trap or not. Even though she didn't know what she was doing, she was blindly confident there was a way to get her soul back and stop the Council from destroying everything. She only had to find it. The hundreds of thousands—perhaps millions—of lives on the line depended on her figuring out something. Three separate worlds filled with innocents, two of which she loved dearly for their own reasons.

And for me and Michael. I cannot allow myself to forget. Not ever.

Angela had been so wrapped up in her own thoughts that she was already at the bottom of the stone steps. The cave floor was almost level, and it seemed like the smells of the last century had lingered, commingled, and settled down in that cave. Oil-burning fires and smoke, damp moss-covered stone, nose-tingling incense, and the occasional waft of something sizzling in a pan. The faint aroma of feces.

The Dalkhu led Angela to the edge of the small homes. Some people roamed the streets in rags, others wore tunics and robes, and a few congregated over the comfort of an open fire on the side of the street. Angela cast her head downward as she passed open windows with watching eyes. With the hood shielding her face and blindly following the Dalkhu, she missed many things she wished she could have stopped to study.

Angela lifted her head at the first sight of the two dozen steps up to the Kissum's doors. Each arch, spire, and pictogram seemed to be carved from one massive stone and polished to a glossy finish. The five bulbous domes were colored with veins of yellow and white that trickled down to the steps. The double doors alone were nearly four times taller than her. Angela was awestruck.

She made her way up the brown stairs as quietly as her boots would allow, watching the structure grow and loom over her. At the top, the doors were propped open by hardened clay ornaments shaped like vases, and Angela saw a mass had begun to form just inside.

At least thirty Dalkhu all stood close to one another,

talking. With her head down, Angela barely noticed that the carved surfaces of the huge doors were scraped and damaged as she passed, and she wondered what had happened to them.

The hall was loud enough that Angela didn't worry about the weapons under her robe; she was more worried that someone would notice she was a woman. In her fourteen years of service, Angela had never seen a woman Dalkhu in battle. She only knew from others that the Dalkhu seldom taught their women to fight and that they weren't allowed to wear the same black robes that men did. Being seen would raise questions, so Angela did her best to stick to the outer edges of the room and kept her head down.

The room was circular underneath one of the Kissum's five domes, and it looked just as exotic on the inside as it did on the outside. Pillars circled the outer wall and held up the bowled roof. The colors of the stone varied between blacks and browns, but all of it had streaks or tiny speckles of gold and white throughout. As far as her eyes could tell, all of the stonework had been polished. She swore she could have spit on the floor and slid ten yards if she were barefoot.

Then, with the company of the soul humming inside her, Angela saw Udug enter the room through a small doorway. He was the only man there covered in soul-fire, and his arrival in the room silenced the others. Accompanied by the few other remaining councilmen, the middle-aged man walked front and center before the crowd. Angela recognized two of them; the one with the beard was Ruchin, and the unnamed one with pierced eyebrows had fought at his side on Earth. A limping man removed his hood, and Angela saw that Shedim was with them, too.

Udug's gaze swept over the room, and luckily for Angela, he either didn't notice her or didn't care she was there. The councilmen stood quietly for a moment as a few more people entered the room, and then Udug spoke.

"Greetings." His voice, amplified by the stone structure around them, boomed in a strange duality of voices, like two people were talking at once. "I'm sure that most of you have already heard of what has happened. Some of you may even know what is about to happen. So let me begin by confirming your suspicions. As you can see by your souls' clarifying senses, I have attempted the forbidden and undergone changes I had not expected. The rumors are true: I made an effort to possess the body of an Anunnaki."

The room stirred with whispers.

"You may wonder why I have not received punishment for my misdeeds and why I still stand before you." Udug took a half step backward and motioned with his arms. "Councilman Ruchin will provide that answer."

The old man stepped forward, running his hand down his beard once and clearing his throat. With a gruff voice he said, "The Council has decided it is unnecessary to reprimand Councilman Udug Hul for his actions. It may confuse you as to why he is allowed such leniency, so allow me to explain what has transpired these last few days so that you may understand and so any rumors may be quashed. With his brash methods, Udug managed to draw a large number of Anunnaki to the Adrift while simultaneously planting a thief and spy in their city. The battle was short and still took lives of our own, but we have managed a more crippling blow than any other I can remember."

Ruchin motioned to Udug, who approached the crowd again with a leather bag. He raised a handful of glowing crystals above his head. The flames of his soul, erupting from his palms and fingers, licked their colored surfaces and sparkled.

Udug smiled as he said, "With these crystals, we stand one step closer to Dalkhu dominance and the end of a battle fought for millennia. We, the Council, hereby announce Shedim, the spy whose fight was vital in our recent victory and my own esteemed pupil, as councilman with the title of the Restorer."

He turned and held the sack to Shedim, who looked anxious. "Do you accept the responsibility to protect the shards of the Anchor and keep them from those who would use them to harm us? Do you swear to oversee the reconstruction of the Anchor itself and reunite the worlds and the people in them when the time comes?"

"I do," Shedim said. He bowed his head and took the bag with open palms. He clutched it tightly to his chest, stepped back, and smiled humbly.

Angela groaned internally. *Now I have to find a way to both the teacher and the pupil. Great.* A pit of despair opened up inside her.

"We have made great strides this day," Udug said. "But we have one more thing to—"

The sound of running feet filled the room, stopping Udug mid-sentence. The crowd murmured, and heads spun, looking for the source of it. Hood blown down to his shoulders, Namtar pushed his way through the crowd. Angela tensed and dropped her head, watching as he walked to Udug with fists clenched and whispered in his ear. Udug pulled back and looked at him, flames jutting from an open mouth as he whispered and then nodded.

Namtar shrunk back, stepping to the side with his head down. He reached up and wiped a finger just below his eyes.

"We've dealt a crippling blow to the Anunnaki," Udug said, his voice deep and bold. "But it is one from which they can recover. This day, we take control of our destiny by continuing the use of unconventional methods. We strike Dingir with all of our strength."

The quiet whispers erupted into worried conversation. People shuffled against one another. Every muscle in Angela's body tightened and her heart surged with rage. Dingir was in incredible danger and she was the only Anunnaki who knew what was coming, yet she had no way to warn them.

Ruchin stepped forward and held his palms over the crowd. His voice cracked with age as he said, "We have gathered you all here today to launch an attack against their city. We will no longer send soldiers to subterfuge, only to destroy and take!"

A handful of voices in the crowd agreed and a few shouted their approval.

"Dingir has stood in our path toward unity for far too long," Udug bellowed. "Kill every Anunnaki you see and harvest the crystals from their corpses like wheat from a field. Fell their city's towers and ignite their machines so that our children may know a brand-new world!"

The crowd's shouts grew constant. Cheers of joy and roars of redemption rattled Angela's eardrums. They reached upward as they screamed out.

This is their pain, manifested, Angela thought. I *guess, even though I've come this close to Udug, I have to turn away.* With a somber heart, Angela realized, *I can't stand by and let Dingir get torn apart.*

"Go forth to the Anunnaki's dominion and show them the full force of the Dalkhu!" Udug raised his fists into the air and looked at all the faces around him. He could see the pain in all of them—a pain he shared. A smile stretched across his face. He had done the same with the others of the Council: showed them that there was no wrong in war.

Pulses of teleportation blasted against her eardrums, rattling her. She staggered and pushed her palms over her ears. Gusts of wind stirred dirt from the floor and cast it into her eyes.

How could this happen so quickly?

The air vibrated as the Dalkhu disappeared from the room.

I can't leave! Angela realized, eyes blinking through grit and tears as she tried to scan the room. *I don't feel confident I'm well enough to make the journey into another world without a shifter. If I had a crystal, a blue crystal, there's a chance I could make it, but I don't, and it's a small chance at that.*

Angela broke into a sprint. Half of the robed soldiers had already vanished. Her skull throbbed an electrifying pain. People appeared to ebb and flow, elongating, then snapping back as her vision distorted and blurred. Angela dove, stretching out to hook one of them she swore was close enough to. It disappeared at the last second, and Angela crashed onto the floor, her gut roiling. She had to restrain herself from heaving up bile. A sandaled foot was only a yard from her. She rolled and reached for the pair of legs. She touched his skin for a fraction of a second, then disappeared from the Kissum's floor.

They traveled in the silence, attached by Angela's grip on his ankle, his left hand still proudly held upright. She wondered what his face looked like and if he knew she had grabbed onto him to hitch a ride, but he had to have noticed the extra weight. There was a slim chance he didn't and little she could do until they broke through the veil and entered Dingir. So Angela waited, and in a stretch of time that was both far too long and shorter than expected, she took a breath of cold air again.

Clouds and blue sky surrounded her. Torrents of wind whipped her hair around her cheeks and eyes. There were no metal platforms or stone buildings. No city. They were falling, spiraling toward an unknown bottom, and the Dalkhu struggled and glared down at her. He grimaced, pulled up the leg she held onto, and kicked the heel of his foot on her forehead. She slid, clasping onto his foot for life with sweaty palms.

He kicked again. She grabbed his other foot, stilling his blows just long enough for her to pull herself upward. The change in their aerodynamics broke them into a rolling fall, and Angela struggled to hold herself together as they wrestled in the air. The deep boom of teleportation came from the distance. They were close.

Angela guessed which direction Dingir was and grunted as she pushed them both into the veil. Even though they were frozen in the space between worlds, the dizzy feeling inside her still lingered. Getting them both inside the veil was all she could manage, and she relaxed and let the unnamed Dalkhu steer them the rest of the way. Angela only hoped that he understood what she was trying to convey.

In time, they burst out of the veil again, and Angela could see a big blurry shape of browns and yellows and a series of reflections whizzing past her. It was too large to be anything other than Dingir. In the midst of their fighting, the Dalkhu pushed them into the veil again, understanding that they needed to get closer to some form of solid land to stand on or neither of them would have a chance at winning the fight.

They appeared again, falling just past the lip of the city. Angela could make out the sharp plates of metal along the city's edge. As she spun, she could see pipes running up and down the moisture-condensing towers, fires in the distance, puffs of either cloud or smoke, and, again, the edge of the platform below. They were narrowly going to fall past it.

She knew she had to do something, but with the struggle of keeping herself together as they fell, she couldn't think of anything. The Dalkhu released her shoulder and reached for something in his robe. The guard of a crude iron dagger shimmered in his hand.

Angela ran her fingers through the brass knuckles at her waist, trying to move faster than him. She struck at his torso and slammed her thumb on the device. It sparked and connected with him. The Dalkhu tensed and his expression contorted in pain as every muscle in his body tightened. Then he relaxed and he fell unconscious. She pushed herself away with her knee so they drifted apart, but he would soon recover. Rerouting the cable, she aimed her tether gun at the passing city.

The gun wouldn't have enough power to pierce thick metal, so she aimed for a space between a pipe and the bottom side of the platform and fired. The spike flew where she wanted it to, and the cable wrapped itself around the under-city piping and anchored her to the city. The cable extended to its full length, and all of her body's downward momentum pulled on her arms and shoulders and she screamed. Her arms tried to separate from her torso as she swung, but she held on for life and fought the searing pain.

The steelwork of the under-city rushed up to greet her. She flew past pipes and boilers until her legs crashed into the railing of a catwalk, bucking her feet over her head and smashing her against the metal grated walkway. Angela let the gun go and lay there.

"Wings—" Angela muttered weakly to herself, wishing she still had them.

She caught her breath and groaned as she pushed herself to her feet. It felt good to roll her shoulders and stretch her back. The tether gun was swinging thirty feet off the catwalk and over the blue expanse below. She sighed, braced herself against the howling winds, and left it behind.

When Angela found a ladder, climbed it, and pushed the manhole cover open, the sunlight gleamed off the streets and right into her eyes. She winced and shielded herself with a hand as she rose to city level. Screams came from almost every direction, and blasts of concussive thunder were only blocks away. Angela couldn't tell if the fires she saw were physical and real or spirit-produced, so she moved her way up a nearby fire escape. At the top, two stories off the ground, she saw what she expected to see.

The fires that were real produced a crisp black smoke that faded into the endless sky. A half-mile away, Etlus soared like flaming hawks above the Ascendancy. There were droves of scattering people on the streets. She saw rocks thrown and shattered glass knives as the common Anunnaki fought in the feeblest of ways. Dalkhu were breaking down doors, slitting throats, and leaving the corpses on roadsides.

People disappeared to places where they could only die. The bodies of flying soldiers would strike buildings and streets in scorching balls of fire. Blown-apart limbs lay scattered like sprinkles. Torrents of elements burst through the veil, a sign that some of the Dalkhu didn't bother closing the holes they punctured in the barrier. They were killing Dingir in every way possible.

One Dalkhu was too slow to move out of the way of a tether gun. Soon he lay face-down on the street, blood oozing from the hole in his skull and filled with lightning. Even the Anunnaki wasted no time abandoning their tradition of retaining at least some sense of respect in battle. It was kill or be killed; the fastest method won. The gloves were off, and they were soaked in blood.

Angela shuddered at every blood-curdling scream of agony. This wasn't an honorable fight between two different peoples; Dingir was now a kill-box where anything capable of dealing death was used to that effect. There was no code of honor and little she could do to stop the fighting. Bloodshed was everywhere, but there was only one Udug, and Angela spotted him, the only flame-cloaked person amid a group of calm Dalkhu. She curled her fist and leapt from the roof, not yet knowing how to end it all.

CHAPTER SIXTEEN

"**G**et inside!" Kushiel yelled. He waved his arms, motioning people through the doorway.

A young couple in the embroidered tunics and black ankle-laced pants of alchemists ran across the front lawn of the Ascendancy. Sweat beaded on their foreheads. It was war out there. Hell, even. He'd never seen the Dalkhu so brutal, let alone witnessed such a large attack on Dingir.

He had tried to stay positive and focus on improving the situation, but the massacre reminded him that *everything* was out of his control. A spear of stone broke through the veil, abruptly entering the atmosphere. The young alchemist tried to avoid it, but in the snap of a finger, it pierced his throat. He looked up to the sky and gargled blood. Then flesh tore and he fell to the ground. The woman screamed and dropped to her knees. Her nails clawed her cheeks, and she, too, was killed.

Kushiel slammed the door and pulled the lockbar down. Curses rolled off his tongue and he struck the door with an open palm. A hand touched the base of his neck and he paused.

"Calm yourself," a voice said from behind him. It was Ja'noel's, and he shook him gently.

Kushiel spun around and threw his arms in the air. "They show no mercy! Rip open holes in the veil and leave them tearing! They have no honor and abide by no codes!"

"I know," he said.

"They are slaughtering us! Common folk, too! How can you be so calm?"

Ja'noel pointed and said, "Because *you* are not! Until we have a plan, we can't do anything, and if I can't depend on you to be rational, I'll find someone else to act in your place. Do you understand?"

Kushiel glared and thought about warning him not to contradict his orders when he gave them, but he realized that a dozen others stood behind Ja'noel—soldiers destined to live or die by their command. The last thing the city needed was infighting. He shifted his weight to his other leg, breathed deep, and said, "You're right."

"I need you to keep yourself composed," Ja'noel said. "Losing your head isn't going to help."

"I know." Kushiel rubbed at his eyes and temples.

Ja'noel relaxed, but his eyes remained wary.

"We should start by moving the injured and the civilians from the infirmary to the prison cells below," Kushiel said. "It will be safer and easier to protect them down there if the Ascendancy is attacked."

Ja'noel smiled thinly and patted his shoulder. "That's more like it. I will need more soldiers than usual to hold the Ascendancy, however. There are still open holes that haven't been repaired from the explosions. I don't want to leave those unguarded."

They began to walk, pushing through the other soldiers and into the hallway. The enlisted followed with their heads down like lost dogs.

"Give me a rough figure," Kushiel said over clomping boots.

"I could do with fourteen, although twenty would alleviate a lot of worry."

Kushiel laughed. "How many Uri Gallus do we have on premise?"

Ja'noel looked at Kushiel bleakly. "Eighteen. Most are off duty, but more should be on the way. It's just a matter of time before they get here."

Kushiel thought of the alchemists outside. "Let's hope so. I can give you five, bringing you to sixteen, but the rest are mine."

Grief washed over his expression, yet Ja'noel had no choice but to take what he could get. They turned down a different hall and halted at each wooden doorway to stick their heads inside and give orders. The healers began to scramble about, gathering herbs, tools, and blankets. They watched them struggle to pick up injured men and women on stretchers, some only sick, others bleeding grievously. Cuffs on his wrists, Donny lay covered in a lightly red-stained sheet. The healers lifted his stretcher and carried him off toward the prison steps as he slept. Once the halls settled, Ja'noel turned to Kushiel again.

"Why do you need so many men?" he asked. "There are innocent people here, too."

Kushiel shook his head. "I haven't decided yet. Just give me a moment longer. It's obvious we have a huge problem. The Dalkhu are after the crystals, but we're so thinly spread that we aren't in a position to do much. There are a dozen crystal caches all over the city. It's not possible for us to reach and defend all of them."

"They won't find too many. The majority of crystals we would lose would be those looted from fallen soldiers. We need to be more assertive in protecting the people in the Ascendancy."

Kushiel looked into Ja'noel's eyes and saw a somber reflection of himself. "I would expect the worst, Ja'noel," he said. "What happens if we allow the Dalkhu to control the majority of our city? How long will we be penned inside this building until they come inside and kill the rest of us? Will they leave when they've torn a hole in the veil large enough to swallow the entire city or when they take three-fourths of our crystals? We wouldn't be able to hold a camp on Earth to save our lives. We'd be trapped in what's left of the city and there would be no more tradesmen to gather supplies and rebuild. Dingir would fall apart." Kushiel shrugged. "We fight to live now or we die later."

Ja'noel's head drooped as he said, "You're right. This fight has been a long time coming. If we hide from it now, we'll fall in the long run."

Kushiel nodded, then froze, speechless as an idea struck him.

Ja'noel raised an eyebrow. "What?"

He pointed toward the doorway down the hall, the one that led to the prisons. "The Dubah. We need Sarosha." Kushiel spun and raced down the hall, leaving Ja'noel to catch up with him. "The Dalkhu are too spread out across the city for me to send my men out to each cache. They'll be picked off. But if we covertly clear out a portion of the city as much as we can..." Kushiel paused, eying Ja'noel's expression. "We can cut off sections of the city and let them fall. Shrink the battlefield and seal the crystals away from the Dalkhu."

"Are you mad?" Ja'noel asked. He jerked Kushiel by the shoulder and shoved his back against the wall. Despite his partner's shorter size, he could overpower him. "You want to unhinge the city? We'd be casting our own people to an eternal fall! There is no possible way that we could get everyone off of those platforms."

"I know," Kushiel said, nodding and trying to gently push Ja'noel off him. "But if we allow the Dalkhu all the time in the world to find where the crystals are stashed, they will. We would only need to drop one or two portions. It would be enough to send a signal. One where they will know we are not going to allow them to take everything we've worked centuries for. Not to mention we would be forcing the Dalkhu into a smaller area. At least then we would be better able to counter with force."

"No," Ja'noel said, shaking his head. Drops of sweat were forming on his forehead. "We can't do that."

"What else do we have? I will take a squad out to the residential platform nearest the sun, and you will go to the moisture towers and warehouses nearby. Save those you can. Direct them to the Ascendancy and recover what crystals you can."

"I-I don't like it," Ja'noel said.

Kushiel placed a hand on his shoulder. "I don't like it, either, but it would be better to lose those crystals and our people to the expanse below than to the Dalkhu."

The sigh Ja'noel loosed was filled with regret, even though he hadn't done anything yet. "I'll find Sarosha and tell her to send workers to the undercity. They'll need a few soldiers with them, but I imagine it won't take them long to find the most vital supports and begin cutting them."

Kushiel nodded, patting his partner's shoulder as though to thank him. "That squad will come from me. Tell Sarosha to drop the city anyway if we do not return within one hour. We might not make it back."

Ja'noel shrugged Kushiel's hands from him and glared, uncertain and worried. He felt sorry for him and wondered if their years of leading Dingir as part of a trio were coming to an end.

ANGELA JOGGED DOWN THE STREET, HER HEAD SWIVELING in all directions. Caution would see her through the haze of the battle, allow her to sneak to the head of the snake and kill it. She advanced slowly, never moving around a corner or onto a street without first deeming it safe. Should the Dalkhu recognize her, they would certainly try to kill her on sight. And the Anunnaki wouldn't know the difference between her and the Dalkhu, so Angela stayed to the alley-ways as much as she could. The last time she had seen Udug was nearly ten minutes ago, and he had been three blocks away.

Shouting from around the corner of a limestone building slowed her jog to a walk. Angela crept along the wall with her back to it, and as she neared the corner, she peered around. A handful of Dalkhu had gathered thirty feet down the street, and they were screaming at one another when a sudden jet of flame appeared out of the air.

They staggered back, gasping and watching the tear in the veil rip open wider. The fire was a beam of pure heat, stretching out over the street and touching rock and metal. The building began to liquefy as the fire spread. Even from her distance, Angela could feel the heat of it on her face.

The Dalkhu locked hands and froze with their eyes closed. Slowly, the torrent of flame grew thinner as they struggled to close the hole. Udug was not among them.

The clapping sound of approaching footsteps on metal plates came from behind. Angela spun against the wall and reached for the tether gun at her waist. In that second, she realized two things: Namtar was only a pace and a half away from her and she had left her gun hanging beneath the city. The knuckles of his left hand collided with her cheekbone, turning her head the other way. Before she could regain herself, another blow landed on her shoulder, then her forehead. Backed against the wall, Angela threw her arms up.

Something slashed her wrist, and warm blood rolled down her forearms. Her brain told her to move. She couldn't see him but knew he had a knife. Staggering to the side and breaking forward only to get away for a brief reprieve, Angela felt something worse than any knife. The muscles in her legs froze, and she gasped for air in the space between worlds.

In an instant, she had been pushed from Dingir so quickly and so easily that by the time she realized what was happening, she couldn't stop it. Namtar's mind clutched onto her so tightly that she couldn't shake him; the strength of his soul was much too strong for her.

The iciness disappeared. What was once a layer of frost settling into her skin was now a warm, buffering sensation that pressed against her from every direction. Water rushed into her nose and mouth, and she was lucky she had a full breath of air. She used her arms as paddles and spun herself, but she couldn't tell which way was up or down. There was no variation in color in any direction. No true up or down. No air and no explainable source of light. Angela was trapped in a never-ending expanse of cloudy blue water.

It wasn't the water that was crushing her—it was Namtar. The pressure was him, holding her and keeping her in that world. It was one of four places where nothing but a single element existed, making it entirely uninhabitable. Her lungs began to burn. Panic set in. Angela watched bubbles slip from her mouth and then lazily float away like wind had pushed them. Namtar was going to drown her, and there was nothing she could do. Even though things hadn't gone her way in a long time, she had never been entirely subject to someone else's whim. She'd never been powerless, and it scared her.

A shockwave beat against her body like she was a liquid drum, reverberating in every part of her. There was light, something hard hitting her side, the sound of splashing water. Then she heard herself cough. Angela wiped the clumps of sopping hair off her face and tried to suck in as much air as she could. Her eyelids flickered, and she saw the golden streets again. The wind was freezing her to the bone.

Something wrenched her by the throat and tossed her onto her back. Namtar climbed on top of her, his silhouette vaguely recognizable with the sun behind him shining brighter than usual, and just as she began to catch her breath, his grip tightened around her neck. Angela's arms felt like rubber bands as she tried to pry his hands off her. She pushed against his shoulders and hit his elbows, but he never budged. Her vision blurred.

Over her choking and the pounding of her heart, she could barely hear Namtar say, "I told you. I told you I'd kill you!"

Angela struck out with her knee and he shot upright,

releasing her throat and howling. He rolled, crumpling on the ground weakly to clutch his groin. She swallowed and gasped at the air as she crawled over him on her hands and knees. Her left hand found the curved skinning knife at the small of her back and placed the edge on his neck. His arms were pinned underneath her. He groaned and tears welled in his eyes as he struggled to cover his most sensitive parts. It took a few moments, but Angela caught her breath and Namtar returned to his senses enough to realize the knife on his neck.

His skin seemed pale as water dripped from Angela's hair and onto his cheeks. "I warned you," he croaked.

A guilty sorrow swelled inside Angela, and she shook her head. "It was an accident, I swear. I wouldn't intentionally kill someone that didn't deserve it."

Namtar scoffed. "Doesn't matter. One of us isn't going to make it out of Dingir today, so do I deserve it?"

"Please, Namtar. Don't force me to do this."

"Then you shouldn't have killed my wife." He smiled, and Angela could feel his mind wrapping around her again.

Angela tightened her grip on the knife, pressing it harder. "Dammit, Namtar," she said.

He half smiled. "Maybe there are reasons for me to follow Udug more feverously now. Knowing your city is crushed would please me." He sighed and looked up at the blue sky behind her. "I suppose this is what I get for trusting an Anunnaki. Yes, I will be satisfied when your world and every last Anunnaki soul is destroyed."

Angela's eyes began to water. Her hands shook. "You stupid fool. I didn't mean to."

It was now or never; it wouldn't be long before he got the idea to kill them both. He'd send them to inferno and they'd die together. Angela shook her head, looked into his copper eyes one last time, bit her lip, and turned away as she locked her elbow straight.

"You'd leave my son an orphan?" he asked.

Neti.

There was a clacking noise of something hard bouncing, then something metal rolling closer. An oblong device made of thin corrugated iron stopped on a crack between the golden bricks. A red circle in the center of it stared at Angela like a big eye. It flashed twice, and Angela rolled off Namtar. She clutched his robes and pulled him onto his side, placing him between her and it. He was confused at first. Then pain rippled through his face as the device pounded the air with one devastating explosion.

It was louder and hit harder than any thud of teleportation she had ever been near. It made her head spin. Spit and blood dribbled from Namtar's mouth, and his pupils rolled up behind his eyelids. His neck went limp, and his head rested against the street.

Angela wobbled to her knees. The buzz in her ears made her dizzy, and nothing around her seemed to be real. She half believed she was in a dream as she rolled Namtar forward and shook him by the shoulders. Then she saw the blood pooling behind his skull and her fogged mind realized he was gone. She slumped there in a moment of silence and thought of Ardat, the dead father in front of her, and Neti.

Nothing in her dream seemed real. Not the screams, the burning homes around her, or the choices she had to make. She didn't wake until the winged soldier who threw the grenade, blurred by the speed of his flight, swooped toward her. He landed on her with his feet plowing into her shoulders, bending her knees and driving her into the ground. The impact shot pain through her legs. The flaming soldier stood with one foot on her chest and one on her shoulder. The polished barrel of a gun pointing straight at her face glimmered in the light of both the flames of his soul and that of the sun. Through the distortion of his heat, Angela saw long hair that reached his shoulders and thought lines on his face.

"If you have to, kill me quickly," Angela said. "Please. I'm in so much pain."

The glove that held the gun creaked as it tightened.

"It hurts everywhere, every fiber. You wouldn't understand the suffering I feel. It's like my insides are on fire."

A deep breath.

"I've lost everything. Even my city is gone. They're afraid that I'm not who I say I am."

"Tell me one thing that only Angela would know," the soldier asked.

Angela thought for a moment, and she wished she could reach up and wipe the water from her cheeks. Angela searched her memories for the best possible answer, and she said, "Earth. Fourteen years ago. Do you remember?"

Nothing.

"We were making our way through an uncharted region, searching for human occupation in a rocky canyon and the surrounding area, if I remember correctly. Very hilly place with sparse greenery, and on a different continent than usual. The air was hot, but it didn't hamper the marvelous sight of the place. Such a big place. I was still training, spending day after day at your side, and you were constantly correcting my mistakes and saving my foolish ass."

Angela laughed. "I was so completely taken aback by the beauty of the place and the things that you had done for me that I began to fall in love with you. Every day that went by, I only wanted to be a part of your life more and more."

The man's expression softened, and he stepped off her and looked away.

Pushing herself to her knees, Angela groaned and looked at his turned back. She could see that remembering hurt him, too.

"We grew close for those few months, didn't we?" Angela asked.

A quick nod.

"At the pinnacle of our relationship, we snuck from camp on dark nights and embraced one another. But as we neared the end, you grew guilty and told me we couldn't go on." Angela laughed. "I'll admit, I was dumb and I should have known better than to fall for a married man, but it still happened."

Kushiel turned around, and even through the flames of his soul, Angela could see that his sorrow matched hers. There was still something—she could feel it—but neither of them could acknowledge it or make decisions based on it. They had to ignore it. They had to fight to move past it every single day. He was stronger than she was, even as far back as she could remember. He was the first to realize that what they had was simply an urge. It was a passionate one, but urges were not enough for a relationship to survive on. It wouldn't thrive, and it was a mistake that they had made together.

His eyes were wary, and his breaths were ragged. He holstered his gun. "I'm sorry for what I did to you."

Angela shrugged. "I know, but don't be. I understand why you left, and I was the one who started it. I never would have considered starting something with Michael if it didn't happen the way it did, so thank you." Angela chuckled. "Even back then he was brash and overprotective, but I knew that he loved me deeply and he always meant the best for me. A part of me craved that protection. I just wish that I could start this over—that neither of us were so stubborn. Maybe he'd still be here and I wouldn't have had to fight like this."

Angela sighed. Her eyes found her fingertips. She flexed them, scrutinized the dirt underneath her nails, and wished that she could move on from Michael like Kushiel had moved on from her. She wondered how something as undeniably sensitive as a heart could survive a bruising such as hers. A smile stretched across her cheeks.

Because it had to. Because that was what made her a great person. Because that was what made her strong. People around her might come and go, and she'd miss some of them, but none of them would have such a hold on her that she couldn't move on. If Angela could continue after Kushiel, she could move on after Michael. That strength was inside her. It didn't come from other people; it came from her heart, her mind, and her soul. Her soul. Oh, a spark to fire.

Udug. That bastard is going to pay. Even though my people turned against me, I will still fight to protect them and so many others. Donny, Michael, Namtar, and Ardat, all of them have passed because of me in one shape or another. I won't let anyone else go because of me.

No, not because of me. Because of Udug. He did this. I have to stop him from collecting our shards, from rebuilding his Anchor. Get my soul back, too. But how?

Worlds and the souls born in them… They're one and the same. Aspects, aetherical energy in each world, a soul's energy. Donny told me outside the tea shop just down the street. Anunnaki and Dalkhu. Dingir and Kur. Souls are aligned to their place of birth and crystals are affected by the same energies of a dimension. Crystals and souls of the same attunement. That's it.

"Kushiel," Angela said, wincing as she rose to her feet.

Lost in thought, he glanced up.

"I need one thing of you: a blue crystal."

His head tilted to the side.

She held out a hand, shaking it eagerly. "Trust me. Just one."

Kushiel shrugged and reached into the pouch on his waist, then handed her a single crystal that pulsed two tints of blue. "Whatever you're going to do," he said, "do it quickly."

"All right," Angela said with a single nod. "Best of luck, Kushiel, if we ever meet again."

"Yeah. You too," he said softly.

HE WATCHED HER EYES LINGER ON HIM AS SHE TURNED away, clutching the crystal in her palm. Even though the fire of his soul and hers added a layer of ambiguity between them, he could still discern a bittersweet expression on her face, and he was sure she saw his, too. He had never felt so much regret.

When Angela was out of sight, Kushiel turned to walk his own way. He entered an alleyway and somberly trudged through the apartment complex's back courtyard a second time. He figured he had left the Ascendancy around half an hour ago. That would leave him enough time to search a few more of the larger buildings for civilians. Perhaps he could even find the time to jump into the Agaric House and retrieve what crystals were stored there.

Kushiel called out into the building one time, just to be sure that he had emptied it. There was no response, and he left, walking past the courtyard benches. Frost-covered bushes and grasses sat in a raised garden in the center. He stared at the hardy plants for a moment, mind wandering, then exited through the archway in the wall that separated the yard from the alley.

A man in a black robe stepped out in front of him. Startled, they drew weapons of steel and mind.

"GET IN HERE, NOW!" JA'NOEL SHOUTED.

He ushered people, both common and soldiers, through the oaken doors of the Ascendancy with swoops of his hands. Frenzied men and women pushed and shoved one another as he held the door open for them to pass. He barked at a few of them to stop, but after a few tries, he noted that his words had no effect on the panicked people. So he waited until the last few had trickled into the structure, then let the iron bar lock the door behind them.

The soldiers, only half of whom he knew by name, followed him as he continued to herd people toward the steps that led into the protective crust of rock underneath the Ascendancy. There was dirt and blood on their faces. Anxiety filled their eyes. He was worried, too.

As difficult as it was, the officials of the Ascendancy stayed strong and steered the people farther in, like shepherds. People trickled down the spiral metal steps in a line and gathered on cell floors. The doors were propped open with crates in case a child accidentally closed them, and when the sounds of the hallways changed from crying to quiet murmurs, Ja'noel left.

Back on the main level, he gave instructions to a few men who appeared to be lost, then resumed his walk. After knocking three times on a wooden door and hearing a beckon from the inside, he stepped into Sarosha's office.

"News?" Sarosha asked. There was cold sweat on her forehead.

Ja'noel shook his head.

She leaned back. "I got an update ten minutes ago. All beams that can be unbolted and dismantled are, and all work is stalled until given the final word."

Ja'noel cursed. "Kushiel hasn't returned yet."

"How long has it been?"

Ja'noel's forehead wrinkled. "Forty, maybe fifty minutes. I'm not sure." He paused, looked away from Sarosha, then reached for the door handle. "Maybe I should go out there and find him."

"Noey," she called, rising from her chair.

Ja'noel immediately spun back around, holding up a finger and glaring at her. "I've told you not to call me that. It's not my name."

She parted her dark hair and tucked it behind her ear, nodding. "Y-Yeah, sorry. It's a habit at a bad time... But you can't go out there. Kushiel knew the risks. If I had a choice I'd rather only lose one of you: if both of you go disappearing on me, I'll have to take charge of everything, and I'm not prepared to do that." She walked around the big desk and stood next to him.

Ja'noel bounced his head in half agreement.

"I don't have combat experience like you two. I just tell people to fix stuff." She held out her hands as if to hug him. Her eyes sparkled, but there was hope in them, too.

He took her hands in his and gently pushed them to her sides. "I'll be fine. *We'll* be fine. Trust me, and no matter what, drop at least one platform. Give them the idea that we'll do anything to stop them."

Sarosha shifted her weight to the other leg, eyes looking to the floor. Ja'noel expected her to argue with him more, but he was pleasantly surprised when she said, "All right. Go, but for the love of sweetbread, just come back."

Ja'noel smiled, then left the office. As he resumed his jaunt down the hallway he pointed to two Etlus who lingered near the infirmary doors. "You two are with me," he ordered.

One, a proud woman with a sharply angled jawline, quickly pushed herself from her rest on the floor and began to follow him with haste. The other, a man with wiry red hair tossed in a bun on the back of his head, asked, "Where to, sir?"

"We have to find Kushiel," Ja'noel said as they stepped outside. They stood on the grass, and the sunlight was warm on his cheeks. The winds were favorable and calm, and he reached behind himself and pressed a button. The extending metal arms of the wings jolted his body. The burst of the linen created a rush of wind that blew his hair. Ja'noel took a deep breath. He had ten minutes, twenty at the most, to find out what had happened to Kushiel.

"Have you searched the outlying storehouses?" Udug asked, running his hand over his graying hair to smooth it back.

A scrawny Dalkhu in the circle of many tipped his head up, looking out from under his hood. "Yes," he said.

Udug nodded, then tossed a sack made of blue silk and red lace drawstrings into the air. He smiled as he caught it;

the sound of crystals clacking and rubbing against one another pleased him. After an entire lifetime of struggle and pain, all it took to end it was a few broken rules. Now they gathered there in the market square to plot their final strike. Or so he hoped.

"Lamid Piristi," a familiar voice said.

Udug turned.

An older pupil from ten years past stepped forward, and with open palms he said, "Should we not send someone home to deliver those to the Restorer? We can ill afford to lose them now."

Udug looked to the bag once, then back. "Yes. I believe that would be good." He held out the bag. "Here."

The pupil's eyes grew wide and he began to fidget with his hands as he contemplated taking it.

Udug shook the bag, impatient and motioning him to take it again. "You can assure me that it will reach him?"

He nodded frantically. "Yes. Do not fret. I'll see by risk of my own life that they make it to Shedim." He bowed, then took it and stepped back. A moment after he closed his eyes, he vanished. The boom of his exit ruffled the cloaks of the others, and a few winced and covered their ears.

The group resumed their conversations: what buildings they had not yet searched, the likelihood of more Anunnaki resistance, and how the other attack groups were faring. When the sound of clomping boots reached their ears, they paused and turned to see a woman cloaked in fire running into the market square.

Udug smiled widely. He held out his hands in a warm greeting and said, "Angela, I was wondering when you'd find your way to me."

She was quiet and stopped only a few feet from him.

Her eyes were black coal in a pool of liquid magma. *How very fitting of her*, he thought.

"I felt your presence in Kur. What did you think of my home?" Udug asked.

Angela shrugged and glanced at each of the Dalkhu's faces. They were stricken and tense, unsure of her presence and uncomfortable seeing an Anunnaki without flame.

"It was an experience, I suppose," Angela said. "The Kissum was a marvelous structure for sure, and the glowing ceiling of the cave—how is that done?"

Udug smiled. "It's not an intentional creation. Simply moss and plant life in our caves." Udug turned, realizing Angela's eyes kept returning to the men behind him. A few of them had their hands in their robes. Grabbing the hilts of their daggers, assuredly. His eyes hardened. "Steady yourselves and remove your hands. She is not foolish enough to be a threat."

A soldier half his age slowly removed his hand from his robe. "But she's Anunnaki," the Dalkhu said. "Certainly—"

"No," Udug said. "She has seen things with our eyes for some time now. Angela has experienced a pain you never will. If there ever was or will be a sympathetic Anunnaki, it is her." He raised an eyebrow at her. "Am I correct?"

"No," she said. "I am an ally to anyone who will barter with me."

Udug smiled, incredulous. "Barter? What is there to barter?"

Angela had a blue crystal between her pointer finger and thumb. "Here," she said, and she held it out for him to take it.

His eyes narrowed. "I'm surprised. Even somewhat untrusting."

She rolled her eyes and shook her hand once more.

Udug hummed in thought. He glanced into her eyes, at the crystal in her hand, then back at her again. *What a curious creature*, he thought.

"Very well," Udug said, and he stepped forward to take it from her. "What is it you think you can—"

As the tips of his fingers touched the crystal, Angela closed her eyes and it began to pulse with blue light. The councilman froze. Something grabbed him by the soul and *pulled*. Lightly, at first, then harder until his face contorted and pain rippled through his chest. His mouth agape and his muscles stiff, he moaned as the crystal vibrated between their fingers. The air around them crackled with energy, twirled about them, and blew.

"What... are you..." The words wouldn't come. His chest hurt so much it paralyzed him.

Angela smiled and said, "Taking my soul back."

The fire in her eyes faded to green as her mind grappled with Udug's soul inside her and pushed it harder than she ever had before. She could feel it writhing, fighting her every step of the way, but she would break it. With all her will, she poured energy into the blue crystal in her hand and felt it devour every drop she gave it. The crystal took on a life of its own, taking her energy and multiplying it. She had never seen that before. Burning away every bit of fuel she gave it, the crystal became a magnet of Dingir's aspect to draw out her Anunnaki soul.

The platform beneath her feet groaned and shifted. Metal cracked and bent, shaking them. The ground fell out from under her, then stopped abruptly, sloping as the edge of the city began to dip lower. She slipped on ice and slammed onto her back. The buildings grumbled as the stones mashed and rubbed together. Some cracked and began to crumble, sending chunks of debris onto streets with loud crashes against the metal ground.

Angela shook her head and propped her legs, stopping herself from skidding across the ground. She sat up and realized she dropped the crystal somewhere. The city's platform had tilted at least thirty degrees, and all the Dalkhu around her had fallen over. The blue shard skidded and bounced four feet from her, moving farther away before getting caught in a crack between steel sheets.

As she bent to reach for it, the ground shook violently again, screaming out one last groan as metal ripped through the streets and vertigo filled her stomach. Angela, the Dalkhu, the market stalls, chunks of broken buildings, and the crystal all began to levitate and float as the platform beneath them broke free of the rock that held Dingir together. Angela watched the rest of the city grow smaller above her, and it felt like a dream.

She snapped out of it, and with one outstretched arm she pushed herself off the ground, glided across the metal platform, weightless as she fell with it. She reached out with an open palm and snatched the blue crystal from the air. Then, over the sound of a hurricane, she faintly heard someone yelling.

Something brown grew larger in the corner of her eye. A stone spear six inches in diameter jutted out of a hole in the veil and raced toward her. Without anything to stabilize herself, she jerked her arms and legs in unison, spinning herself enough to avoid being pierced in the torso. But the spear nicked her shin, not only cutting her slightly but sending her spinning even more wildly.

Angela reached out, and something rough brushed against the back of her fingers. She latched onto it. Her body was immediately jerked in another direction, and she pulled herself to hug it. When her head stopped spinning, she realized she was holding the stone spear. It was twenty feet long before the hole in the veil was closed and it stopped growing. She was only a few feet from the end that had burrowed itself into a building.

In the middle of the market square, Udug held onto a metal sheet as his legs and robe pulled him upward. His teeth gritted and his knuckles were white as he held on for his life, the edge of the sheet cutting into his fingers.

Angela pulled herself with the spear, placed her feet on the platform, and began to walk toward Udug through the buffeting torrents of howling wind. They locked gazes. His lip curled, baring his teeth, as another shout bellowed from his lungs. Another spike of rock erupted from thin air and darted toward her.

She ducked underneath it without missing a single step and pushed herself harder against the fatigue in her legs and the whipping wind. The closer she got to Udug, the more desperate he became. She was a threat now. A danger not only to his goals but to his life, and it felt wonderful. She pushed forward with her head down, avoiding every spear he threw at her until she was only a few feet away. Her soul was so close, and she knew she could end it. What she had felt just seconds before she dropped the crystal had been too intense of an experience to deny; using the crystal as a magnet would work, and it was within her power to set things right. For Michael and for herself.

Angela bent her knees and launched herself forward, free of the safety of the stone pole she used as a handrail. Udug roared again, anger rippling across his brow and the muscles in his jaw tensing. He watched Angela approach in slow motion and felt his fingers give way as she latched onto his back and tugged him away from the platform.

They wrestled as they floated up and away from the only thing around them that seemed stationary. They twisted and fought against one another until they met eyes. The skin-to-skin contact burned and she could smell their flesh smoking.

Angela growled through the pain, determined to finish this even if it was going to kill her. She tore Udug's robes and slammed the crystal into his chest, the fires of his soul enveloping her hand. Blue light flared between them. The crystal vibrated and pulled. She screamed, giving it everything she had.

And Udug's hold on her soul gave way.

He grew limp, mouth agape, and began to fall away from her. His expression relaxed, lifeless. He was a spiritual being, now with no spirit.

Angela's head snapped back like the crack of a whip. Her soul was there, inside her, safe where it belonged, but his soul was still there, too. They clashed against one another, fighting over the space in her chest, but like chaos and order, Dalkhu and Anunnaki, water and lightning, two opposite things could exist together in the right conditions.

Angela clutched her shoulders and held her legs close to her chest as a sensation unlike any other overtook her body and her being. She continued to fall, locked in a peaceful trance.

Ja'noel stood at the edge of the Ascendancy lawn, looking down and seeing nothing but blue sky where the falling section of the city had disappeared into the distance. Two chunks of stone buildings and metal platform had shrunk to dots some time ago. It was a pity. A damn tragedy. And the worst part about it was that Kushiel, the man who helped him get Dingir into the best shape it had ever been, wasn't there anymore. And that made the city a lot emptier than it was before.

"Goodbye," he murmured.

He had forgotten he wasn't alone until one of the Etlus standing next to him said, "You can't be certain he's gone, sir. He could have escaped."

It was the younger, red-headed Etlu who spoke.

Ja'noel shook his head. "I can just feel it. He's gone."

The soldier sighed. "Well, what now, though, sir?"

He turned and began walking toward the Ascendancy, his eyes cast low. "While we haven't likely staved off all the Dalkhu, we've at least brought them to a pause. We should move forward and secure the rest of the city. If we are lucky, those remaining will flee. If we aren't, all of the ones we cast to fall will now be on the other side of the city and be moving their way toward us."

"A victory with a price, it seems," the red-haired Etlu behind him said.

Ja'noel nodded. "Regardless, we should—"

An ear-splitting screech blared right behind them. The soldiers clutched the sides of their heads and dropped to the ground in fright. Ja'noel grabbed the brass knuckles in his left hand and the tether gun in his right and spun to see nothing but the blue and white expanse of sky. Yet the sound continued, and as the seconds passed, it grew quieter.

"There!" The soldier pointed upward.

A blurred figure raced through the air until it slowed to a stop three stories above the Ascendancy's roof. Ja'noel squinted, trying to discern the fantastic quality that made its flight seem so queer, and he noticed that wings of lightning sprouted from its back. Crackling sounds of energy and a feeling of vibration filled the air.

"Listen," it said. The voice boomed louder than what was natural. It cascaded down on the city's streets and echoed throughout, garnering the attention of every person in Dingir. It was robust and comprised multiple tones as though three people spoke from the same body. Somehow low and average in pitch at once.

"What is that?" the red-haired Etlu asked, grabbing Ja'noel's arm and shaking it.

The Grand Uri Gallu shrugged and said, "That's Angela."

"I WILL ONLY STATE THIS ONCE," SHE SAID FROM ABOVE THE city. "So try hard to remember what I say. Anunnaki, Dalkhu, beings of war and prejudice, I know you both. I look on the city that was my home and I see you for what you are. I see the colors of your souls and know that there may never be a time of peace between you.

"To the Dalkhu, I say that you have wronged me. You allowed your own laws to be broken and did not keep your own knowledge in check. There are spells that have no proper use or moral implication. If I ever hear that someone else has become a victim of the same spell as I have, you will see me in your tunnels.

"To the Anunnaki, you have wronged me more. Over the ages you have taught yourselves that the importance of peace through control outweighs the value of freedom and the connections between people, and when you could not control or understand me, you ostracized me. Chased me. There is no place for you in my heart. Therefore, I relinquish any affiliations and any relationships that tie us together. I am me, and I stand only for myself."

Faintly, underneath the blowing wind, Angela could hear whispers below her. The Dalkhu three blocks down the street held expressions of confusion, bitterness. They were conspiring among themselves. Councilman Ruchin was among them, and his hands were clenched as he stared at her.

"It's her," one of the other councilmen said.

Ruchin turned. "Of course it is."

"What happened?" another voice asked.

"I don't know," Ruchin said. He ran his fingers through his beard as his mind searched for answers. When he couldn't find any, he turned around. "I have no knowledge of this, but I can feel that something unnatural has happened. Join me, Councilmen. Let us push her out of this world. Only fire will cleanse this."

The other councilmen nodded, and they took seats on the gold-brick street and began a low hum.

Angela resumed. "Peace between the Anunnaki and the Dalkhu is impossible. You are two beings with two different visions for the worlds. Not only do you kill each other, but you kill those not involved in your war: humans. They are little in your eyes, and they hold no value. I have seen you kill humans, today and before, with little remorse."

A force pushed on her, willing her to go away. The veil settled around her like she was sinking into water. Their push was strong. Her body stiffened and it took her attention. But at the same time, it was nothing. Her souls gave her anchor and fueled her with power through their synergy.

There was something about the two souls of opposite

auras coming together. A feeling Angela couldn't name. It was almost as if she didn't realize what she was missing for all the years of her life, and now that she had Anunnaki and Dalkhu in her, something felt *complete*. Like how it was supposed to be, she admitted.

Looking inside, she imagined the two souls as orbs in her chest. They rotated and swiveled around one another. One red, the other blue. They danced in her with a sense of serenity, but occasionally they would clack against each other and spark. With her will, she had formed this energy into the shape of wings and pushed against the air below her feet, giving her flight. Now she funneled and compressed it into her right palm with her mind. It took the form of a sphere, and it swelled in size as she concentrated. It flashed blue and red, then turned purple as she willed it to, crackling like lightning in her palm.

Angela smiled, drew her arm back, and threw it. The sphere left her fingertips with a zipping sound and its light pulsated as it tore through the air like an arrow. It never slowed or fell in an arc, and it crashed into the ground a short distance in front of the councilmen. The sphere erupted into a field of flashing light and arching energy.

The Dalkhu jumped to their feet and tried to rush from the epicenter. Ruchin, the oldest, was also the slowest, and a finger of lightning burned through his cloak and licked his shoulder. The skin cauterized instantly, and he howled, falling to his knees and clutching the wound. The others dashed to his side, but he shoved them away.

Angela grinned. The councilmen would at least think a second time before trying to cast another possession spell. She waited for the orb to flicker and dispel its energy, and when all eyes had returned to her, she spoke.

"Today, it stops. Here and now, I state that any celestial

being that brings death to Earth will face me first. You will wage war, but no harm will come to humanity. Dalkhu, cease your reunion of the crystal Anchor. Anunnaki, stop your expansion. This is my declaration."

Angela looked down on Dingir one last time. There was no soul-flame from the people below her or from the world itself. There were crowds of normal people in the streets. While she could discern the aura of the peoples' souls, none were a threatening source of scalding heat. It was beautiful, and Angela smiled. She thought about everything that had happened. If there was one person she owed thanks to, it would be Donny, but considering he wasn't there any longer, maybe the one who taught him would suffice.

Angela felt a tang of sorrow. She missed Michael and always would, but she told herself once more that if she had the ability to break free of heartbreak once before, she could again. Heartbreak. It reminded her of her long-gone parents and the parents whose lives she had taken, and she felt guilty. Angela sighed, then pushed herself into the veil, setting out for Kur to make things right.

CHAPTER SEVENTEEN

"Come on, Neti. We've got a long way to walk before night."

The boy looked at the carved oxen in his hands for a moment longer. The wheeled toy was curious to him. He had probably never seen a trinket like it, but he placed the toy back on the stand without a word. The shopkeeper smiled as Neti moseyed closer, and Angela, knowing the boy was disheartened, placed a hand on his shoulder as they turned away.

"It'll be better when we get there, I promise," Angela said.

He shoved her hand from his shoulder and continued walking.

At the edge of the city, Angela retrieved a roll of parchment from a pocket in her dirtied cotton pants and looked over the map Donny had given her one last time. Over dust and sand, highlands and mountains, and the water of lake and sea, their destination awaited them. They had already come quite far, and Angela was certain they were within the final third of the journey.

"This is the right way," Angela said, tucking the map away.

She looked down to Neti, his auburn hair blowing in the wind. "We should be there within a few days," Angela said, trying yet again to hear Neti speak, but he was silent.

They traveled through desert into the cold fall of night, and there was little comfort other than a shawl Angela had traded for. She had given Neti a pair of goggles, knowing that they would help him see through the sand-whipping wind, and he never thanked her. It would take a while before the boy would open up to her, but she hadn't imagined that he would be silent. It made making up with him much more challenging and the grief more painful.

What am I doing? And can I even hope to make it up to him?

Within the first few hours of entering Earth, Angela noticed that something was slowly leaving her. Her wings faded first. Then her vision returned to normal. She could no longer look at Neti and see the aura of a Dalkhu about him or at the black and white simplicity of the humans around her. It was as though some part of her mind was stopping her, like she was her biggest weakness. For nearly a week now, she had tried to reinvigorate herself in the combined energy of the two souls but to no avail, and she wondered what had changed.

As they walked, she wished time and time again that she could bring herself to teleport them, but her batteries were dry and she could not break through the veil. She tried to harness and push her souls' energy while Neti slept, but she couldn't manage it. Every time she tried to get a grip on the energy, her souls seemed to freeze up, refuse her, and it infuriated her to no end.

For the next few days, they passed through the last of

the desert and entered lands where small shrubs and tufts of grass grew. Rocky outcrops had given way to rain, creating trickling streams that led to the sea's shore. The smell of saltwater was heavy in the air.

In a seaside village, Angela found a seaman and they took to water on a shabby sailboat. It was a short journey across the water, yet it did not pass by quickly enough. Angela was bored and Neti's struggle with seasickness made the trip much more miserable.

A small village, squat on a hill just above the sea's beach, grew restless as their ship approached. The wind carried the villagers' shouts down the shore as men emerged from homes and from just beyond the crest of the hill, followed by curious women and children. They stood around their hovels, watching in caution.

The men worked to fold the sails and slow the boat with long oars as the ship glided over the water and came to a stop at the waterlogged dock. The sailors threw the boarding planks onto the dock, and Angela paid the captain with silver.

Taking Neti by the hand, she crossed over the plank and the water below. A man sitting in a rowboat just a few dozen yards away watched them with a harsh and piercing gaze, and she wondered if he was unaccustomed to seeing a woman and a child traveling from across the sea. His eyes returned to the fishing net in his hands as they took to the sandy beach and began climbing the footpath on the grassy hillside. By the time they reached the top, the villagers had retreated into their homes or back to their work.

From atop the seaside hill, Angela could see for miles. Green hills rolled over the land, and small patches of trees not easily considered forests were sporadic. The snow-capped mountains, though, were one of the most marvelous things Angela had ever seen.

A handful of pigs and goats bleated and snorted from behind a wooden fence near the center of the hamlet. Neti took a few steps toward the animals, placed his hands on the barrier, and stared at them.

He's bold when it comes to curious new things, Angela thought.

She dropped the two sacks she carried on her shoulder, then reached into her pocket and inspected her map. Small shapes signaled human settlements, and while names were not listed, she was certain where they stood. Dots were speckled along the shoreline, and just above the one they stood in, there was the circle that Donny had scrawled.

Angela struggled to discern any precise topographical information from the map when a gentle voice drew her attention upward. A woman wearing a purple and red woolen robe stood on the other side of Neti. Her cheekbone and the creases of her hands were dirty, her hair knotted from the wind, and Angela wondered if she looked the same way. Wrinkles beneath the woman's eyes signaled that she was of a relatively old age for a human, but her smile was still youthful and warm.

The woman said something, motioning to the animals with a bony hand, and Neti looked up to Angela for translation, but all she could do was shrug. The stranger nodded and smashed her lips together, recognizing the obstacle they faced. Bending on one fragile knee, she pointed at Neti, then moved her hands in a way that resembled stroking before pointing at the animals. He thought about it for a moment, then quickly shook his head no.

The old woman stood, humming in thought, before her frown was replaced with a sparkle in her eyes. She smiled as she rubbed her stomach, pointing to both Neti and Angela.

"Do you want to eat, Neti?" Angela asked.

Neti nodded and the old woman smiled. She looked to Angela, touching the tips of her index finger and thumb together to form a circle.

"Of course," Angela said, forgetting that the woman could not understand her. She searched through their bags and produced a small silver coin and handed it to the woman.

They followed her into a door-less hovel made of mud bricks and straw. A sheet of lumber held together by crude iron nails lay on the floor. A small pit in one wall had an open shaft on the other side and was filled to the brim with ash. The old woman seated them at a small table in the corner, then took two clay bowls to a pot next to the fire pit and dunked them inside.

The gray, unheated soup reeked of fish, and small pieces of what Angela guessed was grain floated atop a thin layer of film. The bread the woman gave them was hard and dry. Not a minute had passed when Angela noticed that Neti had already devoured half of his own soup. She wasn't sure if she was impressed with the boy's appetite or disgusted. He ripped off chunks of bread and soaked up the last of the liquid.

When the woman sat down with them, Angela pointed to the bowl and gently scooted it away, shaking her head. The woman shrugged, pulled the bowl closer, and began eating it herself.

She was wishing she could tell her "thanks anyway" when a thought came to her. Angela retrieved the map from her pocket and spun it on the table so the woman could see it. Pointing to the circle and speaking as slowly as possible in the hopes that the woman would understand, she asked, "Do you know Teshub?"

The woman's eyebrows rose, and Angela wasn't sure if she was confused or concerned. "Teshub?" the woman repeated in another dialect.

Angela nodded, ecstatic.

The woman stood suddenly, shaking her head and waving her arms. She pointed at Angela as she spoke, then at Neti until her voice broke into shouting. Angela leaned back in her seat just to get a bit farther from her.

What about Teshub is making her so mad? Did I say it right?

Angela raised her palms, trying to gesture that she didn't understand, but the woman wouldn't stop rattling off nonsense. She bent over the table and snatched the half-eaten bread out of Neti's hand, pointing it at his sad eyes as she yelled.

"Time to go," Angela said, pulling Neti to his feet.

The woman followed them outside, still muttering and shaking her head. When Angela turned and tried to thank the woman, she was silenced by a finger pointing north of town. Other villagers had emerged from their homes to investigate the ruckus, so Angela simply bowed, took Neti by the arm, and pulled him away from the village.

At a quiet spot a fair distance away, Angela stopped to sit on a rock and think. Neti crouched low to the ground, watching a six-legged bug make its way across a leaf. She watched him use a stick to prop up the bug when it nearly toppled from its perch, and once the insect was saved, Angela sighed and said, "Come, Neti. Let's get going. I don't know how far we have left, so we'd best keep moving."

The boy straightened, and with an overdramatic expression of fatigue and unwillingness, he clomped toward Angela and pumped his fists as he groaned.

Angela laughed at him. "I know. I'm tired, too," she said, and she finally saw a smile stretch across his face. Without another word, they were off.

Later that day, as they passed between two mountains and began stepping down into a valley filled with trees, Angela spotted something peculiar. Atop one of the white-peaked giants to her left was a dark spot that moved.

"Wait, Neti," Angela said. She held out her hand behind her.

Her eyes scrutinized the mountain's top and watched for movement until she could make out a silhouette. A man stood amidst the ice and snow. Tattered strips of black, red, blue, and brown cloth wrapped around an underlying layer of wool clothes. A scarf billowed over his red cheeks and nose.

He did not move, and Angela suspected he had noticed them as well. They had locked gazes, evaluating one another from a distance. A shiver ran down her spine when she felt the back of a phantom's hand brush against her mind and soul.

Angela steeled herself. *He's feeling me out. And he's a Dalkhu.*

And he was gone. She scanned to see where he went, and seconds later she heard the *thump* from his teleportation. Then a second rumble reached her ear, but it was quieter, and the valley around her filled with echoes.

"He's still in the area," Angela said. "If he would have went anywhere on the other side of the mountains, we wouldn't have heard that."

Neti stood next to her quietly, huddling behind her and peering past her leg.

Curious, yet cautious. "Don't worry," she said. "He's not dangerous to us." *I hope.*

Neti looked nervous, but he followed her down the hillside without a word. The ground leveled out on the valley floor and they were standing in a pine forest. Beyond the chirps of birds, the chatter of squirrels, and the rustles of leaves, the woods were quiet. Angela continued to scan the mountaintops through the trees around them, waiting for the stranger to reappear, but he did not.

The ground opened into a sinkhole. It was almost a perfect circle and at least one hundred meters wide and fifty meters deep. Below in the center was a garden of flowers and trees, and she could even see red fruit growing on shrubs. The sinkhole's wall was a straight drop for almost half of the way down, then angled outward. The bottom floor extended beneath the ground she stood on. There were at least two openings along the outer edge, and the light of a fire flickered from somewhere below.

The way down was a great distance, and while she was relatively certain that she could withstand the impact if she aimed for the trees below, she decided against jumping when she considered the fright it would give Neti.

"We need to get down there, okay?" Angela said.

He glanced down the hole, then stepped back.

"I need you to grab onto my back and I'll climb us down there. It'll be okay, I promise."

He looked uncertain but nodded. Angela tied their bags around her waist, then bent her knees and turned away from the boy so he could wrap his arms and legs around her torso.

"I don't think I need to say this, but hold on, Neti," Angela said as she brought her heels to the edge. Gripping a tree's root, she lowered her feet into the hole. It didn't take too long to find the footing she needed, and she began their descent down the side of the sinkhole. After the tenth step, she could feel Neti jerking his head about to look underneath them.

"Isn't it beautiful?" Angela asked. "The way the trees below aren't touched by the wind?"

Angela's foot slipped on a stone, shaking them, and Neti clutched her tightly and wailed in fear.

"H-Hey. It's all right. Just think about how the trees down here are safe. They get all the sunlight they need, and I bet when it rains their leaves get cold and shiver."

He stilled as he thought about it, and Angela resumed their climb down. It took them a few more minutes to reach what Angela guessed was the halfway point.

Angela tilted her head up and said, "Now look at how beautiful the sun's glare against the stone is."

He shifted his weight and was occupied for yet another moment, and Angela continued to distract him as they got lower and lower. But when they reached the top of the trees, they had no easy surface to climb down. The walls stretched outward and sank underneath the ground into the caves, and she doubted she could hang onto the ceiling and monkey-bar their way down.

"We're going to have to fall the rest of the way, all right?" Angela asked. "Just stay still, hold on tight, and we'll land on our feet."

Neti hugged Angela's back tighter, and she let go. They dropped away from the rocky wall and landed on the ground a few seconds after. Angela bent her knees, absorbing the impact and ending in a squat.

"There," she said. "Not so bad."

He released her slowly and stood on his own, only slightly shaken by the fall.

They walked around the circular garden, through the glimmers of light breaking through the leaves, until they found that the flickering light they had seen from above came from a cave's opening.

"Stay close," Angela whispered.

The tunnel turned downward and angled slightly. The yellow and brown rock showed signs that it had either been dug entirely by hand or at least widened to accompany people. The closer she got to the turn, the brighter it became until it opened into a room.

A bed was pushed against one wall, and baskets sat on the ground next to it. Tiny pockets were carved into one side of the chamber's walls and stuffed with hundreds of books and scrolls. A small fire sat in the center of the room, and the man Angela had seen earlier stood next to it.

His shoulder was facing her, and the scarf around his face had been removed; his eyes were heavily set with wrinkles, his hair gray and cropped short, and the stubble on his cheeks was the color of salt and pepper. She could almost hear his bones creak as he scooped a handful of snow from a leather bag and dropped it into a pot that hung over the fire. The snow sizzled as it began to melt.

"What do you want?" the man asked. His voice rumbled and croaked.

Angela wondered if this was the oldest person she had ever met. Now that she had made it here, she was uncertain what she should say to the stranger. "I-I, uh," she sputtered. "I don't really know, I guess. Simply, I've come here to pay respect to a friend that told me to come to you and has since passed."

The man was quiet.

"My name's Angela, and I owe you thanks. If you hadn't met my friend, it's unlikely I'd be here today."

"What's the name?" the Dalkhu asked, tossing more snow into the pot.

"Donny. From Dingir. It sounded like you two knew each other. You even taught him some things about his soul." Angela paused. "You *are* Teshub, aren't you?"

The man turned, his eyes a pale blue and nearly white with the fire's reflection. "Yes," he said. "Why is the boy with you? He is Dalkhu."

Angela glanced at Neti. "Y-Yes. He's an orphan. I sort of owe him a decent upbringing…"

Teshub was quiet, eyes examining her. Finally, he said, "So you've said your thanks. I assume you'll be leaving now?"

Angela's gaze drifted to the fire. "Well…" She sighed. "I was hoping you'd be willing to help me."

Teshub turned his attention back to the fire. He poured and shook the rest of the snow from the bag into the pot. "With what?"

She shrugged. "I have some mistakes to make up for. To Neti, and a promise to uphold. I'm not who I was. Some—"

"I know. I felt it."

Teshub walked across the room, crumpling the bag in his hand and tossing it onto the ground next to the bed. He returned to the fire with a wooden spoon and began to stir what little snow was left in the pot, accelerating its melting.

"Your aura has a striking resemblance, let me say. But you are not one of them."

"One of what?"

"The Nephilim. I'm sure you've heard of them before. Your aura is close, very close, but you are not of the same proficiency or physique."

"So they were real?"

"Yes. I was there, one of the first Dalkhu and probably the oldest still alive. My father was owned by one of them, and I saw the creature when I was a boy. But I know what you are really looking for: better control over the souls inside you, like a Dalkhu has. You wouldn't be seeking an ex-councilman if it were otherwise. But first I must ask you what trouble my pupil Udug brought you, and how did you come about his soul?"

Angela shifted her weight, shocked that he could identify the soul inside her. "He attempted to possess my body as a way to enter Dingir undetected. He failed, and our souls were traded, so I took mine back."

Teshub applied a spin to the bubbling water with the spoon as he thought. "He was brash when I knew him, taught him, and I'm not surprised that he would have gone to great lengths to try old Nephilim magic." He looked up to her. "I apologize for his actions. I fear it was my doing that made him who he became."

He turned to the carved holes in the wall and retrieved three cups. His hands shook as he dipped each into the pot of water, careful not to burn himself, and handed them to Neti and her. She welcomed the radiating heat into her hands as he slunk back to the fire.

"What now?" Angela asked.

Teshub smacked his lips and breathed slowly. "As a gesture of guilt, I will teach you what I know, and you will tell no one that I am here." His blue eyes grew hard. "You will not interfere with anything I do."

Angela felt uncomfortable, wondering if his reputation with the seaside village preceded him. "Okay… And what about Neti?"

"He is welcome as well. I can show him things of his heritage not so extreme and more honest than what he would have been exposed to in Kur." Teshub's eyes returned to Angela. "You are a warrior. I can feel it. See it when I look at you. There is power in you, and nature did not intend for two separate souls to belong in a single being. You may very well be coalesced with Udug now, who was equally as vicious. Tension emanates from you, and it worries me."

Angela took a drink, unsure of what to say.

"So tell me, what is it that you want most? To be strong? Or something else?"

She thought about it, but it was hard to pinpoint exactly what she wanted most. At one point in her life she had wanted love more than anything else. At others she had wanted to serve Dingir the most, but now everything was up in the air. She had acquired her soul again, and now she felt she was something—*someone*—entirely different. A person even she didn't know.

Angela shrugged and said, "I want to protect the weak and helpless and punish anyone who threatens their peace. Because Dalkhu, Anunnaki, or human, we're all people that have a right to a free life in our own worlds."

The Dalkhu sighed. "Very well."

EPILOGUE

The platform broke into fragments as it tumbled downward. Pieces of metal and stone ripped apart and collided with others to create more rubble. Only one building between torn sections of golden street still stood whole. It spun and twisted behind all the others. The last piece.

Kushiel's fingers had grown weary. His wrists and forearms ached from his death-clench on the pipe that jutted from the side of the stone building. He had almost passed out from his constant rolling twice, and his legs had slipped from the pipe and tried to float away. Nothing but his hands kept him attached, and he had thought about letting go. He was going to die, regardless, but the thought of being sideswiped by debris or smashed between two buildings horrified him.

The platform had rotated in a way that he could look at the pieces below him. He watched the chunks of Dingir bump against one another and spew rock and metal outward like a slow-motion explosion. Occasionally, he passed bodies. Most were Anunnaki, but at least only a few of them were screaming.

A building disappeared from his view, and he strained his eyes in confusion. He swore it was there just a second ago, but he couldn't spot it again. Then he saw the same phenomenon a second time.

Over just a few seconds, a section of sparkling golden street faded until it was transparent. Kushiel puzzled over it. He hadn't been crazy. Next, a second building, traveling at the bottom of the cluster, disappeared into nothingness like something had swallowed it.

No, he realized.

The clouds all around him were like spiraling tendrils, reaching downward into a central point where he was falling. He watched as piece after piece disappeared once it reached an epicenter of vibrant white light.

He forgot about his aching arms and pulled himself closer to the building. Before long, he, too, closed in on the singularity. The building he clutched so tightly began to vanish, but he could still feel it under his fading fingertips. Everything turned white, and he shut his eyes. In the end, he was more upset that he didn't understand how he was going to die, not that he assuredly was. He felt fear, then peace.

Moments passed, and he took a breath. Then another. He didn't feel any different; his shoulders were still sore and his fingers ached. He opened his eyes.

The white was all around him, and his feet had somehow found something to stand on even though there was nothing he could perceive beneath them. There was no ground, no sky, just an empty expanse. The pipe he had clutched was gone, and he could see his hands in front of him again. There were black dots of various sizes in the distance, like drops of ink on a white canvas as large as a world.

Wondering what they were, he looked to his feet and stepped forward. Once again, his foot found hold on nothing but air. Out of caution, he tested his weight against the invisible surface, found it fine, and began to walk toward the black dots on what he guessed was a horizon.

Kushiel wasn't sure how long he trudged forward, but he eventually came to realize that the dots were not dots at all; they were the buildings and platforms that had fallen from Dingir. It was almost as though they had been gently placed upright by large, powerful hands on the same invisible plane that he stood on.

While most of the buildings were heavily damaged, some still loomed over him as he walked over rubble and heaps of scrap and torn gold.

"Hello?" he yelled out.

It was quiet and breezeless.

"I can't be the only one!"

But there was no answer to his call. He continued on, navigating his way through what used to be a city street. Walking through the silent ruins of Dingir made him grow anxious.

Is this a dream?

This place was not the city he loved and it was not Earth or Kur, yet it seemed habitable. He didn't know the name of the world, so he called it the Void.

Something tugged at his waist, and he watched the drawstrings of his leather bag untie by themselves. Crystals of blue, red, and green flew out of the bag and floated lazily above his head for a moment.

"What is—"

The half dozen crystals moved on ahead of him, and

Kushiel followed them, clambering his way through broken windows, up crumbling stairs, and through missing walls. He climbed rubble and saw a mass of swirling colors atop the mound. His crystals joined a spiraling ensemble unlike anything he'd ever seen before, and in the center of them all was a black crystal five times his size. The smaller pieces floating around it connected with the larger one like puzzle pieces, then solidified in a flash of light and lost all of their color.

He looked at the spectacle in wonder. It was like the crystals were orchestrated, too profound and organized in their flight to be unguided. A feeling deep in Kushiel's gut told him the crystalline structure was alive.

Who are you?

A LETTER FROM THE AUTHOR

What could I possibly write here that would make you feel a fraction of how happy I am that this book is in your hands, or on your device, and that you've read it all the way through? I don't think I can, but I'm thrilled you're here, and if you take the time to leave a review online, I will be eternally grateful.

In addition to the readers, I'd like to thank my editor, designer, Pam, Angela, Rebekah, and all the others who helped make this book possible. Since the initial conception of the world with my best creative buddy, William Byrne, in 2016, I've spent countless hours rehashing scenes and chapters because I knew Angela had more to show. I've rewritten this book time and time again because it just would not let me go. I'm not sure if that's a good thing or if I'm just overly obsessive and paranoid, but letting it go into the wild finally is relaxing and frightening at the same time.

So believe me when I say I am so happy you've finished it. I hope you enjoyed it. I'm excited (and terrified) to show you the rest of Angela's story.

AR

ABOUT THE AUTHOR

Until recently, Austen Rodgers was happily plotting his newest series. However, after spending a weekend attempting to advertise this book, he's been admitted to a mental health facility for his own safety.

You're still reading? Nice. This is the part where I tell you about things I've accomplished, but I hate talking about myself. So here's the quick version: in 2015 I self-published my apocalyptic novel *The Book of a Few* and earned my BFA in Creative Writing from Full Sail University in 2016. In 2019 I switched gears and launched my fantasy series The Crystal Mythos. Which genre do I like more? The one with that asks 'what if?'.

Never miss a book when you join my reading club:
https://mailchi.mp/99b2e1331082/signup-page

Or, read my books early by visiting me on Patreon:
www.patreon.com/austenrodgers

Or find my other works on my website:
www.austenrodgers.com

52585981R00190

Made in the USA
Lexington, KY
17 September 2019